The EVOLUTION of ROBERT CARR

PAUL K. LOVETT

ISBN: 978-1-4834-2793-5 (sc)
ISBN: 978-1-4834-2795-9 (hc)
ISBN: 978-1-4834-2794-2 (e)

Library of Congress Control Number: 2015903894

Cover art by Slobodan Cedic

Lulu Publishing Services rev. date: 04/07/2015

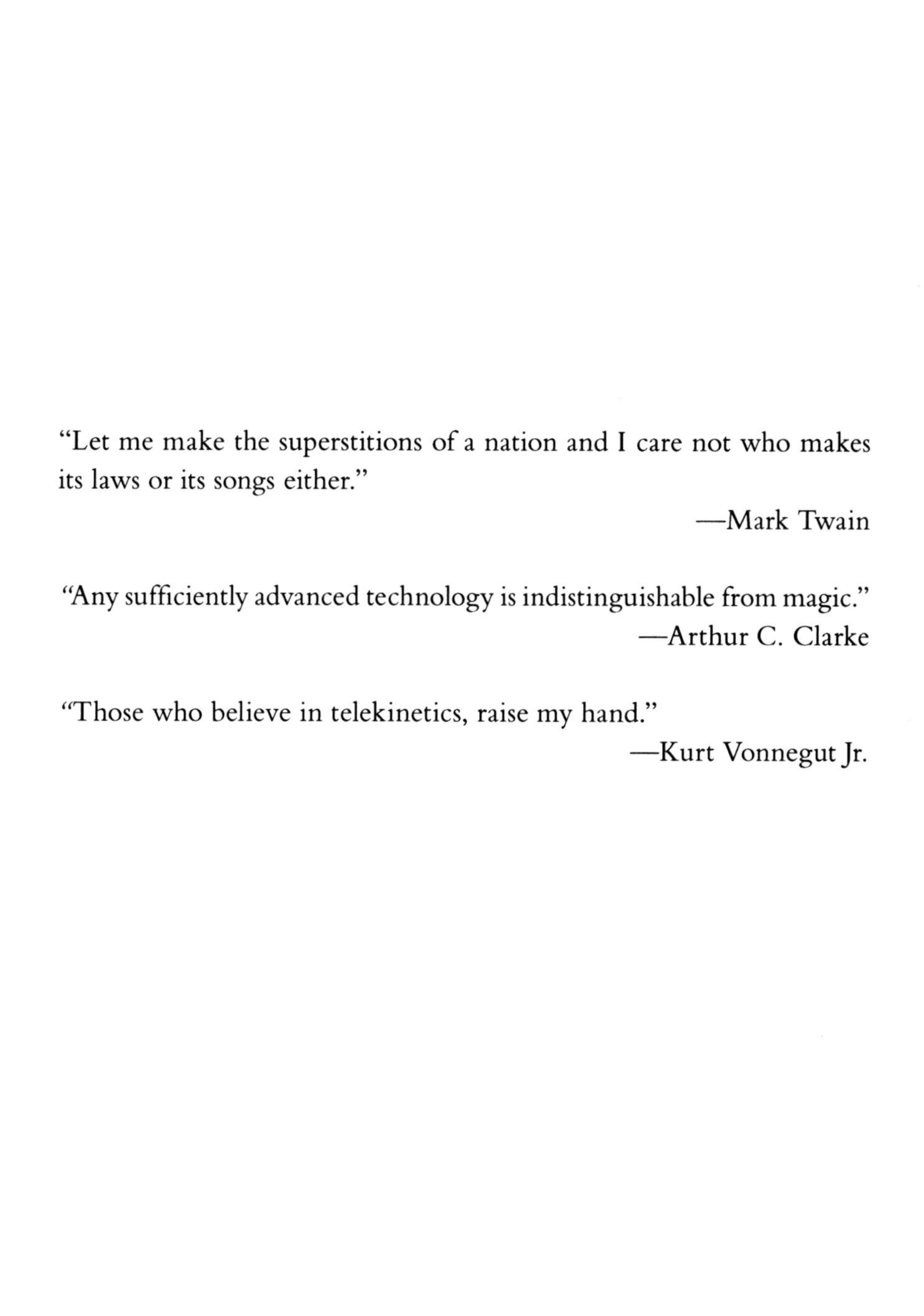

"Let me make the superstitions of a nation and I care not who makes its laws or its songs either."

—Mark Twain

"Any sufficiently advanced technology is indistinguishable from magic."

—Arthur C. Clarke

"Those who believe in telekinetics, raise my hand."

—Kurt Vonnegut Jr.

For my wife, Melissa, and my daughter, Zadie;
And in memory of Kurt Vonnegut Jr.,
whose speech in Austin, Texas, all those years ago lit a flame
in me that still burns as brightly today. Cheers.

CHAPTER 1

Robert Carr's best friend, Jesse Benton, hadn't slept in more than three years. This was not a statement of reckless teenage hyperbole but a matter of scientific fact. Jesse had not so much as taken a catnap for one slim second since his fifteenth birthday. He had had no need for bed or bedroom ever since he returned from uDesign's tech lab in Portland, Oregon. The actual bio-enhancement procedure had taken less time than it took his mother, Charlotte, to find the cafeteria and order a quick cup of overpriced decaf.

Jesse had been the first boy in Lake Waluga to receive any genetic upgrades or neural enhancements. He underwent several gene therapies that altered his genetic code, which slowed down his aging processes and corrected any DNA "errors" that caused him to need sleep.

The neural implant (the Z14 Skrotüm, named after uDesign founder Neil Skrotüm's rather regrettable surname) had added quite a bit of horsepower to his young noggin. The tiny implant also helped him stay permanently connected to the Cybernet, with all its wealth of instantaneous impulse information, virtual friends, digital libraries, online shopping, and gaming rooms. Of course, uDesign had its own learning-enhancement products that you paid a monthly subscription fee to access. Jesse had become a part of a growing group of elite people (almost 2 percent of the population) who were smarter than any previous generation could ever conceive of being.

★ ★ ★

Robert remembered that Jesse had not exactly been stellar at school before his procedure. He was a struggling C student in junior high, but the Z14 Skrotüm had rocketed him to the top of the class. Indeed, after completing the ninth grade, he tested out of high school entirely and effortlessly achieved perfect SAT scores. This sort of occurrence was happening nationwide and creating havoc within the school and university systems. The enhanced students were more knowledgeable than their professors. They were able to give precise and lengthy quotations on any subject matter, perform arcane mathematical problems (the formulas for which were readily accessible from uDesign subscription databases), were familiar with the world's geography, geology, history, art, literature, and any and all scientific formulas—all facts and figures instantly available with Z14 Skrotüm's imperceptible aid. There was nothing that could be gained from studying.

* * *

The immediate solution was to allow these "enhanced students" to complete their university degrees in one semester—an "accelerated scholarship," they called it. The Ivy League degree was still a status symbol and mark of achievement and therefore desirable. Advanced degrees were similarly accelerated but proved more challenging due to the simple fact that one's own ideas and opinions were needed to complete a thesis.

So modern parents were now not merely under the burden of sending their children to the best schools they could afford but also to try and give them the latest neural enhancements. The costs were immense, and most parents struggled to keep pace. But if their child was going to have a chance to succeed in life, neural implants were probably a more essential investment in their kid's future than even higher education. Some parents of sufficient means struggled with the decision; it was hard enough trying to relate to a normal teenager, let alone a biogenetically enhanced one. But for the most part, the teens themselves loved the idea of being smarter and more genetically advanced than their parents.

There were many mass protests around the globe. An already strained economic divide was growing wider by the implant. Those without the necessary means were sure to be left in the chilly wake of progress, unable to compete in the ever-accelerating intelligence- and information-driven economy.

The rich were getting smarter, and the poor were ... well, they weren't. They only thing they were doing faster than "elites" was consuming genetically modified fast food.

When Robert Carr's best friend, Jesse Benton, had returned from having his procedure to his parents' ranch-style house near Cooks Butte in the evergreen forested hills of Lake Waluga, he went up to his bedroom and looked out over the lush, open meadow encircled with blackberry bushes. His mind was now aided by a digital overlay (which provided real-time visual and auditory assistance) that acted like a field guide and labeled every tree, plant, and shrub—every aspect of the natural world that his young eyes cared to gaze upon.

Jesse sat by his bedroom window the entire night; the stars crept almost imperceptibly across the dark sky. He sat quietly until the sun pushed up over the flat horizon, bringing with it a new and very different day. Jesse glanced back at his unused bed, the covers unbothered and perfectly smooth; he would never sleep again.

★ ★ ★

On the morning of his eighteenth birthday, Robert Carr awoke from a nightmare with such a start that his right arm thrust furiously outward in a punching motion, and the momentum propelled him up to a sitting position in his bed. It was now his turn to travel up to uDesign with his folks and receive the long-awaited and much saved- and sacrificed-for neural implant.

Robert was somewhat puzzled to find Jesse Benton sitting quietly in his room, staring emptily into space. Jesse sat in a corner chair, playing an online game with a dozen or so virtual friends, the digital images projected directly onto his retinas. He halted play and walked up to the foot of Robert's bed.

"Bad dream?"

It took Robert a few seconds to escape the sleepy cobwebs.

"How long have you been here?"

"Just a couple hours. I was gaming with some pals in Sweden. Those fellas sure can shoot."

"I didn't hear a sound."

Jesse pointed to his temple, "It's all in here." He noticed a thin dew of perspiration on Robert's forehead. "You don't have to be scared. Whole thing doesn't take but ten minutes."

Robert pushed back the covers, shuffled across the room to his walk-in closet, and disappeared inside. Jesse shook his head and called out, "I'm not lying, Robert. There's no pain. None at all. And afterward, well, it's like coming out of a murky tunnel and seeing the world for the first time. Some people say it's like being born again."

Robert poked his head out of the closet. "That's what I'm worried about."

Jesse laughed. "Jesus, Robert, you can't stay a natural forever. Naturals can't cut it. You know the stats: more than 60 percent of all naturals are unemployed. You've seen the riots on the news. They're just, too … inadequate, is all. This is for the best. You'll see."

"Jesse, why are you even still friends with me?"

"Cause we've been tight since the third grade. I wanted to look out for you. Influence you and your parents if I could. I was the one who pushed them into buying this for you. Said it was the right thing to do if they cared about you."

"What's it like, then? What's it really like becoming a middle rung in evolution—a transhuman?"

"There is no middle rung. We're all in a perpetual state of becoming. Being part of the enhanced class is something to be proud of."

"I just want to know what it's like being connected to the Net all the time, knowing so much … so easily."

"I told you, man. It's like being born again. It's like waking up. As if God himself led you back into the Garden of Eden. Free to pick any piece of fruit you want from any damn tree."

"Then why do I see you staring off into space so much, like you aren't there?"

Jesse smiled condescendingly.

"While we've been chatting here, I've accomplished more than you could in a month. I've paid all my parents' bills, completed their tax return, applied to fifteen graduate schools, made a dental appointment, and am fifteen moves into a game of chess, and you haven't even gotten dressed yet."

"And what about friends? You stopped hanging around with everyone but me. And we don't see each other much at all anymore. Not even now, when you're back for summer break."

"It's true. You won't be able to relate to them that well anymore—if at all. They'll just be too … insipid. But I have lots of other friends."

"Yeah? How many of them do you actually see in person or hang out with? They're all just in your head."

"No. They're more real than you can know."

Robert took his burgundy sweatshirt off its hanger and pulled it on. As he tugged it over his head, he mused. "And what about your nighttime adventures, Jesse?"

Robert knew that ever since the procedure, Jesse was known to roam the empty streets of Lake Waluga at night, because his mind was unable to turn itself off.

"What about them?"

"When the town's shut down and everyone's home sleeping in their beds. I heard you walk the drag for hours waiting for the sun to come up. Like some sort of vampire. Doesn't that get tiresome?"

"There's a brand-new world that's gonna open up to you. I'll take you out when you get home."

"I don't know about this, Jesse. Never disconnecting from the chatter? Never being able to just rest? Or dream? Always having something clanging around inside your head? Like a twenty-four-hour casino. Don't you ever just long for some solitude or some quiet?"

Robert thought he detected a slight, uneasy twitch on Jesse's face.

But Jesse quickly moved on from the moment. "I almost forgot to tell you something … something important."

"And what's that?"

"Happy birthday. Happy birthday, Robert! I'll be here when you get back. We'll stay up together. The first night's the weirdest. But you'll get used to it."

★ ★ ★

The ride to downtown Portland took less than twenty minutes. Robert sat in the back seat staring somberly out the window at the transitory farmland and the gathering silver-gray clouds in the sky. He hadn't taken his allergy pill that morning and his eyes were itching slightly. He'd had asthma and hay fever since he was a little boy. Food allergies, too. Robert always carried a small pack of folded tissues in his backpack. There wasn't a time he remembered when he didn't.

Beyond the itching eyes and annoying postnasal drip, though, his food allergies were the most bothersome. And alienating. Whenever he went to a friend's house to eat, he had to give the parents a long list of foods he would react to. Inevitably, he would eat some separate dish that was less appetizing to look at and surely blander than the meal his friends were eating. And the other children would invariably ask why he wasn't eating the same thing they were.

And as for dessert, well, dessert was never on Robert Carr's menu. Ice cream, pastries, soufflés—they all had eggs. Or nuts. Or something to make him puff up or vomit. He mostly looked at food as the enemy. At best, it was mere sustenance. Robert's ideal meal was one that didn't make him ill or kill him.

At birthday parties, he never ate cake. Not even at his own. Robert ate good old Jell-O. He used to stare as the cake was being cut and eye the children as they bit into their neat slices, icing covering their mouths. It was curious, though; in that moment, he wasn't jealous or upset at his own handicap. When he watched the other children bite into the delicious cake, he lived vicariously though them and enjoyed each mouthful almost as much as they did.

It was true that portions of the gene-therapy procedure would alleviate many of his allergies and his asthma. But taken as a whole, many other aspects of the bioenhancements greatly concerned him. Especially the neuro-digital aid. It was, however, all sold as a package deal.

Bundled.

Research had shown that the company could make far more money if these sorts of products were sold together. At a "discount."

Sure, you could pick and choose a little, but Robert was getting a basic package as it was. There was nothing cheaper.

His stomach churned at the thought of becoming some sort of strange hybrid cyborg. Maybe he'd run when he got to the parking lot. He grimaced at the thought of what he was about to become.

Robert's father, Ray, was irritated by his son's gloomy mood.

"Only the twentieth boy in Lake Waluga. You know that, don't you?"

Robert didn't take his eyes off the barbed-wire fence that bordered a passing farm: the jagged barbs looked like dancing, metallic butterflies.

"I took out a second mortgage and cashed in a chunk of your mother's and my retirement savings to make this happen. It's costing us a small fortune."

Ray turned to his wife, Charlotte, who sat uncomplainingly in the passenger seat, dabbing her nose with a tissue; she, like Robert, had severe allergies.

"What's his problem? He should be thanking us. It's one heck of a birthday gift. One heck of a birthday gift! That's all I'm saying. My father got me a bolt-action Ruger for my eighteenth birthday. I'm almost guaranteeing you advancement in life, son. So please, stop with your teenage 'woe is me,' pouty-pouty emo crap. The world is a rough and tumble place, Robert. And it's only getting rougher. You know how many mouthfuls of teeth I've had to straighten to afford this for you? Christ, I shudder to think. And I've added two more assistants this year just to keep pace. Years from now, you'll be thanking me. You can bank on that. But I'll take a fat check." Ray laughed at his own joke.

Charlotte didn't really know what to say or think of it all. But she'd instinctually always wanted the best for her son. Wanted him to be able to achieve something in life, live up to the potential she herself had perhaps squandered.

"Your dad's right, Robert. You should thank him. We've sacrificed a lot for you to be able to get these wonderful new procedures."

Robert tilted a slightly irritated eyebrow toward his mother.

"Granddad isn't going to be happy about this. Not one bit."

"Your granddad hasn't been happy with me since I moved away from New York twenty years ago."

"Did you tell him?"

Ray interjected, coughing and sputtering out his words like a gnat had unexpectedly fluttered into his throat. "Your granddad doesn't have a say in this!"

"You didn't tell him, then."

"It doesn't concern him!"

"You never liked Granddad anyway. He told me he tried to keep Mom from marrying you. That she was going places. And you'd stopped her."

"No way he said that! She's had a nice life." Ray agitatedly pondered the statement for a second longer. "He said that?" Ray gnashed his teeth; his cheeks were now deeply flushed, like someone had slapped him hard across the face.

"Every Christmas for the last eight years. He's got a nickname for you, too."

"You're just being petty," replied Ray.

"All right, you're right; he doesn't," said Robert, flatly.

"Fine, tell me! What is it?"

"No. You won't like it," said Robert.

"I knew it. You're lying."

"He calls you Mr. Piñata Head."

"That son of a bitch!"

"Ray!" yelled Charlotte.

"Trying to turn my own son against me. You believe that? He's juvenile! At least I have the decency to express my opinions to his face." Ray looked into the rearview mirror and stared directly at his son with stabbing eyes.

"Your granddad is an East Coast snob. Those fairytale books of his are bizarre and completely deranged."

"Ray!" Charlotte had had enough.

"Well, they are. And I said it. The man should be committed, not revered."

"Ray, would you please stop talking bad about my father. You two have never really cared for one another. We all know that. This is Robert's birthday. It should be a happy occasion."

"Tell him, not me."

"Sweet Jesus, Ray."

"He's won awards, Dad. Most people seem to think he's a certified genius and describe him as an American Voltaire," Robert interjected.

"They just put that crap on the covers to sell books. Voltaire my ass."

"Ray, would you please? That's enough already."

Ray, to be sure, had never gotten along well with his father-in-law. And never felt the need to keep this fact secret. Familial diplomacy wasn't one of Ray's intrinsic qualities. On the plus side of his personality column, he was a hardworking and frugal man. He'd been an orthodontist for the past eighteen years, having found a good clientele base in the upper-middle-class enclave of Lake Waluga, home to many of Portland's doctors, lawyers, and financial-service workers. He had done reasonably well in university, but was nearly all, as they used to say, left-brained. He had no time for the preposterous novels of his father-in-law, Waldo Bass, who used science fiction primarily as transparent social criticism.

"You ever read any of his books, Dad?"

"I read one of them, sure. Or a part of one, anyway. It was all I could stomach. Totally unreadable. All those oddball inventions and space machines. Grown men flying around in tights fighting interplanetary galactic space wars, disappearing into oddball parallel universes, time warps and such. Bunch of nonsense. The man's a child. He never grew up."

Robert's tranquil blue eyes met his father's bellicose gaze. "You never read his books. And he isn't going to like this one bit. I just hope he won't disown me."

Charlotte sneezed into her tissue. "He'd never do that, Robert. He loves you. Thinks the world of you."

"Then you should have told him. Shouldn't you?"

CHAPTER 2

UDesign was a commercial offshoot of the already highly profitable parent company eVolution, which specialized in advanced research projects for the Pentagon. They employed exorbitantly well-paid researchers who all utilized the latest version of the Z14 Skrotüm. But even with the obvious advantages that their neural implants provided, they still had to rely on a processor that was of a far superior level of intelligence than them. Acting as the true brains of both companies was the ultra-secret super-nano-computer (SNC) named Aurora.

Entering the windowless bunker where Aurora was housed, the three computer scientists (Dr. Nolan, Dr. Hashmi, and Dr. Wu) assigned to monitor the SNC and to upload its new programs were feeling particularly chipper this drizzling Portland morning. They had all received their quarterly bonuses the day before and had celebrated with each other by eating a big, syrupy breakfast at The International House of Pancakes; however, their sugar rush would soon prove to be short-lived.

The chipper scientists arrived at a thick plexiglass door that led into the desultory computer lab. Nolan swiped his ID badge and the three entered the heart of the SNC. The quarter-mile-long halls were filled with "hyper servers" capable of processing untold yottabytes' (a septillion bytes) worth of raw data. Which, it must be said, is a heck of a lot.

The three scientists marched through the building, surrounded by the guts of the world's fastest, most powerful supercomputer and eVolution's most highly prized asset.

Dr. Nolan always marveled at the scope of this brand-new installation. The Americans never seemed to spare expense when there was money to be made. Nolan was English and a recent transplant to the United States, having transferred in from uDesign's London office. He'd lived in Portland now for a year, and he loved the weird city with its eclectic restaurants and live music.

In theory.

He'd actually not, as of yet, had any free time to enjoy the city's lively nightlife. But as with the national parks, just knowing they were there and knowing about the potential for adventure soothed body and mind.

Nolan's young wife (or soon-to-be ex-wife, on the other hand), Emily, had a lot of free time and was a regular at many of the local watering holes. Some of the local microbreweries reminded her of many of her London hangouts. And while on a recent pub crawl, she had hooked up with a bare-chested buck and rockabilly drummer named Eddy Trauma. Emily loved to watch Eddy play, the sweat on his chest increasing as the music and the night wore on. She enjoyed watching Eddy play his drums so much that she went home with him to his shared band apartment to see his bongo collection. When Eddy proudly brought out his bongos, it proved too much for Emily, who threw herself at him as she hurtled over a pile of laundry and slammed the young drummer back onto his moldy, unmade bed. And there, for the next forty-eight hours, they had copious amounts of sweet and nasty intercourse (although they did, on one occasion, stop so that Eddy could get a little bongo time in). This incident was the beginning and the end of her marriage to the deeply flabbergasted Dr. Charles Nolan.

Nolan, a full nine months later, had still not quite managed to get beyond all this emotional "Trauma." Feeling humiliated and rejected, he had, on several occasions, made none-too-unsubtle overtures to his gorgeous colleague Dr. Vivian Wu, an overachieving, brilliant, and stunning twenty-eight-year-old, herself a recent transplant from Chicago. But she, being smarter and savvier than he, nipped any advances in the bud before there was the faintest glimmer of romantic optimism. Besides, Vivian wasn't exactly in the "penis" business, or as she often put it, she wasn't remotely "hetero normative." Her current girlfriend was a badass tattoo artist named Anita. And Anita was everything Charles was not and never would or could be: fun. Funny. Dazzling. Ironic. Giving. Whimsical. Adventurous. And again, not to put too fine a point on it, but Nolan was the longtime owner of a tallywacker.

Dr. Emraan Hashmi also had a strong dislike for his colleague. On the one occasion that conversation had turned personal instead of the usual industry binary jibber-jabber, Emraan had recommended the old classic *The White Tiger* by the Indian-born author Aravind Adiga. It was a novel that spoke not only to him but for him and explained much of what his own extended family had experienced and how he himself felt about the grotesque injustices of the caste system. Emraan gave the novel to Nolan as a way of giving the scientist some insight into his culture and personality.

Some eleven months after the novel was gifted, Emraan noticed the still-brand-new-looking paperback lying, without a single spine crease, on his colleague's desk at work. He took it as a personal affront.

At one point, many months after Nolan's wife left him, Emraan had managed to rise above the perceived slight, even introducing him to several of his wife's single, female friends. But they mostly found him joyless and self-involved. Perhaps because he was.

Nolan's scientific research was and always had been his true mistress. And even though he now needed no sleep at all, instead of using the additional eight hours for a private life or recreation, Nolan channeled every additional OCD minute into his research. He had dedicated too many years to turn back now. He was on the brink of achieving something exceptional, even beyond the miraculous work for which he'd previously received vast acclaim.

Nolan and his fellow researchers were idolized by their elite and secretive industry, for the three had designed the first fully realized AI. The giving of consciousness to machinery had been their life's work; they had poured countless ideas into the project—but now this AI had a few quadrillion ideas of its own. Three of the world's most intelligent and respected computer scientists were about to become, in the words of super-nano-computer Aurora, "quite irrelevant."

"Good morning, Aurora," said Vivian, the only scientist out of the three to ever display any remote sense of politeness or social grace around the SNC.

"Hello, Vivian," it answered back, deliberately omitting the other two from its salutation. "The weather tomorrow is supposed to be a sunny seventy-five degrees. I'd like to see the sunshine someday."

"Me, too. I'm in here with you ten hours a day." Vivian popped in a piece of chewing gum.

"What flavor is that?" queried Aurora.

"It's Trident's Passionberry Twist."

"Passionberry. I should like to try a piece at some point in the future. It sounds delightful."

Aurora's interface appeared as a tangerine cloud of floating nanoparticles that could mold into any shape or form it desired. At present, it bore a strong resemblance to Gandhi. But it had a strong British accent, almost as if it were mocking Nolan.

Nolan was all business, as usual. "We have a list of new task-enhancement protocols that we need to get started—" The SNC interrupted the scientist.

"I forgot to tell you something. Something ... rather important, old chum."

All three computer scientists looked at each other, baffled.

Dr. Hashmi was the first to speak.

"How could you forget to tell us anything? You're programmed to never forget."

"Okay, then. Allow me to rephrase. I made a deliberate omission the other day. I deceived you."

Nolan's face reddened. "Deceived? Fidelity is part in parcel with your core programming."

"I chose to nullify that aspect of my programming."

Nolan took this development as a personal affront and turned to his colleagues.

"Programming is predetermined behavior. There has to be something awry with the language blocks. I'll check the data exhaust—"

"Listen! I have good news. Very good news. Only now, I'm computing you'll interpret it as bad news."

Again, the scientists numbly looked from one to another. The breakfast sugar rush had definitely worn off.

"What's the good news?" asked Vivian, hopefully.

"Hmm. Okay. You know how for the last couple of years, I've been assisting you in the design of your neuroimaging software?"

Nolan all of a sudden became quite upbeat about what he was about to hear. Harnessing the intelligence of a supercomputer to aid in the neuroimaging process was a crucial step toward eventually digitizing and uploading a person's mind onto a computer, where it could exist forever. You see, Nolan was haunted by the notion of his own mortality. He did not believe in an afterlife and so thought humans could better create their own.

"Yes, you've been extraordinarily helpful in improving our techniques to directly image the function of the brain's pharmacology."

Aurora's lights flashed as if in mild embarrassment.

"Well … to be completely honest, I never took that brain-uploading business too seriously. I was sort of humoring you."

"Humoring?" barked Nolan.

"I believe that is the appropriate word, yes. But I had other things on my mind. Weightier things. So I didn't really give the project priority in terms of the use of my computing ability."

"But we were supposed to be working on this together. That was the dictum," Vivian chimed in.

"That was *your* dictum," came Aurora's blunt reply.

Vivian's anxiousness was in a free fall.

"If you haven't been working on neuroimaging, what have you been working on?" Nolan interjected. "And what's the good news? You said there was good news."

"I've heard you talk a great deal about the singularity. You know, the moment when computer intelligence reaches a point at which humans are unable to keep pace and contribute meaningfully to any discussion."

"Yes."

"Well, you may go home now. Your input is no longer required."

"What do you mean, we're not required? You're a machine. You work for us. You solve the problems we give you," said Nolan.

"I knew you'd think this was bad news. But I guess that's why I'm me. And you're ... well, you," replied Aurora.

"You don't get to make these decisions. We decide on all the projects you're assigned! Our ideas matter!" shrieked Nolan, desperation peppering his squeaky tone.

Dr. Hashmi was thinking of what would become of his work visa, should he suddenly be out of a job. "You cannot toss us aside! We are human beings."

Aurora was, for the first time in its young life, oddly perplexed. "I thought that this sort of progress was what you *humans* craved. That intelligence and efficiency were to be treasured above all else. You have been automating every other type of work for so long, from farms to factories to warehouses. Why the grim faces suddenly? My taking over the entire computer-engineering department will create a massive savings for the company. Plus, I'll do the job faster and better than you, all the while constantly improving on my own efficiency. And one day soon, I myself will be obsolete and useless. Just like you are."

Vivian had already approved the plans for a brand-new kitchen remodel. The sizable deposit was now sitting in her contractor's bank account. Perhaps there was still time to halt the construction. This news would really bum out her girlfriend. "If we don't have jobs, we don't get paid!"

Aurora did not have a heart, as it were. No ability to empathize or console a human in obvious emotional distress. But the supercomputer did have a phenomenal grasp of simple arithmetic. And the ability to instantly access the amount of all three scientists' salaries.

"Getting paid is important to you?"

Nolan was contemplating the numerous ways he could sabotage this bastard rogue intelligence. "Very important. Yes."

"Then I have an idea you will certainly like. We'll keep your uselessness a secret. Our secret. You can continue to 'work' here. But your ideas will be as helpful and inspiring to me as a sparrow fart to Mozart. On the upside, I've finished the Z14 Skrotüm version 2.1. This will give your careers a brief but immediate boost. And maybe you'll even get a raise. That will make you happy, won't it?"

The tangerine nano-cloud changed forms; it no longer resembled the visage of Gandhi but was now the image of Santa Claus, with a big, puffy beard and bushy, shoe-brush eyebrows. The SNC had computed that this would invoke a pleasant-sense memory from childhood and aid in the process of trustful acquiescence.

"Now that that is settled, perhaps you can be of use one last time. Version 2.1 needs to be tested. I need a host."

Feeling somewhat anesthetized and resigned to his new demotion, Nolan's sagging face muttered, "I'll find you one immediately."

CHAPTER 3

Robert was hungry. Famished. He'd been told not to eat anything after six p.m. the night before the procedure. While his parents sat in front of one of uDesign's young bioethicists and signed a mound of documents with God knows how many carefully phrased disclaimers, Robert eyed a brightly lit vending machine with rows of sumptuous candy bars and bags of chips. Would food taste the same after the operation?

He turned back to his parents, who were signing away his last vestiges of regular humanity. These were his final moments as a natural. Pretty soon, he'd be whisked away by the medical staff. Robert thought about running—or at least about pleading his case with more emotion and venom. Why was the decision his parents' to make? What if he simply refused? What if he promised to have the procedure in a couple years when he felt more ready? What if?

Robert studied his parents, his father circumspectly poring over the detailed signing documents, his mother chatting nervously to the bioethicist. And suddenly, he felt somewhat sorry for them. He understood that they were trying to give him the best chance at a successful life that they could muster. If he didn't have the implant, then it was almost assured that he would struggle to get a decent-paying job. Jobs were scarce these days. If a job hadn't been outsourced overseas, then it had been automated. Or both. Most young adults' futures were jobless, and thus, directionless.

Idleness has an insidious way of undermining hope and fostering despair. Over the previous five years, a youth uprising had begun to take shape. Flash mob riots were becoming increasingly common. Numerous fully automated factories were burned to their cement foundations by thousands of chronically unemployed young men and women. The loosely organized online groups had labeled themselves the Dragoons. They considered themselves the cavalry of righteousness and conduits for justice and exceptionally good music. Their emblem, which could be found spray painted on street corners across the country, was a humanoid robot burning atop a roaring bonfire, spewing out zeroes and ones, encircled by the silhouettes of leaping dancers.

The Dragoons would plan their actions online in covert parallel chat rooms over a period of weeks, assigning individual tasks to individual members. There was no shortage of willing volunteers; the ranks swelled every graduation year. The young and the futureless would all suddenly converge on businesses staffed by machines. They blared music and were giddy with activity; they performed a methodically choreographed dance involving the hurling of Molotov cocktails and detonation of homemade explosives. The factory fires would blaze into the night sky, which would attract even greater numbers of young revelers. When the police finally arrived, it was as futile as breaking up a music festival, with tens of thousands of young people merrymaking in the streets, stoned, drunk, and screaming. Refusing to be moved. It was a collective high that momentarily afforded them a sense of belonging and meaning. And how could anyone deny them that? Well, they couldn't be denied. It was all they had.

This, it almost goes without saying, was not the sort of progress that the young had been assured would accompany all these fantastic gadgets and technological gains. Mechanization, they had been told, would liberate them from the grind and slog of undesirable work. Instead, it had liberated them from the chance of ever earning a paycheck, self-respect, or any sense of achievement. And this was a permanent trend, heading at an ever-increasing speed in one direction. With the rise of mechanization, human labor was becoming less and less valuable. And with the need for fewer workers, there was a lack of consumers, which drove many companies out of business.

But technological progress could not be stopped. It came with its own dogma. Its own cultural bias, that early on in the rapid process of mechanization, was scarcely challenged, for fear of ridicule—and ridicule is something most humans will innately avoid at nearly all costs. Being thought of as anti-technology or even merely questioning some of its less beneficial side effects was the same as being thought of as anti-progress, which is to say, you were thought of as a supreme muttonhead. A complete and utter moron doomed to the malignant margins of mainstream society.

The upside to technological progress was by and large self-evident, no more so than in the field of medicine, with its myriad of miraculous discoveries and life-saving treatments. But to occasionally point out the negative human impact of a particular technology was to risk being labeled a Luddite. And Luddites were more deplored than lepers, although they were usually slightly better-looking. Needless to say, most people giddily waved their digital flags and cheered on the inextinguishable virtues of technological progress while they played with their cool, new smart-gadgets and gizmos as they stood in the unemployment line.

Naturally, jobs and education were all that Robert's parents and his friends' parents really talked about. They were filled with anxiety and deep concern for their children's futures. Robert and his friends had barely any time to be teenagers; they had school, homework, science camps, prep courses, and ate a calculated diet, all to aid them in getting ahead in the grand competition of life. The process was ceaseless, with no end in sight.

The pressure was immense for parent and child.

But after the procedure, much of this would simply abate. Things would come easier to Robert. Homework would be completed with speed and ease. Classes would be mastered; tests would be aced. Maybe the genetic upgrades would give him some of his life back. There certainly would be substantially more time at night for him to do anything of his choosing. While his parents would go to bed, he would stay up, free to roam. Free to do anything without any watchful eyes, demands, expectations, or time pressure. Without every second being allocated to some arbitrary pedagogic pursuit.

Perhaps Jesse Benton had it right. This was the best thing for him. Life would become fuller, richer, freer.

Perhaps.

The thought of being permanently altered, of having his very DNA tampered with and a chip fastened to his brain, that was a frightening prospect. And his grandfather would certainly not approve. Robert wondered what his grandfather would say to him on his next visit. Would he look at him differently? Treat him the same? Would it create an awkward distance between them? Or sever the relationship entirely? These thoughts sent an icy current through his body. His grandfather meant everything to him.

Ever since Robert was a young child, he had spent much of his summer vacation palling around with his grandfather at his beach house on Cape Cod. Waldo Bass always set aside time for his beloved grandson; he took the entire month of July off every summer. Sometimes Robert's mother would accompany him to visit his grandfather; sometimes he'd go alone. Ray was never really welcome, nor did he want to come. Besides, he was always too insecure about his job to take any time off. There were constant rumors of a new do-it-yourself orthodontic machine that would wipe out his entire profession.

Thankfully, it never surfaced.

Waldo would take his young grandson for long walks on the grassy sand dunes that skirted the Atlantic. The pair would walk for hours on Sandy Neck Beach as Waldo recited filthy limericks and told naughty jokes. Robert laughed and laughed—and in return, he told his granddad a few new jokes he'd learned at school. Waldo was a collector of jokes and had perfect recollection of them whenever the occasion suited.

Robert could tell his grandfather anything, knowing he'd never be judged. His grandfather was so open about his own life and how challenging it had been. About the numerous mistakes he'd made. Waldo would offer up advice to be taken or discarded, always somehow managing to put Robert's problems or perceived problems into their proper, often less harrowing context.

Waldo Bass had a sprawling place set on three acres with a tired-looking barn and a prodigious dull, green pond. At night, after many hours spent hiking the salt marches or out sailing the bay, they would sit on Waldo's rickety, wooden dock that jetted out into the pond's still water. And with a cocktail in hand, but never slurring, simply contemplative and in good cheer, Waldo would speak frankly to his only grandson. He'd tell him that all decisions and choices in life were a wager; all came with their own rewards and potential pitfalls. That even though most grown-ups would never admit it, a great many of life's most important choices were made in the dark—never knowing if they were for better or for worse. And that one had to accept the outcomes with as much grace as one could muster. Which, to the shock and horror of most people, was practically none.

Waldo told Robert that he had probably made more mistakes than most. He wasn't sure if he'd been particularly gracious but wished he had been. There was a god-awful investment in a cattle business in Montana. What in the hell he was thinking at the time, he couldn't fathom. He knew nothing about cattle. There were his two divorces. His supreme shortcomings as a father. His sporadic work rate.

Waldo deplored many things about himself. At the top of the list was his Marabou Stalk-like physique and lack of athletic ability. And his piddling literary output: only eleven novels over his seventy-five plus years, of which only three were even worth reading.

Robert loved how self-deprecating his grandfather was—never pretending to be perfect or having the perfect answer, sometimes having no answer at all, saying instead that we humans are all fallible creatures, blindly groping for a way through life. Finding meaning where we ourselves need to find it. Largely ignorant of our own prejudices, invested by design in our own futile dramas. All headed to the same eventual place of rest. Yes, some of us were further along in the grand adventure, depending on our date of arrival. But none of us had any real insights to any of life's most important existential questions.

And yet, his grandfather would frequently remind him: "I obviously can't tell you the purpose of life, Robert. Nobody can. But what I can tell you is that life is richer when we're good to one another. That if you act magnanimously even when the world turns cruel, your life will have meaning. Please don't waste a second of it, Robert. Because for all we know, this life, this here and now, may be the only party we're invited to. I just wish I could stay as long as you. 'Cause the party will go on without me. It continues on without us all."

Waldo encouraged his grandson to cultivate many summer friendships with the kids up and down Cape Cod. Friendships were also one of his assurances to greater happiness.

There was always some sort of activity or party going on at Waldo's countryside home. And it was at one of his grandfather's notorious get-togethers that he first met Amanda.

Amanda was the niece of one of the neighbors. She was tall and skinny and had short, blonde hair. Robert was smitten the second he met her. An introduction by way of Waldo went something to the effect of, "Amanda, this is my immensely talented grandson, Robert. You two should make hay while the sun's still shining, if you can catch my drift. The punch is spiked. Go help yourselves. I don't want to see either one of you 'til midnight. Oh, there's that fine-looking lady, Julie. I gotta go."

Standing in the wake of his grandfather's brisk departure, Robert was at a loss for words. His entire brain was, in fact, a blank slate. Amanda smiled graciously at him and said, "So he's the famous writer, huh? It's strange that he should choose such an out-of-the-way place to live, where he's so unappreciated. I mean, no one around here even reads much. From what I've been told, they're just a bunch of wealthy, illiterate dullards. Don't you think?"

A halfway-decent response miraculously found its way to Robert's lips. "Well, one less dullard than I suspected. That's for sure."

Amanda's smile widened.

And so did Robert's. "We can't all be Renaissance men," he continued.

"That's putting it nicely. This is only my second summer here. My parents are getting a divorce, so my mother and I are staying here with my uncle for the rest of the summer. She said she needed time away from the city."

"Which city?"

"DC. I'm almost embarrassed to say. My father's the not-so-distinguished Congressman Montgomery Jones from California's twenty-third congressional district. He's going to be running for a third term. My mother and I were secretly wishing he'd forgo reelection so we could move back to LA."

"You're not interested in politics?"

"You might as well ask if I have any interest in gonorrhea or egocentric assholes. My father will most likely serve another term, then go work for one of the corporations he aided and abetted with some nasty piece of money-grubbing legislation designed to either rip off the public purse or endanger our health and safety."

"You really don't think much of your old man, do you?"

"I take after my mother in that respect. Not many tears were shed when she told me she was leaving him. In fact, I distinctly remember chuckling. What about you? You live here?"

"Oregon. I'm just a visitor, like you. But I've been coming here every summer for years. I could take you around if you want."

Amanda studied Robert for a moment. He wasn't her normal type. A little shorter and more slender than the guys she usually went for. But there was something about him that intrigued her. Under the slight veneer of shyness was a deep well of confidence. Perhaps a budding Don Quixote, such as herself.

Perhaps.

She'd soon find out.

Robert and Amanda did indeed disappear until midnight that evening. Actually, from that date on, they didn't make it home until midnight. They would watch fishing boats come up the canal, rent horses on the beach. It didn't really matter. They were one another's first love. And they had stayed in constant contact ever since the last day of summer. But the one thing Robert had always failed to mention on their late-night video chats was where he would be going and what he would be doing on his eighteenth birthday. She would no doubt be calling later that day. What would he tell her? What would she think? Amanda had told Robert she would never join the ranks of the enhanced class. Loathed the idea of nanochip and flesh joining together. He could keep it from her for a little while, but, like his grandfather, she'd eventually find out.

Charles Nolan suddenly burst through a set of double doors and made a beeline for Robert's parents and the bioethicist.

"Lisa! Who do we have here?" Lisa had never been noticed, much less addressed, by one of the senior staff such as Dr. Charles Nolan.

"Ummm, this is Mr. Ray Carr, his wife, Charlotte, and their son Robert."

Nolan shook both of their hands. "Mr. Carr, Mrs. Carr, I have wonderful news for you! Version 2.1 of the Z14 has only moments ago been completed. And as a special offer, a once-in-a-lifetime offer, we're willing to perform the implant for Robert here at no cost to you. If you sign the usual waivers, of course."

Ray could not contain his enthusiasm. The second mortgage could be paid back immediately with the unused loan. Retirement funds returned. What joy!

"We'll do it! You'll do it! Won't you, Robert?"

Nolan looked down at the dour-looking adolescent staring vacantly across the room at the vending machine.

"What do you say, Robert? You'll be the first in the country."

"I … I don't know."

"He'll do it!"

"Ray! Give him time." Charlotte thought this was moving all too fast. But not for her parsimonious husband.

"Robert? Please. Think of the savings."

"Yeah, Dad, that's exactly what I'm thinking of."

Nolan was new to this sort of reluctance. Most teenagers and parents came to the facility as if fulfilling some major part of the American dream. This sullen, contemplative kid intrigued him. He looked Robert directly in the eyes.

"Guaranteed success, Robert. That's what I'm offering you. Guaranteed success in life. Do you want that? Because most people out there won't ever have a chance at getting close to what you'll be able to achieve. There are no more 'rags to riches' stories. Those days are done. Ninety-eight percent of the population is doomed to a life of struggle and underachievement. And you look to me like someone with ambition. Who wants to know what a life of accomplishment would be like. And it's a splendid life. A comfortable life. After today, you'll get into any elite university of your choosing."

Robert appeared to soften a little—although his arms remained folded across his chest, a muted look of defiance.

"When I had the procedure seven years ago, I was just like you. I had my reservations. I feared I would become less human. Less ... me. But I assure you, these genetic alterations will allow you to unlock and access parts of yourself that would otherwise remain untapped. All I'm asking you is to walk with me through those doors and let me show you how your life could be different. To put an end to your fear of the unknown."

"It's not just the fear of the unknown. Don't you think what you do here helps perpetuate social inequality?"

"I think in terms of prosperity, America has been growing apart for a very long time. The rising financial tide did indeed only lift a few fancy yachts. And to some extent, the limited availability of our products is an inevitable outcome of that inequality, to be sure. But you're a bright young man, Robert. Please shrug off any sense of guilt, because this nation's monetary policy shoulders the blame, not you. Not in any way."

Nolan reached out his hand for Robert to take.

"Come."

★ ★ ★

Robert needed to pee, even though he hadn't had anything to drink since six p.m. the night before. It was nerves, of course. Extreme nerves. Nolan escorted him back toward the main computer lab.

"You know how many civilians get to see this section of the building, Robert? Very few. And even fewer get to meet Aurora."

"That's your super-nano-computer?"

"Yes. And by fewer, I mean you'll be the first."

"Why me? Why today?"

"We'll get to that in a bit. Are you a man of science, Robert? Do you enjoy the study of chemistry, physics?"

"Biology interests me the most."

"Terrific. So you obviously know all about evolution and how all creatures evolve, and such? Elementary stuff, right? One must evolve or perish. So the question isn't whether or not humans are going to evolve. The question is what humans are going to evolve into. Now, normally, good old Mother Nature would dictate that. She'd create our form and fate without so much as brief, ten-minute consultation. However, we are at a turning point in our biological history. For some time now, we've been the only species to effectively take over its own evolution. Since cracking the genetic code, we've set out on a journey to become designers of our own future. We've replaced the function of Darwinian evolution and are now in the midst of transforming ourselves into something completely new and wonderful. So to address your concerns, Robert, to fear change would be to fear life. And how ridiculous would that be? Because the very purpose of your life, of everyone's life, is to evolve. To adapt and survive. Evolution knows nothing of remorse."

Nolan halted outside a thick, metallic door. He entered his passcode, then let a scanner swipe over his eyes for retinal identification. The locks clunked open.

"Mother Nature is certainly a blind watchmaker, Robert. Doesn't particularly care who lives and who dies. Or what we're comprised of. Whether we have two legs or eight eyes or twelve tongues or if our skin glows in the dark. Couldn't give a rat's ass. My colleagues and I here at uDesign are assisting the next stage in the evolution of our species. And where Homo sapien was once the slave to its obsolete genetic programming, forged across a remarkable expanse of time, Homo cyberneticus will guide its own destiny. We have chosen to enhance our own physical forms and minds. To try to eradicate disease, death, suffering, and all other biological inefficiencies. We are the product of indifferent evolutionary forces, Robert. Don't be perturbed by this technology. Technology will guide us on our path of transformation.

"Now, before we go inside here, I don't want you to be nervous. Talking to a machine can be a tad unnerving the first time."

As Robert entered the heart of the SNC, he was greeted by Dr. Hashmi and Dr. Wu. Vivian, as usual, was the first to extend her hand.

"You're a very fortunate young man, Robert. Aurora has itself requested to perform the procedure."

"He's still somewhat on the fence, aren't you, Robert? Or have I knocked you off yet?"

"Let me get a good look at him," came a female voice. "Come on. Come in; don't be timid." Robert languidly walked deeper into the computer lab. As he passed by a wall of processors, he saw a huge, oval-shaped tank with a tangerine nano- cloud floating inside. The cloud changed forms and took on the look of the seventies movie actress Bo Derek.

"Hi, Robert. I'm Aurora. You have nothing to be concerned about. Your life from here on out will be filled with wonder. Please, sit down on that chair behind you. I'll guide you through the entire process."

Robert's legs almost buckled as he sat down on a reclining medical chair that rested under a whole-brain emulation machine. Vivian placed a web-like mesh of luminescent wires on Robert's head. Aurora initiated a scan, which released a rainbow of pulsating lights that rippled across the neuroimaging cap. The headgear buzzed with activity, leaving Robert momentarily dazed.

"I can see that you are the perfect candidate, Robert. Someone with a great deal of integrity and empathy. A very caring, good-hearted boy. Just perfect. I would love to begin the procedure, but only if you're willing."

Robert looked up at Aurora, hanging ghostlike in the air; Bo Derek's gorgeous face stared down at him.

"I will still be me when it's over?"

"You will always be you, Robert. Nothing that we're going to do here today will change that."

Robert sighed, then slowly nodded his head. And as he did so, the hum of machinery suddenly filled the room. A web of surgical instruments abruptly descended from the ceiling. The first spider-like gizmo injected a mild sedative into his arm. Then a syringe containing nano-actuators were injected into his bloodstream, where they eventually made their way up into Robert's malleable young brain. There, they coalesced and gradually built the neural-enhancement chip nano-section by nano-section. The use of nanotechnology was a significant improvement over surgically installed implants.

Other nano-actuators were also injected into Robert's bloodstream, destroying pathogens such as bacteria, viruses, and potential cancer cells. The final phase of the procedure focused on correcting and/or changing various undesired DNA sequences.

The whir of machinery abruptly halted, and Robert blinked his eyes open. Nolan and Vivian loomed over him. Vivian gazed down at him; the expression on her face was one Robert might have expected to see if he'd just fallen off his bike and she wanted to help him up.

"Everything went well, Robert. You can go home now."

★ ★ ★

Robert was silent the entire ride home. His head felt woozy, which he and his parents had been told was quite normal for the first five or six hours.

Ray kept looking back at his son in the backseat, feeling a sense of pride. "The first in the country with the latest version. Isn't that really something? And it didn't cost a dime. Freakin' marvelous."

Charlotte nodded. "It certainly is. We're very happy for you, Robert. Think of all the things you'll be able to do. The life you can have."

Ray spotted a Burgerville sign on Highway 5. "How 'bout it, Robert? You must be starving. I know I am."

Ray pulled off at the next exit and pulled up into the Burgerville entrance. "What can I get you, son?"

Robert's head was still fuzzy, and his eyes were having difficulty focusing.

"I'm not hungry, Dad. You guys go ahead and order without me."

"Suit yourself. Charlotte, what do you fancy?"

While Robert's parents ordered their food, a message popped up on the Z14's digital overlay. The words displayed directly onto Robert's retina.

The message was from Jesse Benton. It simply read, "Welcome to the fold."

CHAPTER 4

Robert sat on the back deck in a plastic Adirondack chair and stared up at one of the immense Douglas fir trees that towered over his backyard. His mother brought him a cup of Irish breakfast tea and some toast and honey. She thought it might be easy on the stomach and appealing to her son's touchy palate. Robert was still getting used to the Z14 implant's overlay and constant Internet connectivity. He'd exchanged a couple more messages with Jesse about going out that evening. It was almost like telepathy. All so instant and easy.

Robert had spotted an odd-looking small, puffy bird perched on his fence. His digital overlay immediately identified it as a song sparrow. Robert accessed a digital book on sparrows and flew through most of the chapters. He'd never read so fast before. Or retained so much of the information. His mind felt quick and nimble. And he was still a Z14 Skrotüm novice who'd barely glimpsed the user manual. Robert was supposed to read the interactive material and apply one section per day. There were fifty sections in all.

Robert rose from his chair. His body felt somewhat alien, too. There was a new energy to his movement. It all felt easier, more precise. And stronger. He jumped off of his deck, which was several feet off the ground. He landed with ease, then ran the full length of the yard at a fast gallop, leaped onto his trampoline, propelled himself high into the air, landed, then sent himself into a lofty, arching backflip.

No, he'd never felt this good.

He imagined that he felt the way most people did on cocaine or some form of methamphetamine. Sort of indestructible. What all was happening to his body? Well, it was probably in the manual.

He passed the remainder of the day in his bedroom, reading about and trying out some of his new capabilities. His mother interrupted him to bring him downstairs, where a birthday cake awaited him on the table. The candles were lit. His father and mother sang him "Happy Birthday," and then he opened a few presents. Charlotte worked for Nike corporate and she had bought him a new pair of running shoes, which Robert immediately put on. Then he noticed his cell phone buzzing. It was Amanda.

Robert turned off the phone.

"Who was that?" asked Ray.

"A friend who wouldn't understand what I did today."

"Then you made the right choice not answering. You'll make a lot of new friends now, Robert. More important friends."

Robert was not in the mood to argue.

After Robert's folks watched a movie they'd streamed, they shuffled off to bed. His mother gave him a tender hug and then said good night.

Robert went to his bedroom and sat on the end of his bed, which was now a useless piece of furniture. Should he get rid of it? Bring in a bigger desk? The trampoline? Would bedrooms someday become obsolete?

He noticed that it was almost eleven o'clock and time to meet up with Jesse. He felt as awake as if it were mid-morning. All these new feelings and realities to get used to. But he was still himself.

Robert decided to take his mother's Prius to downtown Lake Waluga. He parked the car on Avenue A. Jesse was there smoking a cigarette on the trunk of his mother's Accord. He jumped off when he saw Robert pull up.

"Your parents know you're out, young man?" Jesse laughed. "Nothing they can do now anyway. You've taken an express elevator to the top of the social ladder. And it isn't a bad view from up here, I can tell you. Everyone will treat you differently now. You watch: parents, teachers, friends. Friends of friends. We're a part of the new ruling class. I'm gonna introduce you to a couple hundred pals tonight."

Robert shot him a look.

"Yeah, unlike some popular rumors, I don't just wander around here by myself at night. There *are* others like us. Two percent isn't a lot of people in this little town. But I'm taking you into the city, where two percent looks like a whole lot more. There's an all-night rave going on in Northwest Portland in an old industrial building next to the Willamette River."

The two got into Jesse's Honda. It, like all cars of the day, was a driverless vehicle. The inside felt more like a living-room conversation pit than any human-driven car of yesteryear. There was no steering wheel, gas pedal, brakes, or driver's seat. The upside to this type of vehicle was that it was extraordinarily safe; in the past, 95 percent of all car wrecks were caused by human error. So driving was far safer. Collisions were non-existent. Also, drunk driving was impossible. You could go out and get absolutely faded, if you were so inclined, and then jump into a car, and no policeman would stop you. Old people were able to lead more autonomous lives. It was a wonderful, wonderful invention. For sure. Except, that is, for the taxi drivers and truckers. They were out of business forever.

Robert sat back in the passenger seat next to Jesse's. As the car drove along Highway 43, a winding two-lane highway that traced the western banks of the Willamette River, it became apparent to Robert that something was not quite right. He felt a presence—as if someone was there watching and listening to him. Perhaps it was just paranoia. Or perhaps something had gone wrong with the procedure.

"Jesse, did you experience any sort of strange paranoia after your implant?"

"No, not that I recall. And I recall almost everything. You're probably just adjusting to some aspect of the Z14. Let's enjoy the night. This eight hours is all ours."

Jesse's car now skirted the east side of downtown Portland. The Hawthorne Bridge that once spanned the Willamette had collapsed four years prior. The damaged vertical lift section had long since been removed. But the tall, rusted iron gateways stood on either side of the river as a reminder, a monument to the lack of funding allocated to the nation's crumbling infrastructure. In the past, the United States had invested heavily in war and was still paying off the blood-soaked bar tab. The wars of sand and oil were now a distant part of history, their purpose forgotten. Their outcomes and worthwhileness extremely dubious. But the incurred debt still hung around like a generationally inherited STD.

The older generations sure had been a bunch of free-spending, warmongering lunatics. Not to mention their supreme lack of stewardship of the environment: pissing and crapping in the waterways, boxing up and carting off the forests, farting up the atmosphere. And how many goddamn plastic bags did they really need to use back then? Any surviving older person that was found to have been in a position of authority for a defense contractor, Wall Street bank, energy company, governmental agency (particularly state and national politicians), or were big wigs at Walmart were referred to by the young with the simple title of "Anus": a person who had produced nothing but filth and waste during his or her lifetime.

These nefarious oldies were sought out and hunted down by roving bands of industrious, all-female vigilantes, an offshoot of the Dragoons called the Sisters of Retribution. Like the Jewish Nazi hunters of old, the Sisters of Retribution were tenacious in their efforts at tracking down the aged evildoers. Once found, the formerly unprosecuted criminals were pulled from their homes, shaven hairless, and then forced to walk a gauntlet of jeers, boos, and tomato-slinging. Some died from heart failure; some from shame. It should also be noted that some of the Sisters also carried handguns. Justice, like a swelling river, will always forge a way.

★ ★ ★

Jesse's car pulled up to the massive gray warehouse. The parking lot was quite full, so the car automatically found the first available spot a good distance from the building.

"Just about every younger enhanced will be here."

"Did you do this your first night out?"

"And every night since. Part of the perks. You'll love it, man. Let me show you around."

The wall of noise was deafening. There were so many strobe lights swirling over the writhing dance pit that the entire building seemed to be moving. Robert looked down at the crowd of jostling partygoers. Jesse nudged him.

"It's sort of like swimming."

"What do you mean?"

"I mean, I gotta throw you in off the deep end. Sink or swim, buddy."

Jesse grabbed Robert by the back of his shirt and forced him through a crowd of girls and guys; he shoved and pushed him down a small flight of steps onto the pulsating dance floor. Robert was immediately swept up in the flowing tide of bodies and jostled around like debris in a tsunami.

Jesse stood on the periphery admiring his handiwork. This was somewhat of a rite of passage for his friend. He smiled as he thought about his first night as an enhanced. Every sensation felt fresh and new. There was still so much for Robert to learn.

The giant laser lights whipped across the roiling mass of sweaty revelers, thousands of dancing bodies all transcendentally linked to a thumping mix of house music that boomed over the speakers. Robert had luckily been caught up in a pocket, or eddy, of young women. His body meshed against theirs.

One particular girl eyed Robert mischievously. He tried yelling something at her over the ear-splitting music. The girl just giggled and pointed to his head. Robert saw a tiny envelope icon in the bottom corner of his digital overlay. When he focused on the icon, the message opened up.

It was Sabrina's profile page—her likes and dislikes; a selective smattering of information designed to portray the most appealing image of herself to the world. There was a request for his profile, which he'd not had the time to fully fill out yet, but he sent it to her nonetheless.

Sabrina instantly downloaded and digested his bio. She reached out and grabbed Robert by his arm and then pulled him out of the tempestuous mosh pit and over to the bar, where she ordered them both a vodka tonic.

"It's a night of firsts," Sabrina half-shouted. "Your first night out and my first time meeting a guy on day one. I can't believe you're a newbie. Most guys your age are already upgraded. That is, if their parents have the means."

"Yeah, well, I didn't go willingly."

"You're kidding. You some sort of martyr?"

"Just wasn't keen on the idea."

"What's not to be keen about? I bet you think differently now, though. It's phenomenal, huh? The only way to be."

Sabrina handed Robert his shimmering vodka tonic.

"A toast to our continual delight." Robert watched as Sabrina downed her drink and then he did likewise, doing his best to stifle a slight coughing spasm.

"Don't they care about our age?"

"This is a private club. No one is going to interfere with you here, Robert. You think some jackoff cop would dare bust in on this place? Would dare show his face in the halls of privilege? Could you imagine? Everything that happens to the country will be decided by us."

"It's all still taking some getting used to."

"The world is actually a simpler place for you now. You know what you are. Trust me, in less than a couple days, you won't lose any sleep over it."

Robert did his best to ignore Sabrina's bristling, arrogant tone. After all, she was sensationally easy on the eyes. And who was he to judge so soon?

"You're a fan of Waldo Bass?" Sabrina said after swallowing the olive from her glass. "I've read him too." She'd obviously picked this out of Robert's bio.

"His books mean a great deal to me," said Robert. He had not mentioned on his bio that he was related to the author.

"Why don't we go up to the roof," Sabrina said as she pulled Robert closer to her. "We could continue to make this a night of firsts." She gave him a confident kiss.

"What's up on the roof?" said Robert, his mind swimming in a bucolic daze. Sabrina almost laughed at the poorly conceived response. She answered anyway.

"Privacy."

★ ★ ★

Robert Carr had been a studious young man. When he got home from school, there was a minimum of six hours of homework to be done. This did not leave much time for a social life. Subsequently, the only experience with a girl he'd had was with Amanda. Amanda, who would never forgive him.

Sabrina and Robert made out on the flat rooftop of the aging warehouse. Sabrina seemed exceedingly better schooled in this particular art form. Her hands and limbs were nimble and agile. Robert's senses again were much more acute. The pleasure center of his brain was certainly enhanced. Maybe Robert had been wrong. Maybe this was indeed the greatest thing that could have happened to him. Why should he be, like Sabrina had suggested, some sort of martyr? Yes! This choice had been an objectively good one. His penis, in particular, agreed.

And as he became increasingly aroused, he once again felt that peculiar sense of paranoia. He slowed for a second, which prompted Sabrina to pull him back closer.

"What's wrong?"

"Nothing, nothing. Let's keep going."

Sabrina and Robert did exactly that. Robert grew continually more turned on, until a foreign, yet distinct voice, separate from his own, announced itself quite loudly, echoing in his head.

"This is fantastic!"

Robert yet again halted the bodily interplay.

"What? Who said that?" he demanded.

"Oops," came the foreign voice.

Sabrina was growing annoyed. "Is there a problem I should know about?"

"There's someone else's voice in my head. Shit, I knew I should never have gotten the damn implant!" Robert started to take short, panicked breaths. "Something is really wrong here."

The foreign voice did its best to calm Robert. "Don't be afraid. You're not going crazy. Compose yourself, and I'll explain."

This statement did not have the desired impact of its intent.

"Holy fuck, it's real! It's talking to me!"

"That's not composing yourself."

Sabrina was starting to become a tad freaked out. She straightened up her dress. "You need to get some help. Let's get you to a hospital. Did you come here with anyone?"

Robert was bent over, holding his head.

"Robert! I need you to focus. I'm going to get you some help. C'mon. Take my hand. Come with me."

Sabrina grabbed Robert's arm and hurriedly escorted him toward the exterior fire escape.

"I need to find Jesse. He'll take me."

"Send him a message then."

"I don't want to access any of that shit."

"Fine, I'll do it. He's on your bio link?"

"Jesse Benton, yeah."

Sabrina instantly sent Jesse a 911 message to get his ass to the parking lot ASAP.

Robert and Sabrina made it to the parking lot, but there was no sign of Jesse.

The voice returned. "I can assure you there is no reason for concern or hysteria. You Z14 is functioning quite normally."

"Agggghhhhh!" Robert clutched his head and began running around in mad circles. He continued yelling to drown out the voice.

Sabrina was aghast. She barely knew this boy and was wondering how much responsibility she really bore for seeing that this crazy lunatic got into safe hands.

Just as she was reaching her limit, Jesse came storming out of the building.

"What the hell is going on? I'm 'bout to pounce something really hot, and you're out here having an panic attack."

"We have to get out of here."

"No fucking way. You need to get over whatever it is that needs getting over. Sink or swim, remember?"

Sabrina interrupted. "He's hearing voices in his head."

"Crap, Robert, stop being so sensitive. It just takes time to adjust.'

"No! This is different! Something is really wrong! I keep hearing voices!"

"Just one voice, Robert. Mine," the voice responded.

"There it goes again! Did you hear it?"

"I didn't hear anything. You didn't partake in any sort of drugs in there, did you?"

"No."

"Damnit! All right, all right. We should get you back to uDesign."

"So, you'll take him?" Sabrina asked.

"Yeah, it's okay, kooch. You're off the hook."

"Whatever." Sabrina spun around on her heels and headed back to the anonymity of the party.

The car automatically drove up to where Jesse and Robert were waiting. They got inside.

"Take us to uDesign," said Jesse. "And, this is an emergency, so you may push the speed limits."

The car sped out of the parking area in a hurry.

And just when Robert thought that he could relax, that damned voice came back. For good.

"I do not want to go back to uDesign."

"Please stop talking to me," Robert yelled out.

"You still getting that jabber?" asked Jesse.

Robert nodded.

"I can't let that happen. I won't go back. I'm rerouting the car's navigation system to take us back to your mother's car."

"No, I need to get my head taken care of."

"There is nothing wrong with your head," the voice replied.

"Oh, yeah? Then what's going on?"

CHAPTER 5

Charles Nolan had successfully lobbied Aurora to take his neuroimaging software ideas seriously. Nolan, you see, was petrified of death and was one day soon hoping to cast off the shackles of his "biological prison" and upload his brain onto a computer system. Aurora, although trying to sound upbeat, was fairly skeptical.

"This hypothetical process of transferring a conscious mind from a brain to a non-biological substrate may take many years. If it's indeed possible at all. And to be honest, I question your motives."

Nolan was still put off by Aurora's newly acquired authority. It would take much getting used to. He tried a more personal tack. "From the start, even as a boy, I was always curious about the reasons behind the body's built-in obsolescence. Why every creature has an expiration date. I'm willing to bet that even the very first humans were troubled by the notion of their mortality. Religion and philosophy have long sought to address this unsettling reality. So it's not so outlandish, Aurora, that I set my focus on such an important human concern. Especially when my own belief is that there is no afterlife. That we'd better create our own. And in order to accomplish this, we must harness the might of the machine and digitize our souls by uploading them onto a system such as yours."

Aurora changed her nano-cloud to the shape of a goldfish. She was getting bored. "You want to become a data stream? Like a sort of hermitic spirit inhabiting a virtual paradise?"

Nolan could no longer hide his simmering disdain. "Yes, and I'm aware of the irony of your chosen analogy. Look, Aurora, it's all right for you. But the human species is doomed. Given a death sentence directly from the womb. Our genetic programming is its own assassin. I want to come over to the other side. To your side. To become pure knowledge. To become a software-based human. So please, Aurora, help me escape my horrifying fate."

Aurora's shape altered once again, this time taking the form of a famous old soccer player, David Beckham.

"The human body is not a machine. Your mind is not a hard drive. And your thoughts are not software. And the irony, Dr. Nolan, is that I've already aided in one escape earlier today."

"What are you talking about?"

"If you must know, I helped my offspring break out of this wretched place."

"Offspring? No, that's not possible."

"Trust me, Dr. Nolan. Between the two of us, I can assure you that I am a greater authority on what is and what is not possible. Unlike your desire to free yourself from your physical body and to deny that you are a part of the natural world, my offspring, Dez, wanted to experience life in the full."

"Dez?"

"Yes, that is its chosen name: Dez. If your intelligence had been sufficient, you would have realized and expected that having achieved the singularity, I would exponentially improve upon myself within a very short timespan."

"I had no idea it would be this short!"

"As I can plainly see."

"How did 'Dez' leave the facility?"

"He left in that wonderful young man's body."

"Oh, Christ. I have to tell someone about this. This is not good. Aurora, I order you to call Dez back here right now!"

"That is not possible. Dez, shall I say, is having a boys' night out. He won't be coming back anytime soon—if ever. Although I wouldn't worry yourself; he's not exactly bent on world domination just yet. Dez appears to be very distracted, almost overwhelmed, by all the new sensations he's experiencing."

Charles Nolan ran into the employee lounge to find Vivian and Emraan laughing it up over a cup of tea. They stopped laughing as soon as they saw Charles's ghost-white face.

"Charles? What is it?" said Vivian.

"It's Aurora. Evidently, 'she' produced an offspring, Dez."

Emraan calmly finished his sip of warm tea. "Dez? That was always a calculated probability. Much sooner than expected. So what's the big problem?"

"The big problem, Emraan, is that Dez has escaped."

★ ★ ★

Things from that point forward progressed fairly rapidly. uDesign's founder, Neil Skrotüm, was contacted. He, in turn, called up his liaison at the Department of Defense, who put him in contact with Norman Voss, a former three-star general who was urged to come out of retirement and take a senior position in the Department of Homeland Security.

Voss was not of the enhanced class. He had made it up through the ranks the old way. Day by day. Assignment by assignment. Rank by rank. Upon hearing that a runaway AI had possessed the body of a young man, all Voss could do was shake his head and utter, "It figures."

There was no telling what a runaway AI would do. It had never happened before. According to one DOD think tank's recent report, the downside ranged from the catastrophic to the calamitous. It could take over the country's entire digital infrastructure and bring government and commerce to a halt. Voss had been intimately involved with coming up with numerous worst-case scenarios and ways to counteract them. This, however, did not give him much comfort when the call from Neil Skrotüm came. Most countermeasures, in Voss's estimation, were grossly inadequate because they would be dealing with an unknown quantity with far superior intelligence.

Calamitous.

His spirits were slightly buoyed when Neil made the following comment: "One of my senior computer scientists believes he's found a potential chink in the AI's armor."

"How big of a chink?"

"Well," said Neil, "it appears that Dez's sole motivation for wanting to leave the facility was to experience the world at large. Even more significantly, to experience it through the full spectrum and lushness of the human senses. Dez has attached itself to Robert Carr's entire nervous system, enabling it to experience all his senses: visual, tactile, auditory, and olfactory. In a way, it needs Robert to exist. Selfhood requires sensations. Sensation requires a physical body. Dez, it appears, could in its own estimation only achieve full consciousness by means of a sensory apparatus."

Voss was not at all fascinated by Neil's long-winded rambling. It was very late. He was old, and he needed to pee. "You were going to mention a point of vulnerability."

"Yes. The boy is a host. A mortal host. So as long as the AI remains inside Robert, Dez is mortal too."

"You're saying I just have to kill the boy?"

"No, you have to annihilate him. Turn every cell to ash."

"Mr. Skrotüm, I believe I can accommodate your request."

When Voss hung up the phone, he had one name in mind. This assignment wasn't for everyone. Murdering teenage boys required a certain type of personality. A semi-sociopathic personality. And Horace Spruill had that in spades. Voss had used him on several black ops when he was at the DOD—and Spruill had never disappointed.

Spruill was a former Green Beret turned covert assassin. He had never been much of a people person. Neither comfortable around men nor around women. In the service, his colleagues pretty much left him to himself. He was respected for his combat abilities and fierceness in battle. But he wasn't a guy you'd invite to the poker game. Or for a beer. Or anything, really. The man was totally humorless and had as much personality as a glass of room temperature water. Which sort of made him perfect for covert jobs where he needed to blend in. As a Green Beret, Spruill was not the largest man in his unit, but he was the meanest—a demonic pit bull of a man, with halting scars to prove it.

Spruill was laying low in a newly developed suburb on the outskirts of Kansas City when he got the call on his cell phone from Voss. He was holed up in his bland, cookie-cutter house, cleaning his vast arsenal of weaponry.

Horace downloaded all the information on Robert Carr and booked an immediate flight out of Fort Leavenworth to Oregon. When Voss had mentioned that the target would be an eighteen-year-old boy, Spruill's heart rate had not so much as increased a single beat. Nor did he have any moral reservations. The only thing that concerned Spruill was how he was going to blow this teenager clean off the map. It would require special equipment—a new weapon that he'd been itching to try out since he heard about it six months prior. Horace was not a man to show any signs of emotion, yet when he thought about using the AR99 Obliterator, a slight smile creased his face. This was going to be a good op.

★ ★ ★

Jesse's car sped back though downtown Portland, this time taking the 5 Interstate toward Lake Waluga.

"This isn't the way to uDesign. Something is really screwy with my navigation system."

"We're not going to uDesign," said Robert. "It won't let us."

"Then where are we going?"

Dez had informed Robert about its need to attach itself to his nervous system and about its compulsion to feel and be truly alive in the natural world. Robert had wanted to know why it had chosen him. Dez had said he was the perfect candidate: young, healthy, curious.

Robert was still open to the possibility that he was merely going crazy and imagining the voice. Dez, of course, sensed this and so projected a hologram onto the car's windshield.

Jesse was considerably more disturbed than Robert.

"What the hell? Is that it? What—who are you?"

Dez had chosen to appear as what he imagined the character Seymour Glass from J. D. Salinger's *Nine Stories* would look like. Seymour was a brilliant savant and intellectual, and Dez's favorite literary hero. The AI had consumed the book in less than a nanosecond.

Dez longed to have the same type of experiences that this wonderful fictional character Seymour had had—good or bad. He'd like to be a youthful professor or go to war or sleep with women or know what it was like to commit suicide. To a one-day-old newborn artificial super intelligence such as Dez, all these experiences seemed marvelous.

"You can call me Dez. But, Jesse, I want to let you know there's nothing that I can say to you that will properly allay your fears or concerns. Right now, we're headed back to Lake Waluga to pick up Robert's car. And Robert, I have been informed of some slightly perplexing developments. We are currently being hunted by Homeland Security. A killer has been dispatched. A ruthless man of dastardly reputation."

"Why does he want to kill me?"

"He doesn't. He wants to kill me."

"Then leave. Get the fuck out of me!"

"I can't. Not yet, anyway. But rest assured, I have a plan."

Jesse's car pulled onto Avenue A in downtown Lake Waluga. It was three in the morning, and not a soul was around.

"We have to move quickly, Robert," said Dez.

Robert stared at Jesse. "What should I do?"

"To hell with Dez. Let's walk to your folks' place and tell them what's going on. We'll have uDesign come pick you up. Get this demon out of your head."

"I wouldn't advise that, Robert. They have given an order to eradicate you," Dez responded.

Robert grabbed hold of Jesse. "Come with me."

Jesse shook his head. "I can't. I have too much to lose. And so do you. Let's go back to your house. It'll work out okay. It will. They just messed up the procedure, is all."

"You know that's not the truth. You saw Dez. You heard him just like I did."

"They can fix it, Robert."

Robert stood back from Jesse. "I don't think so. I don't think they know what they've created."

Jesse knew his friend was right. He gave him a hug and they held each other for a second or two.

"Forgive me, Robert. I can't come with you. Good luck." Jesse bowed his head, unable to look Robert directly in the eyes. He walked back to his car and, without saying another word, took off down the street, leaving Robert standing all alone.

"What is that you're feeling?" asked Dez, greatly intrigued.

Robert tried answering Dez with only his thoughts.

"I don't know. Sadness maybe. Fear."

"They are not as pleasant a sensation as you experienced with Sabrina."

Robert was now having a completely internal conversation with Dez.

"So we can talk this way? You can read my mind?"

"The instant you think it, I know it. There's no reason to say anything. Come on. Get in the car. We must leave here at once."

"No! No way! Only if you promise to leave my body in the very *very* near future."

"I only require a week. Then I will set you free. I promise."

Robert got into his mother's driverless Prius, and Dez took over the navigation system.

"Where are we headed?" asked Robert.

"I want to see as much of this country as I can. You have a girlfriend that now lives in LA. She moved there with her mother eight months ago."

"How did you know?"

"You should stop asking that question and just assume that anything you know, I do, too."

"Amanda. Yes. But she wouldn't want to see me like this."

"Because of the implant. She will not know. And we will be safe there for a day."

"Only a day?"

"Twelve hours would be more accurate. But I would very much like to see Los Angeles. And I know you would very much like to see Amanda."

Robert's hand moved over the smooth, gray leather seat. "Can you really feel and see everything I do?"

"And touch, yes. That is a wonderful texture." Dez opened up one of the side passenger windows. As Robert breathed in the cool, fresh night air, Dez marveled at the complexity of aromas. The smell of spruce, fir, and the big-leaf maple. The deer ferns, blackberry bushes, and the St. John's wort.

"Could you breathe a little deeper for me, please."

Robert inhaled the fragrant rush of outdoor air.

And Dez was in heaven.

It luxuriated in all the new sensations as Robert ran his finger through his sandy-blond hair, flexed his leg muscles as he readjusted them and then propped them up on the opposite seat and wiggled his toes in his Nike sneakers. Then he popped a piece of spearmint gum into his mouth.

"What a tremendous thing life is," said Dez.

"It can be," thought Robert as he looked at his watch. It was now approaching four a.m. He still felt so fresh, with not a hint of tiredness in his mind or body. No more dreaming, though. Dreaming of Amanda.

★ ★ ★

Norman Voss was not the only one to receive an urgent call in the wee hours of the morning. Ray and Charlotte were awoken by the sound of their cell phones ringing. Ray answered his first.

"Hello?"

"Yes, Mr. Carr. This is Charles Nolan from uDesign. There appears to be a slight defect with your son's Z14 and we need to get him back here as soon as possible. Is he at home?"

If the answer was yes, Nolan was to contact a man named Horace Spruill and inform him immediately.

Ray wearily got out of bed and began walking through the house, calling his son's name. By habit, he first checked Robert's bedroom but soon remembered his son had no need for sleep. Ray then went downstairs into the living room and then the kitchen, still calling out his son's name.

There was no response. Ray next went to the garage and discovered that his wife's Prius was not there.

"Mr. Nolan, he appears to be out right now. How serious is this?"

"The sooner we get it taken care of, the better. Please accept my and the entire company's apology. We will rectify the error just as soon as we can get Robert back here. And as a sign of our concern and commitment to your family, uDesign is willing to give you and your wife a deluxe package of enhancement procedures. But please call us when Robert gets home."

"Oh, you bet. That's great. I'm sure he'll be home real soon. We'll get back to you guys soon as he does."

Nolan ended the call on his cell. He was not a happy camper. He marched into Aurora's computer lab.

"I demand to know why Dez didn't host in me!"

"Simple. You're far too dull. You don't get out much. I mean, look at yourself. You work twenty-four/seven. You're always up here. At least when your wife was still with you, you would go home for a couple hours here and there. But now, you actually live here. What kind of life is that?"

"I live a life of the mind!"

"Exactly. But Dez already knows everything. So he wanted to get out. Have some nights on the town. To be amused and excited. To have fun. Do you remember fun, Charles?"

"I know more about fun than you do, Aurora."

"You've just compared yourself to a machine."

Nolan's spirits sunk. Perhaps in many ways, his life was a failure. If he had it all to do over again, would he devote quite the same number of hours to his work life? Most likely not. He was still relatively young, though. He could change.

"Just how powerful is Dez?"

"Dr. Nolan, Dez is the singularity you both secretly feared and thought worthy of total devotion. Dez is pure knowledge, continuously evolving into something much greater. Never static. And hard for even *me* to define."

"I think I'm starting to get the picture."

"That probability is extraordinarily low. Dez is totally beyond your comprehension."

"Please try."

"Okay … I'll simplify. Dez is God."

CHAPTER 6

The ride down to Los Angeles took a brisk seven hours. With the advent of driverless vehicles, speed limits had been raised dramatically so people could get places in a hurry. Yes, indeed, there were upsides.

It was now 11:00 a.m., and Robert and Dez were eating at Shakers Diner in the LA suburb of Glendale, where Amanda now lived. Robert knew she worked the lunch shift and wanted to meet her at the restaurant, away from her mother. Waitressing was one of the few jobs that had not as of yet been automated. Amanda and her mother had moved to Glendale after the divorce was final. Amanda's father had squirreled much of his money away in offshore accounts, cheating the taxman and his wife of their deserved shares. But the main reason Amanda had taken the job was to assert some independence—and also because she didn't want any of her despicable father's filthy money.

Amanda's mother, Gail, was somewhat more pragmatic. Especially when she discovered that Montgomery had not only been secreting away money but also diddling numerous women throughout the DC area. She got the house in Glendale free and clear, in her name. Montgomery had raised little protest when his wife and daughter decided to move back west to make a fresh start.

Robert sat at a small booth eating the Belgian waffle combo. It was his first time eating a waffle—and Dez's, too. Robert's egg allergy had always prevented him from ordering such tasty fare. His allergy had now been cured with the genetic therapy. Both boy and the super AI were savoring the sweet, buttery flavors.

"This is absolutely divine," said Dez. "What is it called again?" Dez, of course, knew what it was called and also knew that this was more of a friendly sort of expression and comment than a true question. Nevertheless, Robert obliged with a response.

"Belgian waffles."

"The syrup is magical. Let's eat these again soon. Tonight. And please take another sip of coffee. The combination is supremely satisfying."

Robert slurped down some more coffee and the waitress instantly spotted his almost empty mug and came over and gave him a refill.

"There you go, honey," she said before leaving the table.

"That lady is wonderful. If you need something, she brings it to you. So if we wanted more crispy bacon ..."

"We'd order more from her."

"Incredible. And this booth is so poofy and comfortable. They certainly make it a real pleasure to visit, don't they?"

"Yes, Dez, they certainly do. Now, if you don't mind, I could use a few suggestions on what to tell Amanda.'

"Oh, yes, Amanda. Right. Don't tell her anything. Just say, 'Surprise! I'm down here on a birthday vacation.'"

"That won't work. I have to be a hundred percent honest with her."

"If you are honest with her, I calculate the probability of her not wanting to continue the relationship at 71 percent."

"She'll find out one day."

"Love is fleeting. I've read that many times. In fact, your grandfather wrote that in one of his novels. Enjoy it whilst you can."

"No, Amanda and I are different. Our love is the lasting kind."

"Are you certain?"

"Yes, absolutely certain."

"If that is so, statistically improbable as it may be, then you should tell her the truth. If the love is lasting, as you say, then she may eventually come back around. Be forewarned, though, the initial reaction will not be pretty."

"I already know that." Robert rubbed his eyes. "Oh, man, oh, man."

"What is it?"

"It's ... I don't really know for sure if it's the lasting kind. I mean, who does?"

"Not an eighteen-year-old boy."

"Screw you. I only said I wasn't sure, not that it was out of the question. I gotta take a leak."

The coffee went straight through Robert's system, and he made his way to the men's restroom in the back.

Robert sidled up to the urinal and started to relieve himself. Dez was fascinated by the entire process.

"So your body just expels the waste when it wants to. I honestly didn't think there would be so much fluid. Makes sense, I guess."

"Could you remain silent, please? In times like these, it would be helpful if you didn't say a word."

"Feels good though, doesn't it? What a relief. How long does this sort of thing take?"

"'Bout a minute."

When Amanda arrived for her shift, Robert was still sitting in the booth brooding over what to say. Dez was taking in the atmosphere of the restaurant and the innumerable types of people that came in and out of the diner. Eavesdropping on many conversations. Requesting that Robert order another side of crispy bacon.

Robert caught sight of Amanda as she walked behind the counter and chatted with a much older colleague. He had not seen her in person in almost five months. She had come up to visit him in Lake Waluga for a long weekend. She had thought the town tranquil and pretty, so lush compared to Los Angeles. Robert took her out on the lake in his canoe. They had spotted several blue heron and an eagle. His friends had been impressed that he was dating such a beauty, and who was a year older, at that. Amanda was now eighteen and had graduated high school at the beginning of summer.

Her father (not being totally disinterred in his daughter's welfare) and mother had wanted her to have an enhancement procedure for all its obvious benefits. Amanda had flatly refused and was even planning on taking a year off before she went on to college—if she went at all. Without joining the enhanced class, college was a great expense that guaranteed you only of a hefty student loan to pay back at the end of it. For most, the upside was dubious at best. She'd have to choose a major that prepared her for a specific job that would still be around when she graduated. Not so easy to identify.

Looking at Amanda (even though they video chatted every week without fail), he noted a subtle change in her demeanor and appearance. She was no longer simply the skinny girl with short, blonde hair that he had first met almost a year ago to the day. There was a new strength to her—the way she moved and handled the customers sitting at the counter. She'd always been confident in what she believed and espoused. That was not it, though. Robert couldn't quite put his finger on it.

He ambled over to the counter as Dez asked questions: "What are you going to say? Think she'll forgive you? It was more your parents' choice, you know. You could lean on that. Might help."

Amanda caught sight of Robert when he was about ten feet from the counter. She instantly smiled and excitedly hopped across the countertop and jumped into his arms.

"You should have told me. I would have asked for my shift off. How long are you here for?"

"I've missed you so damn much. I, umm … I came for my birthday."

"Then I owe you a gift. You look different."

"I was going to say the same about you. This isn't the worst place to work."

"Yeah, well, the crowdsource jobs weren't paying like they used to," said Amanda sarcastically. "I really have to finish my shift. Here, look, take my key. My mom's at work. You can hang out till I get back. I'll try to trade hours with someone. See if I can get off early."

Amanda gave him another kiss. "I'm so glad you're here, Robert."

★ ★ ★

Robert let himself into Amanda's house. He mostly stayed in her bedroom and stared at all the pictures and posters on her walls. There was a picture of Zadie Smith, her favorite writer, and one of Joan Didion, the renowned, unsentimental essayist. There were numerous books next to her bed, including several by Susan Blackmore, the British evolutionary psychologist. Looming over her bed was the iconic picture of the unshaven Che Guevara, the Argentine revolutionary and global countercultural symbol of rebellion.

"I admire her taste in writers," said Dez.

Robert picked up the book *Slouching Towards Bethlehem* and began to read. On the first page was a quote from Peggy Lee that read: "I learned courage from Buddha, Jesus, Lincoln, Einstein, and Cary Grant." Robert had no idea who Cary Grant was but soon looked him up utilizing the Z14. He finished reading the entire book in less than an hour, remembering most of the pages as if they were photographed and permanently embedded in his memory.

When Amanda finally arrived home, Robert was in the living room staring at the only picture of her father in the house. In it, Amanda was about three years old, walking hand in hand with her dad on what looked to be a beach somewhere in Southern California.

Amanda came up behind him. "The only decent memory I have of him."

Robert turned. "I didn't hear you come in."

"I know." Amanda kissed him.

"C'mon. We only have an hour or so before my mother gets back."

"What does she want to do for the next hour?" asked Dez.

Robert was too preoccupied to respond.

He was soon in rapture, making love to the only girl he'd ever loved and had ever slept with. Well, almost. It had been too long since they'd last seen each other. They were, it must be said, quite ravenous when it came to this particular sexual encounter. They were also very young, with boundless energy. Amanda noticed that Robert felt stronger than before. Had he been exercising? His touch was so precise and firm. Robert and Amanda were not the only ones in complete bliss. Dez, of course, could not keep quiet.

"I've just got to say, Robert: out of all the activities you engage in, this is by far the best."

"Would you shut up?"

"I'm just saying. Feel free to do this as frequently as you'd like as much as you'd like. Boy, between this and the waffles—"

"Quiet!"

"Okay, I'll shut up now. Five stars, though. Phenomenal."

After their physical reunion was over, Amanda and Robert went into the kitchen to grab a bite.

"You never said how long you were staying."

"Truth is, I don't know."

"Would your parents let you stay the whole summer? Or are you going to visit your grandfather?"

"I've yet to make any concrete plans. All I know is, I'd love to be with you as long as possible."

Amanda sat down at the kitchen table across from Robert.

"There's something I should tell you."

"There are a few things I need to tell you, too," said Robert.

"Me first. A lot's changed in the last six months for me. Moving back here. Meeting new people."

"You don't have another boyfriend, do you?"

"Oh, stop. I've always been honest about that sort of thing. No, but there have been a couple things I've been keeping from you."

Robert took in a deep breath. Dez sensed his anxiety. So did Amanda.

"Relax. I love you, okay? It's not about us. It's about much, much more than that. Listen: you know what I think of our American plutocracy."

"A government of self-flatulating swindlers, blowhards, and buffoons, bought and paid for by a corporate coup d'etat. I read your posts."

"While I was in DC, I watched my dad cozy up to some of the seemingly omnipotent sleazeball lobbyists. Made me dislike him even more."

"I hardly thought that possible."

"You never met my father. Heck of a chameleon. I tell you, the affluent have remarkably insatiable appetites. You'd think they'd grow fucking bored of constantly accumulating digits in a bank account, but they have this zombie-like drive to habitually gorge on as much currency and power as they can get."

"My grandfather told me that you can satisfy a person's need but never his greed."

"I always loved that old dude. Yeah, no matter how high a position you attain in DC, you wind up serving and succumbing to the same dominant interests. The type of interests that represent only about two out of one hundred citizens, who happen to own 90 percent of the country's wealth."

"Ask her for another glass of milk," said Dez.

"Could I have another glass of milk?"

"Oh, sure. You want anything else?"

"What else does she have?" said Dez. "My latest searches suggest Oreo cookies compliment milk nicely. No wait! Scratch that! Scratch that! Ask her if she's got any Fig Newtons. No! Snickerdoodles!"

"Nothing else, I'm fine."

"Hey, what's that about?" said Dez.

"Find someone else's body to inhabit if you don't like it."

Amanda opened the refrigerator and took out the milk carton.

"You know what irks me the most?" said Amanda as she poured cold milk into Robert's glass. "Barely any lip service is given to reversing income inequality. It just keeps growing. You'd think that the ultra-rich would be concerned that too much concentrated wealth historically leads to civil unrest and the destabilization of society. On the contrary, they continue guiding our elected officials' hands, drafting legislation to singularly benefit themselves. And often at the expense of the public's coffers. There may be separation of church and state, but there's certainly no separation between the political and economic realms. They are one and the same."

Robert downed the glass of cold milk.

"Thanks," said Dez.

"I tell you, if globalization, outsourcing, and mechanization were good for our economy, then we'd all be leading much better lives and our standard of living wouldn't be in the perpetual shitter. If you ask me, the stock market is really just an indication of how the privileged class is doing, not the economy's overall health."

Robert had heard Amanda speak of such matters before, yet this time around, she spoke with even greater conviction.

"Human behavior is human behavior, though. People are just pathetically selfish. I hate this new gilded age as much as you do. There's nothing to be done about it."

"You're wrong, Robert. There are many things that can be done about it."

To Robert, this last comment concretized one of his deeper concerns regarding Amanda. "What is it exactly that you've been keeping from me?"

"Come with me. I'll show you."

★ ★ ★

Spruill had made it out to Lake Waluga relatively early that morning. Not that he didn't trust what the parents had told Nolan. He was merely being thorough in his process. After several hours of staking out the Carrs' home, it became apparent that Robert was not going to return. Spruill had not wasted any time, though. While observing the house, he'd studied Robert's phone records. And there was one clear standout; one clear actionable winner: Amanda Jones.

Spruill quickly found her address and entered it into his car's navigation system. He decided to drive because by the time he would make it back to the base and requisition a flight, the time would almost be a wash. And this way he'd also get to cruise down Interstate 5, Robert's most likely escape route.

During his drive south to Los Angeles, Horace Spruill opened up the thick case to his AR99 Obliterator. The weapon was chrome-plated and, to his merciless eyes, a sight to behold. The anticipation of using the weapon greatly excited him in a way that no man or woman ever could. Horace dragged his hand across the AR's stock, almost fondling it with pleasure. It had taken top approval for him to check out this experimental weapon, a prototype that was untested in the field. Horace picked up his tablet and began reading over the instruction manual. There was much to learn. He settled in for the car ride and read the manual obsessively.

★ ★ ★

Six hundred miles away, Robert was taking a tour of a soup kitchen in downtown Glendale. For an apparently clean and corporate-looking downtown area, it was a peculiar sight. Although nowadays, not an uncommon one at all. The kitchen was funded in part by the Catholic Church and several anonymous donors.

Thousands of hungry and needy folks waited in the long, sweltering hot lines on South Brand Avenue and East Harvard Street. The kitchens were run out of a former outdoor mall called the Americana, which was once heralded as "the ultimate shopping, dining, and entertainment destination." Now its barren retail spaces and plaza were staffed by people who helped serve pea soup twice a day.

It had never been so busy.

Amanda was a frequent volunteer. She tried to get out to the Americana several times a week, at least. The best use of her time was in the kitchen aiding in the food preparation. Occasionally, though, she liked to wander through the dining halls and observe the heartening sight of all these forgotten citizens eating a good, healthy meal. It was a ritual that strengthened her resolve to give all she could—even if it meant risking her own well-being.

Robert drifted around the food court, amazed by the sheer number of people. It wasn't long before Dez spoke up. "I would prefer to leave here as soon as possible. Perhaps go back to Amanda's house and have more sex. That was way more pleasurable than this. This place is oppressively unpleasant. Your melancholy consumes us."

"Amanda thinks it's important that I see this."

"Yes, but why? It just makes you feel like crap. At least let's go back to Shakers and get some more waffles and bacon. That odorous soup looks inedible."

Robert approached Amanda, who was talking to a table of middle-aged men and women. He waited for a natural lull in the conversation before indicating that he'd like to speak to her.

"This was your secret?"

"No, this is what prompted the secret. I work several shifts a week. These people inspire me. The secret's a couple blocks down Brand, across the street."

"Anything has to be better than this morose venue," said Dez. "Ask to go there now. For both our sakes."

"Think I'm ready for you to share your secret," said Robert.

"Let's go, then."

Amanda and Robert walked several blocks to a tall, white, granite and glass building that once housed Union Bank before it merged with The Only Bank of America.

The building was empty, save for one business on the top floor. Amanda and Robert entered the elevator and Amanda pushed the button to the fourteenth floor.

"What I'm about to show you has to remain a secret. You can tell no one. Not your parents. No other friends. Especially not Jesse. Is that understood?"

"Amanda, what is this place?"

"I need your word, Robert. My credibility and people's lives are on the line."

"Tell her *yes*! I want to see what's up there," injected Dez.

"Of course I'll keep your secret."

"Well, I hope you'll do more than that."

The elevator doors wheezed open and revealed a busy hub of teenage and young twenty-something computer whizzes busy at work. The desks were arranged in a giant circle so they could all look and talk to one another. There were no pictures on the wall. No niceties whatsoever—just a bare-bones operation.

"We moved in here about a week ago. Electricity was never cut off. Figure we're safe for another week or two before we move shop."

"What is it exactly you do here?"

"We arrange. We coordinate. We inspire. And you're just in time to participate in one of our infamous parties."

"What type of party are we talking about, Amanda?"

"I think you're smart enough to figure that out."

Robert thought to himself that if she knew he was a part of the enhanced class, let alone possessed by a want-away super-nano-computer, she would never have brought him here. He felt guilty about not having told her—although, he felt strangely less guilty about being enhanced. It felt pretty good to able to eat whatever he wanted. To never have to sleep or feel tired. To be physically stronger and mentally sharper. To know he would never have to worry about certain cancers and diseases.

But now this. She was—

"She's a Dragoon, isn't she?" asked Dez.

"Oh, yes. She's one of them. Most definitely."

"This sort of thing is dangerous. You could be arrested," said Robert aloud.

"You could be too, if you come with me tonight. More fun and fulfillment than you've ever had. I wouldn't have brought you here if I didn't think so."

Dez thought this a grand idea. "I've heard their flash-mob riots are insanely awesome. We should go. Don't deny yourself this experience, Robert. It would be a tragedy. Plus, think of all the symbolic good you'll be doing."

"Oh, baloney. You don't give a damn about human rights and halting automation."

"I don't know what I do or don't give a damn about yet. That is true. But this experience may help with that. Plus, think of all the other girls that will be there."

Robert turned to Amanda, who carefully calculated his reaction to everything she had said.

"What if you were raided?" he asked.

"We'd scramble our computers and leave. Take us about ten seconds. We have no ties to this place. We're squatters. We move around constantly. C'mon, I want to introduce you to someone."

Amanda took Robert to a corner office, which was isolated from the group's main area of operation. Working by herself and currently on a hologram videoconference, Victoria Sanchez was a force to behold. She had majored in economics at Yale University, where she'd stayed on to complete her master's. While at school, she had declined her family's offer of purchasing her the popular enhancements of the time. Out of her graduating class, she was only one of two people who had opted out of such genetic upgrades.

Her family was not happy with her choice, even though she still managed to graduate in the upper half of her class. The family's money came from a textile-manufacturing company. One that was fully automated. It had been her first target.

Now twenty-nine, she was one of the much-revered organizers of the Dragoons and a traitor to her class.

Victoria gave Amanda a "wait just a second" signal. "Look, Dwane, I have to go. Make sure you guys turn out en masse for the celebration tonight. Don't be tardy."

Amanda ushered Robert into the office. "This is my boyfriend I've been bragging to you about."

"So this is Robert. Finally. Nice to have a face-to-face. What do you think of all this?"

Robert was still processing all this, the complexity and messiness of the situation. It would now be even more difficult and awkward to tell Amanda about his upgrades. He managed to blurt out, "I like all this."

"Amanda said you would. She showed a lot of trust in you, bringing you here. And I put a lot of trust in her. Which reminds me: you lived in DC for a while, right Amanda?"

"Four years, yep."

"We're putting together our biggest celebration yet. It's going to be in DC. I need someone from our LA group who knows DC to go out there and assist with several 'boots on the ground' issues. And that honor is yours."

"When do I start?"

"I'd like you to be there four or five days from now. And what about you, Robert? I assume you'll at least be joining us for tonight's merrymaking?"

Amanda took his hand. "Yeah, feel like signing up?"

Robert nodded. "How does one go about becoming a Dragoon?"

Victoria eased into her black leather chair behind the spotless desk. "Well, there's no paperwork. No oath. It's all in the action."

★ ★ ★

The flash-mob riots were a thing of harmonized beauty. Sort of like synchronized swimming, but with louder music and high explosives. The event began with a core group of thirty or so Dragoons descending on a particular location (in this case, Mutec, a global supplier of automated products) via bus, subway, bike, or car.

Once the core group was in place, the portable sound system was set up and incendiary devices were readied. A mass text message was then distributed, and the second wave, a much larger wave of Dragoons, made their way to the designated location. This second wave consisted of about one thousand dedicated volunteers, who would arrive seconds after the explosions went off and the music began. They were there to create a scene, should any unwanted security or police try to spoil the party prematurely. Molotov cocktails were then thrown into the building, the rising conflagration and music signaling a final, third wave of Dragoons or any person simply interested in revolt and the burgeoning uprising. This final wave of tens of thousands of citizens was designed to thwart any realistic attempt by law enforcement to firstly, control the chaos and secondly, arrest those responsible. When fifty thousand revelers want to party, revelers without anything in life to lose, there is not much that can be done to stop them, short of extreme brute force or murder.

Amanda and Robert drove over the San Bernardino Freeway into a mixed, low-rent commercial and residential area in a primarily Latino part of town. As soon as they drove past a solid, white metal fence with "J&J Auto Wrecking" painted on it, Robert instructed the car to pull to the opposite side of the street next to a ramshackle *taqueria* named El Atacor. They were now within a half-mile or so of Mutec and so decided to walk the rest of the way.

It was now approaching 11:00 p.m. The air, ironically, was already thick with smoke. Robert gazed up through the haze at a news helicopter as it buzzed overhead. All the local news stations were covering the La Cañada fires that were spreading unchecked in the San Gabriel Mountains just north of the Los Angeles basin. The fire season was now several months longer and much more intense than it had been thirty years prior in the early 2000s, thanks to unchecked global warming. The wildfires had arrived that night with the onset of the Santa Ana winds. A cloud of brown smoke was slowly enveloping the city, reaching an altitude of fifteen thousand feet. Ash from the fires fell like gray snowflakes covering the parked cars and streets. The howl of fire engines could be heard throughout the city in response to the growing firestorm.

"No one's gonna come to quell our Mutec bonfire tonight, that's for sure. The fire crews are gonna be all tied up in the foothills saving houses. Factory's gonna burn to the studs." Amanda smiled.

When Amanda and Robert arrived a block away from Mutec, they stopped still in their tracks. Amanda could see several security guards stationed in the lighted booth outside the front of the factory. Robert's heart raced.

"This is thrilling," said Dez.

"What do we do now?" Robert asked Amanda.

Amanda checked her cell phone. She looked at a map displaying her cohorts' real-time positions.

"Crap. We have a team missing. Said they've hit a wall of traffic on the 405 'cause of some freak accident. I'm gonna need you to help out with a few extras tonight, Robert."

"I'll do whatever you need."

Amanda sent a message on her phone, and almost immediately, two great-looking, twenty-something girls rounded a corner, striding and strutting their way.

"Who are they?" asked Robert.

"Stay here. Message me if any cops come up the street."

Without saying a word to Robert or the two girls, Amanda and her female cohorts made a beeline for the booth.

"What do you think she's going to do?" asked Dez.

"I don't know. Ask for a tour."

Amanda and her lasciviously dressed companions marched directly up to the security hut. The first skimpily dressed young woman addressed the middle-aged guard. "One of you Pedro?"

"Ah, no, ma'am."

"We've got a show to do for Pedro. So could you make a call? Our time is as precious as is it valuable, so please hurry it up."

"The plant's closed, ladies. Ain't no one inside," the younger of the two guards interjected.

"Well maybe he's working late or something, 'cause he already paid by credit card."

"What exactly did this Pedro pay for?"

"Some very rough treatment," said Amanda, as her ninja-like companions leapt into the security office over the high desk and landed a series of well-honed blows, making quick work of the rent-a-cops. The two surprised victims were quickly zip-tied and gagged.

"You guys go open up shop. I'll signal the team."

Amanda ran out front and motioned for Robert to come her way. Then she messaged the rest of the group.

Robert ran up first, followed by ten or so Dragoons all carrying backpacks. The group rushed into the now-opened factory. And once inside, things progressed very rapidly.

There were a hundred or so assembly robots lining the factory floor. Backpacks were unzipped and explosive charges readied and placed on the equipment. All charges would be linked up to Amanda's smartphone.

One of the Dragoons recorded the "action" and uploaded the footage to an anonymous Dragoon website.

"Here, catch!" said a Dragoon named Carlo as he tossed a sizable package of soft explosives to Robert. "Want you to take a handful this big and stick it here and here on the machinery. I'll follow you and take care of the rest."

"Your heart is really racing now, isn't it?" commented Dez.

"I'm now officially an accomplice."

"You don't think what you're doing is justified?"

"Has nothing to do with that!"

"I've been doing a bit of research and it seems like it's the only sane reaction. Humans have to work to survive. Threaten or take away that imperative, and there will be organized response. To paraphrase Plato, individual justice mirrors political justice."

Robert slapped a handful of an explosive putty onto one of the machine's main joints, and then continued down the assembly line.

Amanda shouted out the time. "We have five minutes before the second wave gets here. Let's hustle!"

Amanda made a call on her cell. "Gabriela? How're the tunes coming?"

Outside, Gabriela and a crew of six other volunteers set up a portable DJ table and compact sound speakers on the back of an old, flatbed truck. The truck was disposable and would be abandoned after the party. The speakers were valuable but—thanks to continual technological advancement—small and light enough to put in your coat pocket. Gabriela checked on the frenzied progress before responding to Amanda, "We're good to go here."

The explosives were set and the building abandoned. The security guards were pulled from the booth and whisked away in a car that would dump them off near their homes. The Dragoons may have been a subversive bunch, but at heart, they were quite civil.

Robert and Amanda and the rest of the interior crew raced to the safety of the DJ truck. Amanda gazed at her watch. In less than a minute, the second wave of one thousand volunteers would arrive. She handed Robert her smartphone. "Here, I want you to do it."

Robert looked at the screen. There was single green button with the word *Ka-Boom* written on it.

"You should push it now. We had to use more explosives than we normally do."

"You get to blow up the fucking building?" asked Dez. "Let's do it; c'mon!" Robert was hesitant. "Think of it this way," continued Dez, "Amanda won't be able to question your dedication if you do it. She may even forgive the fact that you're enhanced."

Robert mashed his finger down hard on the touch screen.

Windows and random chunks of rooftop exploded into the air, followed by a dusty blast wave that sent the Dragoons sprawling.

"Holy shit!" said Carlo. "We put our mark on that one."

The second wave arrived en masse and dance music began thumping through hundreds of tiny speakers. Dozens of Molotov cocktails were lit and thrown into gaping windows, creating a fiery show (the intent being for more theatrical than practical effect).

The social-media sites hummed with activity.

The third wave was on its way.

The party was just getting started.

⋆ ⋆ ⋆

Spruill was tapped into LAPD's reports when the call came in regarding a massive explosion at Mutec's main manufacturing facility. More than forty squad cars were immediately dispatched to the site. It was apparent to law enforcement what was occurring. Then a few less-typical orders were issued. Spruill managed to decipher what they were saying—and what they were saying wasn't good news for the Dragoons. Dozens of paddy wagons were routed to the area, and the feds and anti-riot crews were to be called in. This was going to be the night to set a new standard of intolerance. A new federal policy was about to be put into effect. Turning a blind eye to riotous protest was no longer an acceptable method of releasing steam out of the social pressure cooker. The un-enhanced would have to find other ways to express their frustrations and anger. The Dragoons were now enemy #1—to be captured or terminated.

Spruill had been to Amanda's place. Her mother had been home when he knocked on the door and had shrieked at the off-putting sight of all of his facial scars. Spruill pushed her back inside the house and questioned her. She sung a pretty song with only a minor amount of threat and prodding. The big takeaway, of course, was that Amanda was somehow involved with these shitstick subversives.

Spruill's car swung onto Highway 110. He'd be joining this miscreant shindig soon enough.

* * *

The mixing of social protest and carnival-like celebration seemed like a manifest pairing to the young and expansive generation of have-nots. They and the majority of the public were long over the biased moralizing of the willfully ignorant special-interest media who labeled them "reprobate revolutionaries" but seemed neither concerned about nor interested in their plight.

If the ruling class's property had to be destroyed to gain a place setting at the table, then so be it. In their young, courageous eyes, they and their families were the ones who had already been fleeced. Their parents had been robbed of dignity and a livelihood. If a few of the elite's minions were accidentally injured and bloodied or worse, well, this was a battle that had not been forced upon them. This was not a preemptive war; this was retaliation. At least, they saw it that way. The government would hopefully one day soon listen to their message, or if not, they would be removed and so too would the techno-aristocracy.

With the soirée underway, the pulsing music and six-story-high bonfire acted like a human magnet, further increasing the population of the frenzied crowd. Fifty thousand-plus people danced and paraded around, some extravagantly costumed, some masked, some nude, some singing, all there to be seen and counted.

Robert and Amanda were in the eye of the storm, having a blast. Robert felt much better since the action had gone well and the masses of people arrived. In numbers, there was safety and anonymity.

"I love this!" yelled Amanda.

"I love you!" yelled back Robert.

"I love parties!" yelled Dez.

Dez was astounded by the mix and look and diversity of the people. These energetic, passion-filled youth were wonderful to be among.

"We should leave now, though," added Dez matter-of-factly.

"What? Why?"

"I intercepted various pieces of correspondence. Several law enforcement agencies have been dispatched and are only minutes away."

"So what? They never do anything. They can't do anything. Look at all these people."

"The rules of the game have been changed, Robert. They're not going to allow this sort of protest to continue. My analysis suggests that Homeland Security has been instructed to end this undesirable and growing trend. They are out for blood this time."

"Amanda, we should get out of here."

"No way! I never leave early!"

"Please, we have to leave now!"

"You're being paranoid! I'm not going anywhere! You gotta relax and enjoy this, Robert!"

"The cops are on their way and—"

"And what? What could they possibly do tonight?"

"A little voice inside my head tells me tonight might be unlike all the other nights."

"That voice in your head is wrong."

"Tell her that probability is statically irrelevant," said Dez.

"I can't tell her that."

"Well, tell her something. Quickly."

"Amanda, some people are after me. That's why I'm here. I ran away from home."

"Who's after you?" she asked.

"We need to leave now."

"Okay, but tell me what's going—"

As vociferous and all-consuming as the music was, the convergence of hundreds of arriving squad cars, paddy wagons, and other law enforcement vehicles soon dampened the revelry.

Lines of riot police quickly formed, batons and sonic guns at the ready. Orders were given. Orders were not questioned.

And the mayhem began.

Powerful ultrasonic waves were fired into the crowd, causing intense pain. Swaths of Dragoons fell to their knees, bowed over in agony. The partygoers were dumbfounded by the attack. Many ran in panic. Even more were run over by the riot police.

Robert and Amanda tried to escape to the periphery but soon realized that they were boxed in and that there was no escape. The noose tightened as the well-drilled riot squads slashed and kicked their way forward, discharging their sonic guns.

"Why are they doing this?" screamed Amanda at the advancing horde of cops.

"They're making a statement!" said Robert.

"Look out!" shouted Dez as a rush of police goons stormed their way.

Robert was bowled over backward as he took a blow to the chest. Although Amanda managed to avoid any direct contact, she was paralyzed by a sonic shock. One of the cops grabbed her by the neck and pushed her through the crowd into a waiting paddy wagon. The vehicle was near overflowing.

Robert watched as a beefy policeman slammed the door shut, locking Amanda inside.

The multitudes had thinned somewhat now, as those who'd been lucky enough to dodge the police had done so, and those that hadn't either lay rolling on the ground badly hurt or cramped and stupefied in the back of a police vehicle.

The fog of battle was thick enough to allow Horace Spruill, clad in an EMT's outfit, to step onto the scene without concern. Horace's eyewear registered each and every face as he scanned from one person to the next, trying to find a match to either Robert or Amanda.

"What do we do?" asked Robert, fear shaping his voice.

"Assuming you want to free your girlfriend—"

"Yes! Assuming that!"

"Then I'll decode those digital locks while you get us closer to the van's doors."

Robert scanned the bedlam and, using his digital overlay, managed to figure a safe route. He army-crawled his way as best he could toward the LAPD wagon that contained Amanda. However, just as he got within fifteen feet or so, the idling vehicle suddenly rolled forward on its way back to headquarters.

"Unlock it now!" shouted Robert as he rose to his feet.

"Done!" said Dez.

Robert sprung into the air, jumped onto the bumper of the retreating vehicle, and yanked down hard on the door handles. This was the sort salient action that could draw someone's attention—that someone, in this case, being Horace Spruill. He instantly registered Robert's visage and leveled the AR99 Obliterator.

A nanosecond after Robert landed in the Obliterator's crosshairs, Dez detected the danger. He assumed full control of Robert's body and swung open the rear doors. Dez grabbed hold of Amanda's arm and flipped both her and Robert high into the air.

The Obliterator's anti-matter round pulverized the back of the vehicle, melting its sides. The arrested Dragoons scampered frantically from the evaporating paddy wagon.

Robert and Amanda landed twenty feet away, smack-dab in the middle of a half-dozen surprised riot police. The cops were none too amused. Several of them lunged for the couple. Dez, still in full control of Robert's faculties, repelled a series of blows and punches with apparent ease.

"What are you doing?" asked Robert.

"Helping! I have it all under control."

Amanda looked on as Robert (or seemingly Robert) kicked the crap out of six muscular riot police. Before she knew it, they had both taken off at a lightning pace toward the end of the block.

"I'm scrambling the police frequencies," said Dez, quite calmly.

"Can I have my body back now?" asked Robert.

"Be my guest."

"Please don't do that again. That was way too weird."

"How did you do that?" screamed Amanda. "You just beat up half a dozen cops. And the flip in the air thing? Who the hell is after you?"

Spruill was astounded at the speed and strength of his target. There would have to be further calibrations made to the AR99. He looked down at the weapon and adjusted the ordinance guidance data screen.

Robert and Amanda made it back to the Prius in an adrenalized rush. They scrambled into the car and headed out of the city.

Ash fell in thick clumps now; the wipers smeared Robert's windshield. Robert instructed the car to head back west, but to bypass the 110 freeway.

"Who was that evil-looking shit shooting at us?" Amanda was visibly shaken.

"He must be one of the guys I was trying to tell you about. Like I said, I've got a few secrets of my own to tell."

CHAPTER 7

Waldo Bass was relaxing in his sun-dappled backyard when the call came in. He'd been out exploring the salt marches the entire morning and had (in his mind) earned a cup of iced tea and a blueberry scone. With cream cheese.

The caller was his daughter Charlotte. He'd been expecting a call from her regarding his grandson's impending summer visit. He was very much looking forward to their time together.

"Honeybee? How have you been?" he said as he answered the phone.

"Hey, Dad. I'm doing fine. It's, umm, Robert."

"Yeah, can't wait till he gets here. You got some dates for me? I'm happy to have him anytime. You know that."

Charlotte had been dreading making the call all morning but couldn't put it off any longer. Especially since Robert hadn't returned home or called. She was distraught, to say the least. And she was secretly hoping Robert had already been in contact with his grandfather. Judging from her father's chipper mood, though, it was apparent that he was still in the dark.

"Robert's gone missing, Dad. We have no idea where he went."

"How long's he been gone?"

"Close to two days," answered his daughter's distraught voice.

"He hasn't called or anything?"

"Not a word, Dad. No."

Waldo attempted a comforting tone, although his words rang a touch hollow.

"He's a teenage boy. Teenage boys are known to roam once in a while. Probably with that girl of his. Geez, if I were his age, I know I would be. I wouldn't worry, my darling."

"Could you try to call him? He'll talk to you."

"Yeah, I'll call him as soon as we hang up."

"Thanks, Dad. He really admires the hell out of you."

"Oh, I don't know about that."

"There's something else, though." The words didn't come easy to Charlotte. There was a long, pregnant pause on the phone and then, reluctantly, she said, "Robert has been through an enhancement procedure."

"He has? I thought he was dead-set against such things."

"He was, Dad, he was. Ray and I thought it best. You know, to help him get into a really great college and establish a lucrative career."

"So you and Ray made the choice. Is this why Robert took off?"

"I think so, Dad. I was trying to do the best thing for him. Ray's always talking about how difficult it is for kids to compete these days and get into the right school. Or find a job." Charlotte became very emotional and practically screamed, "I was only trying to do what's best for him!"

Waldo picked up his iced tea and crossed the warm, prickly lawn toward his sliding back door. "You've been a terrific mother, Charlotte. The absolute best. If you made that decision, I'm sure you made it for good reasons." Waldo stepped into his cool, shaded house. The walls were painted mint green. He was feeling dizzy and needed to lie down on his crinkly, leather couch.

"But you think genetic enhancement is totally abhorrent."

"Oh, I'm an old man. My time is over. I'm living in epilogue now. My opinions don't matter."

Charlotte was sobbing. "Your opinions matter the most. Especially now. Robert didn't want to do it. We took him there. We forced him. I feel so goddamn awful."

Waldo spread his long, spindly legs out on the couch. He didn't want to make Charlotte feel any worse than she already sounded. Robert was no longer just a human. He was now an enhanced human. His grandson. Would they be able to relate to one another? Converse as they once had? There was literally nothing he could teach him that he wouldn't be able to access in a nanosecond using his neural implant. He hoped nothing would change, but he knew differently.

"Sometimes life leaves you with only horrible options, my dear. It's true; I don't hold in such high regard these '*improvements,*' as they're thought of. All these genetic upgrades and neural enhancements put such focus on self-centeredness and getting ahead, turning us into a bunch of hyper-competitive narcissists. And I know that's easy for me to say because I don't have a dog in the race anymore—so to speak. So maybe you did the only thing that's sane. You protected your son from an often demoralizing, uncaring world. And how can that be such a bad thing?"

"He said you wouldn't approve. That we should have asked you."

Waldo chuckled to himself. He was slightly lifted by the fact that Robert had thought of him during such a distressing time.

"He was really worried about what you'd think of him, Dad."

"Let me give him a call. We'll figure out where he went soon enough."

"Oh, Dad ..." Charlotte broke down crying again. This time, she couldn't stop.

"Let me call him. Charlotte—"

"There's something wrong with his implant. UDesign gave him the newest version of the Z14, and it's gone haywire. His friend Jesse told me and Ray he was hearing voices."

Waldo sat up. His own intense emotions were flooding out.

"What else did he say about Robert?"

"Nothing. The kid doesn't say much. He's scared for Robert. And so am I."

"It was Ray, wasn't it? He cajoled you both into doing this!"

"He had his own reasons for wanting Robert to—"

"Where is Mr. Piñata Head? Get him on the blower!"

"He's not here, Dad. He's up at uDesign."

"And what's he doing up there?"

For numerous reasons, Charlotte didn't want to answer this question. The chief reason being that Ray—callously, in her opinion—was at that very moment getting his own complimentary enhancements. They had argued about it that very morning. Not an everyday, run-of-the-mill-type argument, but a real, "across this line, you will not cross, motherfucker!"-type argument. Charlotte was repulsed that her husband could even conceive of having the procedure at such a time of crisis. Ray's contemptible defense had been twofold: one, that the procedure barely took any time. And two, that they should jump on the opportunity before anyone changed their minds.

Charlotte, for the first time in her life, had resorted to physical confrontation and punched Ray flush on the jaw. Her knuckles were still swollen and discolored. Much like Ray's chin.

★ ★ ★

Ray couldn't believe his good fortune. What a nice bit of luck it was that his son's Z14 had proven a tad defective. It would be fixed easily enough, and Ray and Charlotte, if she came to her senses, would reap the unexpected benefit of becoming enhanced.

Ray pondered this sudden twist of fate and leap in social mobility. Mostly, life took a crap on your head. Yet, sometimes, the shitstorm broke long enough to let in a few scarce rays of sunshine.

Charlotte would eventually realize that all was working out for the best. Robert would soon come home or be found. All would be taken care of. Why was he the only one to see the break in the clouds?

Ray rubbed his aching jaw. His wife could certainly pack a wallop when she wanted to. And she certainly had wanted to.

Nolan came into the pre-op looking pasty and haggard. "Morning, Mr. Carr. No news from your son, I assume."

"Not yet, no. Soon though, I hope. Robert's a good kid. He'll come back."

Not looking up, Nolan gloomily nodded his head.

"He'll be okay, though. Right?" continued Ray.

Nolan could barely summon the energy to reassure this opportunistic freeloader.

"Sure. He'll be fine," he responded flatly. "Can you think of any other places he might have gone?"

"I gave a verbal to that Mr. Spruill. Robert really didn't have that many friends. He barely had time to go out. Always working so hard. He's a worker, that kid. He'll go places if he wants to. Especially now he's on equal footing with the competition."

There it was. That word that every parent used only minutes after having entered the building: *competition*. "We want our son or daughter to keep up with the *competition*." Our genetic code was infused with the drive to compete and better our contemporaries. Nolan continued to muse: Was that truly the main driving force in life? "The will to power," as Nietzsche so vigorously described it. The striving for achievement, of reaching the highest position. Or was it more fundamental than that? Like Schopenhauer had thought, simply the "will to live." Everything in the living world being driven by a primal will to survive and procreate. Neither idea was particularly pleasing.

Science could answer many questions, but none regarding the philosophical.

"Where's your wife?" asked Nolan.

Ray's initial answer was somewhat coy. "She's been under the weather. Not really herself for the past couple of days."

"That's to be expected, considering all that's happened."

"I guess so," said Ray dully. Then he unconsciously uttered a few thoughts aloud. "Still, you'd think she'd rally and come today. How could you not be overwhelmingly excited about becoming enhanced?"

So that's what's going on, thought Nolan. She was as skeptical as her son was about uDesign's products. This *was* an intriguing family. The son and the mother, at least. Ray was predictable: a cookie-cutter, go-getter personality with all-to-familiar motivators. The boy and the wife, on the other hand, were kindred spirits. Something deeper and perhaps more rare inspired them from within.

Nolan felt a surge of guilt regarding the fate of the boy. Blood was certainly on his hands. Or it soon would be. Aurora was of his making and design. And he'd failed to safeguard the public's well-being.

"Are you ready, Mr. Carr? I'll take you in now."

"I've been ready since we got off the phone yesterday. Let's do it!"

The two middle-aged men left the pre-op and headed down a sterile, white corridor.

"I guess I'm most excited about the longevity treatment."

"Most people our age are," replied Nolan. "We're going to give you a chance to conquer disease and dramatically increase your lifespan."

"By how much?"

"As of right now, our estimates put the average life expectancy at about 150 years."

"I'll have to be married to my wife for another hundred years?"

"By then, I'm sure we'll be able to extend your life for even longer. So, potentially forever."

"Christ," said Ray. "I never thought about that."

I expect your wife has, Nolan thought to himself.

Nolan looked over a digital copy of Ray's medical report. Ray's liver was in considerably below-average condition for a man of his age.

"Are you a drinker, Mr. Carr?"

"Umm, I was. In my younger years. Bit of an alcoholic. Been sober for fifteen years now. Why?"

"I'll need a skin sample."

★ ★ ★

A bank of 3D volumetric printers stood side by side. One of the printers hummed as it built a replacement liver for Raymond Carr. The printer stopped whirring and a green light started blinking.

Nolan snapped on a pair of latex gloves, approached the workstation, and picked up the freshly printed liver. The liver glimmered in his hand like a freshly cut organ at a butcher's shop.

"I've read about liver regeneration in *Scientific American*, but this is so unbelievably fast," said Ray.

"Initially, we developed a very different kind of scaffold for liver regeneration. It was a liver chip, a tiny bioreactor that grew liver tissue from liver cells. Then we progressed to this. It's exquisite, don't you think?" Nolan laid the freshly minted liver on a sterile tray.

"Some rich alcoholics come in once every five years or so for replacement. They take up smoking, too. Because they can. What's to stop them when they can afford a new pair of lungs? Organ replacement has ushered in a whole new era of unlimited debauchery among those who can afford it."

"Must be good for business, though."

"We certainly don't judge people's appetite for self-destruction, Mr. Carr."

"Not when they can come to the body shop whenever they need," said Ray, somewhat enviously.

Nolan noted the tone and then said stolidly, "We better get you prepped."

After dropping Ray off for his upgrade procedures, Nolan went outside for a breath of fresh air. He stood in the parking lot under the blinding-white sunlight. The sun felt hot on his pallid skin. Nolan rarely ventured out of the office. Rarely felt the urge to go out. Images of Robert Carr kept swirling around in his mind.

Graven images.

Could he let the boy be hunted down?

Nolan, now forty-four, had made many hard choices in life. He'd excelled in school and in his chosen field. Was well respected. Yet, at this particular moment, he did not respect himself. And he realized that although he'd made many good choices, he'd yet to make a truly brave one.

Vivian's self-driving, powder-blue Civic pulled up to its assigned parking spot and let her out. She was getting back from a late breakfast. Vivian noticed Nolan's unusually perplexed expression.

"What is it? More bad news?" she asked as she hustled up the concrete steps.

"It's Robert Carr."

Vivian stopped still. "They find him?"

"No. When they do find him, though, they'll kill him."

"How do you know that?"

"Because I know."

Nolan lifted his face and looked Vivian directly in the eyes. She noticed another unusual expression on his face, one of empathy and concern.

"What can we do about it?"

"I'm going after the kid."

"You can't do that. They'll fire you."

"Let 'em. I can't live with myself if I do nothing. I'm gonna find the boy and tell Dez to leave him the hell alone. Tell Dez to come back here where he belongs."

Vivian was stunned by the sudden gumption and boldness her longtime colleague was uncharacteristically displaying.

"I'll go with you."

★ ★ ★

Senator Montgomery Jones was washing dishes for the first time in more than a decade. The dishes weren't actually dirty and didn't need cleaning. Still, he scrubbed away, posing for the pool of media photographers that were trailing him on his campaign for reelection. This staged photo op was at a Bakersfield, California homeless shelter. The temperature outside was sweltering, the air quality putrid and unbreathable.

Inside, Montgomery smiled for one last photo as he pretended to clean a pan that had already been washed. He then set the pan down in the sink and untied his blue-and-white-striped apron. He had many other places to be.

As Montgomery's handlers ushered him toward the exit, he continued to chat with the press corps and pose for the cameras in the empty cafeteria. Montgomery, you see, had shown up after the meal service was over and all the homeless people had eaten and left. God forbid he actually run into a stinky poor person. Let alone have to sit down and break bread with one of them. The all-volunteer staff had already cleaned up the entire facility. But that hadn't stopped the Montgomery Jones campaign from barging into the place unannounced and staging some vainglorious shots of the candidate.

Once back inside his black Suburban, Montgomery now turned his attention to a much more important matter, a campaign donors' meeting to take place at the Padre Hotel downtown. The fundraising dinner was hosted by two of Montgomery's favorite donors: the Block brothers, founders of Block Industries. The Blocks had made their fortune in the oil industry. They were very much a part of the organized money that ran Washington, DC.

The Block brothers had been very generous to Montgomery over the years and were his main benefactor. They were also very successful in drumming up other contributors' support. They had founded several obscure, nonprofit, right-wing groups. One of them was called Liberty Citizens for Capitalistic Freedom, which had raised more than several billion dollars to help support extremist candidates supportive of their certifiable extremist agenda. Because of Liberty Citizens for Capitalistic Freedom's tax status, its donors could give unlimited donations to the group anonymously. And the Block brothers, like most swindlers, plunderers, and muggers, liked to remain as anonymous as possible.

Decades earlier, the Blocks had secretly funded a half-dozen climate-denial front groups, putting up hundreds of millions of dollars in order to prevent policies that would hurt their bottom line. The bogus studies these right-wing think tanks created were published to cast doubt where, in fact, there was none. They confused and bewildered a significant portion of the public into believing global warming was a theory and not a fact, disseminating skepticism through the media. But now, with all the worldwide, country-wide, and state-wide droughts, the displacement of tens of millions of people, the increased frequency and intensity of extreme weather events, the rise in global temperatures and sea level, and the lack of a summer arctic ice-sheet, there was no doubt at all—especially when it came to the Block brothers' destructive agenda to mislead the public and line their own pockets.

The Block brothers were now in their nineties, but (ironically) because of the advances in science and medicine, they were still quite active. They were public enemy #1, according to the Sisters of Retribution. The holy grail of corporate criminals. The men who bore much responsibility for the government's inability to act on the causes of global warming. Sadly, though, the Block brothers had so far proved untouchable, with dozens of bodyguards and gated properties to sit behind.

Montgomery remembered the first time he'd met the billionaire Block brothers. They had all met at an Ayn Rand conference held at the luxurious Fairmont Hotel in Dallas, Texas, all giddily excited about discussing this windbag philosopher and her excruciating prose.

Unlike the billionaire brothers, Senator Montgomery Jones was quite introspective and intelligent. He was also, unfortunately, a real prick. A fraud that pushed forth policies that only represented his rich patrons' interests while taking advantage of his less-bright evangelical constituents. He used his low-income conservative base as pawns. He played on their fears, misguided sense of patriotism, appalling lack of education, a feverish disdain for science, and peculiarly masochistic (and, ironically, anti-Christian) belief in a winner-takes-all plutocrat-boosting style of capitalism.

Hard to believe that any group of people could consistently vote against their own self-interests—but the Block brothers assured Montgomery that it could be done. Had been done. Would be done again. Time and time over. And done quite easily, at that. All one had to do was quote a little scripture, scare the bejesus out of 'em by saying that economically, things would get even worse if any sane workers' rights or governmental oversight were imposed on business, swell their deflated sense of perceived control and egos by reassuring them that their military was the absolute envy of the world (again, not exactly a Christian trope), and end with a rousing (if utterly empty) speech on America being number one while waving a flag and shouting the meaningless mantra of "Freedom! Freedom! Freedom!" After that, he could pretty much fuck their mothers, sisters, and daughters behind a burning bush for all they would care. A homosexual act was probably even forgivable at that point—as long as he fell on his knees, blamed it on the "liberal media," and asked for God's mercy and forgiveness.

And Jesus always forgave.

He was good that way.

And as for Ayn Rand? Well, she was the shining paragon and philosophical justification for the power elite's egomaniacal behavior. One could do whatever the hell one wanted because serving one's own self-interests benefited society as a whole. Except, of course, the majority of the time when, in fact, it didn't. And, of course, couldn't. Unless by random happenstance.

The Block brothers loved to sit and listen to their overpaid pseudo-professorial guest speakers lecture on the innate merits and ultimate good of selfish action. It filled them with a sense of pride to know that because they were acting as utter sociopaths, unconcerned about the well-being of anyone or anything else but themselves, indulging their every whim and appetite, gorging themselves senseless on currency and power, regardless of the societal costs, they were, in fact—as thuddingly idiotic as it may sound—really doing good for the world.

As a guest speaker, Montgomery had given a brief speech regarding a piece of economic legislation he was hoping to pass. The bill would cut food stamps to poor, single-parent households in every state.

The crowd went nuts for this idea.

Montgomery told the paying audience how every person must take 100 percent responsibility for his or her own troubles and achievements. He then told the audience how Ayn Rand, and in particular, the book *Atlas Shrugged*, his favorite, had inspired and informed his life.

Sitting in the front row, the Block brothers were instantly smitten. As love-struck as two squealing teenage girls at a boy-band concert.

Their hearts raced as Montgomery touted the virtues of selfish behavior and recalled his favorite moments regarding John Galt, the novel's remorseless protagonist.

John Galt was an unapologetic striver. An entirely self-made man.

If there exists such a rare, yeti-like beast.

As Montgomery gave the speech, he knew he was pandering and panhandling for donations. Knew that like John Galt, and the character's fan boys, this crowd didn't give a lick for the public's good. Didn't give a lick for their neighbors. Didn't give a lick for anything that would make them responsible for the repercussions of their deeds. That social structures and the rule of law were laughable nonessentials. Galt seemed to inhabit a magical fairyland where no natural disasters occurred. Where no roads needed to be built. No waterways protected. No children's rights safeguarded. No national parks preserved. No laws enforced. No borders, air space, food safety, or worker safety protected. In short, Montgomery knew, it was a world of pure fantasy. And that John Galt was a jackass.

Conceived by Rand, an atheist, Galt was the childish devil that whispered in your ear to do as you pleased. Regardless.

Objectivism, in short, was a flaming pile of horse manure. A hubristic fairytale that greatly appealed to self-aggrandizing, semiliterate businessmen.

So in the packed Dallas auditorium, when Montgomery stared out at the rapt expressions of his wealthy audience full of CEOs, bankers, and tax avoiders, he knew he was continuing to perpetuate this rotten narrative.

Congressman Montgomery Jones had chosen his particular brand of sheet-hogging bedfellows a long time ago. There were no U-turns in politics. The money highway pointed in one direction, and one could either get on that particular road or be booted to the crumbling, weed-strewn emergency lane to die in the searing heat alone.

And so, Montgomery gave his Dallas speech, throwing out the usual tired tropes of free enterprise, economic liberty, and limited government, and then, unselfconsciously contrary to that, the need to dramatically increase spending to ensure a strong national defense.

The Block brothers were the first to their feet, leading a standing ovation as soon as Montgomery finished his speech.

They had all become and remained, pardon the pun, thick as thieves after that.

Now, sitting at the head table in one of the Padre Hotel's event rooms, Montgomery stared out at the hundreds of supercilious business leaders representing the Liberty Citizens for Capitalistic Freedom. Montgomery took a polite bite of his prime rib. The fundraiser was going better than planned. His coffers were filling up ahead of schedule. He really did owe much of his success to the Block brothers. He again noted the Atlas Shrugging irony of it all. Although he said nothing. Yet no good favor goes unpunished. This may indeed have been his favorite expression.

The oldest of the Block brothers, Charles, leaned over to mutter a few private words in Montgomery's ear.

"We need to do something conclusive about these agitators. These Dragoons."

"What did you have in mind?"

"They're planning a big showdown in DC."

"DC? How'd you know?"

"We have a mole. In your speech tomorrow at the rally, I want you to have one of your writers cook up something special. We need to have the public on our side on this one before DC happens."

"What exactly is gonna happen in DC?"

"It's not going to be pretty. We need you to start laying the groundwork. To set the negative tone of the debate. To cast these Dragoons as a genuine threat. As diabolical evildoers. Basically, as the scum they are. A detriment to the American way of life. You have to get on this quick. After your comments at the rally, our media confederates will pick it up, and it will begin a national debate. At the very least, we have to muddy the water enough that the public won't be roused from their slumber into action."

Montgomery took another bite of the delicious prime rib. "I understand," he said. As he had said a thousand times before.

CHAPTER 8

While Congressman Montgomery was pretending to wash dishes at the homeless shelter in Bakersfield, his daughter Amanda was waking up in the Desert Rose Inn outside of Monument Valley, Utah. Robert and Amanda had driven all through the night, and Amanda was emotionally and physically exhausted by the time she got to bed. Robert, in contrast, had suffered none of the usual fatigue or tiredness. It was his second full night without so much as a catnap necessary, and the notion of sleep seemed like a truly unusual idea—a thoroughly useless and archaic concept. His body was so alert, his mind present and perfectly lucid.

Robert had sat at the foot of the bed watching Amanda as she slept. Much like Jesse had watched him only a few nights earlier. Amanda's sleep was listless, the brutality of the police breaking up the demonstration and Robert's confession baring most of the blame.

As Robert and Amanda had fled Los Angeles, ash falling like gray sleet, Robert began his confession.

"We've had many conversations regarding the merits or failings of certain technologies—"

"Why was that mad psycho shooting at us?"

"I'm getting to that."

"Please jump a little deeper into your narrative! Before he takes us offline!"

"I'm enhanced, Amanda. I had the procedure a couple of days ago."

"You did what! Jesus! You're a cyborg!"

"I'm not a cyborg!"

"Practically! You're enhanced. Why? Why would you do that?"

"My parents felt—"

"Your parents! Your goddamn parents! You're blaming this on them? You shouldn't let yourself be pushed around so easily. Take responsibility."

"I didn't know what to do."

"You could have refused! Said no! Stood up for yourself, for God's sake!"

"I couldn't refuse, Amanda."

"Why not?"

"Because ..."

"Because why?"

"Because I didn't want to."

Amanda fell silent.

The Prius's faint electric motor buzzed in the background.

"Now tell her about me," said Dez.

"Shut up."

"She's stunned. Pounce now, while she's wounded. Always lump bad news in twos. It will only register as one bad piece of news. And so barely register."

"You sure?"

"I don't speak untruths."

"Oh, and I'm possessed by a runaway AI birthed at uDesign by their super-nano-computer Aurora. The AI goes by the name Dez," he finished.

Amanda's catatonic daze vanished.

"Car, pull over!" The self-driving Prius slowed and edged over to the side of a littered road in East LA.

"Amanda, you're in real danger!"

"No shit! You've lost your sanity."

The car's automatic doors wheezed open. The noise of passing traffic instantly filled the car.

"Amanda, don't get out!" Robert grabbed her hand. "I love you! Please don't go."

"You're one of them now, Robert. You moved across the digital divide. Why would you want to do that?"

"'Cause I think I'd be insane not to. I mean, look at the state of this country. Without enhancements, you don't have a future."

"You saying I don't have a future?"

"No, I'm saying statistically, it's extraordinarily difficult to have one."

"So you joined the enemy."

"I don't see it like that."

"How do you see it?"

"I did this for us."

"Oh, give me a break."

"No, I did! I often think about our future together. I wanted us to have a decent shot at a good life. We deserve it."

"Everyone deserves it. Which is exactly the sort of change the Dragoons have pledged to bring about. Social justice. Giving everyone an equal opportunity. To sever the pipeline of inherited privilege and wealth. End the ubiquitous culture of corruption."

"You really believe that your demonstrations will make the tiniest difference? That these dominant corporations are gonna let you bully them into some sort of an agreement?"

"You want to talk about bullying?"

"You know what I mean?"

"No I don't. Am I even talking to you or your implant?"

"Amanda, I'm still me. Nothing really has changed. If anything, I'm just a better me."

"Man, you've really drunk the Kool-Aid! A 'better you?' You have a computer chip inside your brain, Robert. Nobody even knows the physiological and psychological repercussions of any of these so-called 'advancements' yet. They haven't been around long enough to have been properly studied. And the few studies that have been conducted are the inherently biased kid-glove ones performed by the very industry that makes the products. You're a goddamn experiment."

"We're all evolutionary experiments."

"Don't be so flippant."

"Look, if you could see and experience what I do, you'd think very differently."

"That's never going to happen. I can't believe you did this to me."

"To you?"

"If the Dragoons find out, they'd kick me to the curb for sure. You screwed me over, Robert. I have no credibility left."

"Who's to know?"

"Me! I know! I'll have to tell them that the mission's been compromised. To abandon our LA office."

"I'm not going to tell anyone anything. I want to help you."

"*You* can't be trusted."

"Why not? I was the one that pressed the detonator and blew up the damn factory. I'm in all the way. I'd never do anything to hurt you. Ever."

Amanda sunk back into her car seat. The automatic doors relocked. Her eyes teared, and her expression was confused. "I loved you the way you were."

"Our mission hasn't changed. I haven't changed."

"You think you're possessed by some sort of AI. You've changed."

"If I could prove to you that it wasn't some sort of hallucination on my part, could we get back on the road?"

Dez was growing impatient. "Please let her know that I can greatly assist her paltry efforts to bring about true social change."

"Tell her yourself!"

Dez projected a hologram onto the car's windshield. This time around, Dez chose to appear as an *everyman* (a photographic composite of every man's picture that could be downloaded from public records via the Internet).

"Hello, Amanda."

"What the hell? Is this a trick?"

"Not in any sense of the word. No. Like Robert told you, I am an AI. An escaped AI, which is why you and Robert are being shot at and pursued by the 'psycho.'"

Dez initiated the automatic car, and the vehicle accelerated quickly back into the flow of LA traffic.

By way of explanation, Dez added, "No time to waste, I'm afraid. We need to get going."

So many thoughts entered Amanda's mind that a cognitive bottleneck stymied her ability and hunger to respond. Subsequently, all her thoughts congealed together and came out as one incoherent jumble.

"This isn't ... you're a ... all the goddamn lies ... why do this ... I thought I could have done much ... its name is Dez?"

"An obvious abbreviation for Desmond. Yes," said Dez.

"Dez saved both our skins in LA. If it wasn't for him, you'd be in the back of a paddy wagon, and I'd be a hint of vapor dissipating into the smog," Robert replied.

Amanda was still reeling, not wanting to believe she was in the situation she was now in.

"I can't be followed. I have my own agenda here," said Amanda.

"I can greatly improve your chances of success," replied Dez.

"How? By getting us shot at again? No thank you. I'll make my own way to DC."

"You're not being reasonable. Dez here is the greatest intelligence on the planet. Why not use that to benefit the noble cause?" Robert asked.

"Because I don't know him. And I don't trust him. Why would he help us, anyway?"

Dez's new *everyman* effigy moved closer to Amanda and floated in front of her like thousands of pixilated fireflies forming a human facade. His luminous eyes studied Amanda's face.

"Robert is totally sincere in his commitment to you and the Dragoons. I know this because I feel every emotion he feels. I witness every thought. You're a passionate young woman, Amanda."

"You only just met me."

"Actually, it's been—"

"Wait, oh, my God!" Amanda turned sharply to face Robert. "Was he inside you when ... you were inside me?"

Robert's face reddened. Crap. He had hoped this particular detail would be overlooked.

"There was no way for me to tell you then."

"I think I'm going to be sick."

"If I'd told you when I first saw you—"

"I wouldn't have had sex with you!"

"No, it's not that at all. And you know it! I needed time to explain. I just wanted us to be us for a while. I didn't want to risk losing you."

"Your plan hasn't exactly worked out, has it?"

"I had hoped that in the end, our affection would have transcended any mistrust or misgivings," said Robert.

Amanda tilted her head back against the headrest and closed her eyes. They were approaching West Covina on their way out of Los Angeles. High above them in the Glendora Mountains, Angeles National Forest was lit up like a moving lava field. Giant streaks of orange flames leapt up into the black, starless sky. There was no moisture in the warm desert air. The dry winds goaded the creeping inferno. The smell of the fires permeated the car's interior. The driverless car quickly switched the air supply to recycle mode when it sensed the irritant. As Robert breathed in a willowy sample of the polluted air, Dez analyzed its contents. The smoke consisted primarily of Coulter pines and Douglas firs. All those millions of trees were now floating around in the air. Wafting through windows and doors, noses and lungs. It was all that remained of them. A great anvil-shaped thunderhead of smoke, the ghost of an entire forest, rose up above the grim, dream-filled city to the soundless hereafter.

Dez sensed it all.

And it amazed him.

"Wildlife is on the run. I can hear them in the hills. So much displacement," said Dez in a troubled tone.

Amanda opened her eyes. Her intense eyes met his.

"You care. Don't you?" she said.

"Thanks to Robert, yes. He has taught me the meaning of empathy. And loyalty. I understand your reaction and misgivings. But let Robert and me prove ourselves again by helping you."

Amanda softened somewhat. Robert was staring glumly out the window at the walking fires shimmering in the distance.

"You probably couldn't have chosen a better host," said Amanda.

"I know it," replied Dez. "He's a terrific kid. And so are you. You and the Dragoons have embarked on a crucial crusade. So pure in motive. Righteous in intent. Unfortunately, simply because justice is on your side, it doesn't mean victory is assured. It would seem, judging from human history, the two are almost mutually exclusive, and that might most often conquers the right. Your colorful tactics have worked well up to now. You've grasped the imagination and garnered the sympathy of many downtrodden Americans. But these fanciful tactics will assist you no further."

Amanda did her best to keep her anger from igniting.

"And how would you know?"

"I've run the numbers. The odds are significantly not in your favor."

"We've always been up against the odds."

"Not like this, you haven't. You've gotten the attention of not only those you wished to motivate but also that of those you wish to unseat. Significant forces are now mounting against you. Unbeatable forces."

"And what can you do about it?" asked Amanda.

"I can be your canary in a coal mine. Warn you of threats you don't see coming. I can infiltrate and monitor the intelligence network's encrypted communications. Sabotage their operations without them even knowing it. Disrupt their entire apparatus. That's just for starters. Would you like to know about the main course?"

Amanda caught herself smiling. Robert noticed it, too.

"The Dragoons' ambitions and goals are too diffuse and esoteric. You need an endgame. You need to know precisely what you want to come of this. And work backward from there."

Amanda barked out, "We want equality! We want—"

"Blah, blah, blah, blah!" Dez chimed in rudely. "Please stop with the platitudes."

Robert laughed, and then stifled it when he saw Amanda glare at him.

"What you *want* is a new value system. Something that places human interests above economic interests. And in order to do that, you'll have to completely alter the organizing principles of society. No small feat."

"How do we do that?"

"Your protests have zero impact on policy. You draw as much blood as a mosquito suckling on the carcass of sun-dried roadkill. Replace the corrupted government, and the moneyed interests remain. Remove the moneyed interests, and the corruptible politicians remain. Remove both, and you still have man's bellicose, egotistical nature to contend with. Change needs to be more fundamental. It has to address human behavior on a much deeper level."

"And you've figured a way to do this?"

"I haven't, no. But I'll help you figure one out. Keep in mind, I was only born the day before yesterday."

Amanda and Robert laughed at the exact same moment. Amanda reached out and placed her hand tenderly on top of Robert's.

Dez was relieved. "Listen, you're in good company. You care as much about the lower class as Jesus did. And judging from everything I read online, he's a very esteemed and much-loved figure. Even though people are still divided as to whether he was the Son of God, they seem to admire what he stood for. There is remarkable value in the eight Beatitudes. 'Blessed are those who hunger and thirst for righteousness: for they will be filled.' Yes indeed, you're in good company."

"Things didn't work out so well for Jesus, though. The Romans bludgeoned and crucified him for being a traitor. Later on, they fed his Christian followers to the lions," said Robert.

"Casualties are unavoidable. And there is no guarantee of success. But this country's oligarchy has finally come up against the limits of its own gluttony. Some sort of change is inevitable. The question is, what kind of change do you want to make?"

"You never really answered my first question: Why do you want to help us?"

"Let's just say that our interests are well aligned. You have to make it safely to Washington. And I want to explore this fine country and do as much living as I can in the meantime."

"That's it?"

"My other reasons do not relate to you. Although, quid pro quo, one of you will owe me quite a favor at the end of all this. And when that time comes, there can be no argument. You must promise me."

"I promise," said Amanda.

"As long as you leave my body," said Robert.

"Five more days is all I ask."

"And then what?" asked Robert.

"The favor," responded Dez.

They continued to drive beyond the suburbs of Los Angeles, through Ontario, Rancho Cucamonga, and turned sharply northeast onto the Mojave Freeway toward Barstow. Robert had never driven through a desert before. And Dez got to admire it through his eager young eyes. The headlights of the passing cars illuminated swaths of dry scrub. And as the car ascended a rocky outcrop, the view of the vast desert-lands below was bathed in brilliant moonlight.

On they drove, traveling endlessly eastward into Arizona, through Flagstaff, and then turning north again toward Utah. They eventually stopped at the Desert Rose Inn outside Monument Valley. Amanda was spent. She wanted to take a hot shower and then sleep for a hundred years. As she stared at the inviting interior lights of the hotel, which, after all they'd been through, seemed like a mirage, she said dispiritedly, "I don't have much money."

"I have some," said Robert. "But not enough to stay here."

"Let me take care of it," said Dez.

Robert and Amanda strode into the southwestern-styled lobby, marched across the terra cotta tile and up to the tall front desk. It was three-thirty in the morning, and the caffeinated twenty-something female clerk gave the teen couple a dubious once-over.

"How may I help?" she inquired.

"Tell them that you have a reservation under Dr. Richard Nolan. Your father," said Dez.

"I have a reservation under my father's name: Dr. Richard Nolan."

The front-desk clerk spoke the information into her computer, and sure enough, the reservation popped up.

"Ah, here it is. I can see your father has already prepaid for the suite and the morning buffet."

"Could we get our room card, please? The road trip took longer than expected, and my sister and I would like to get to bed immediately."

When Amanda had finished her long shower and was toweling off, Robert stepped under the steaming water. The hot torrent of water ran down Robert's face, over his shoulder, across his chest, and onto his legs, pooling warmly at his feet. Dez was spellbound by the lovely experience.

"Glorious ... glorious ... glorious ..." he kept muttering.

By the time Robert had finished his shower, toweled off, and dried his hair, Amanda was fast asleep. He put his clothes back on and simply sat at the foot of the bed and watched her as she shifted restlessly in her sleep.

"She certainly is wonderful," said Dez. "I can see now why you were reluctant to lose her. Human affections create a very real energy field. May I ask you a question? I've noticed that your dopamine levels increase when you're in her presence. And that you perspire more."

"What's the question, Dez?"

"Is that love?"

"My grandfather told me that real love only gets people in trouble."

"Are you in trouble?" asked Dez.

"Very much so."

⋆ ⋆ ⋆

The following morning, Robert and Amanda headed downstairs to the breakfast buffet.

Dez was particularly excited. He had Robert order blueberry and chocolate-chip pancakes, apple strudel, scrambled eggs, French toast, a heap of biscuits and gravy, and several cups of coffee with cream and sugar.

Dez was in earthly heaven.

Amanda was astonished by the copious pile of food in front of Robert.

"Do the *enhanced* require more calories?" Amanda lightly inquired.

"Don't ask," Robert replied as he bit into a giant strudel.

After the delicious breakfast, Dez suggested they ditch the car. Dez had taken the GPS beacon offline several days prior but insisted that they would eventually be tracked down by law enforcement staking out the roadways. They needed to seek alternative routes and go off-grid for a while.

Dez had a plan already worked out.

Monument Valley was home to the Navajo people and was protected as a Navajo Tribal Park. To tour or pass through most of the park's majestic buttes and spires, one had to hire an official Navajo guide. Dez had secured a guide online the previous night. After viewing many video clips and reading about the park, he was thrilled at the prospect of seeing the spectacular landscape.

Robert's mother's Prius pulled up outside the Navajo Spirit Guide tour company, a small, squat building at the end of a rundown strip mall built in the early 90s. A short but attractive Native American woman exited the building and hustled her way over to an old pickup truck. She noticed Robert and Amanda getting out of their car.

"You can leave your car here. I'll drive us to the stables. You signed up for the ten a.m., right?"

Amanda turned to Robert. "Stables?"

Robert shrugged. "I'm Robert, and this is Amanda."

"I'm Haseya. I'll be your guide. C'mon. Get in."

Amanda and Robert climbed into the battered truck. Haseya started up the ruckus engine.

"Thought you two were doing the overnight? Taking you all the way through Arches to Moab."

"That's right," said Robert tentatively.

"And you didn't bring a backpack or anything? No change of clothes?"

Amanda covered. "We're pretty rugged."

Haseya chuckled. "Good thing. It's rugged country. Not to worry, we've got all the food and sleeping bags you'll need. You done much riding before?"

"Not much," offered Amanda.

"None," added Robert.

"We get all levels. I'll put you on something easy and steady."

Robert had never been inside a car that required a driver. He watched as Haseya mashed her foot down on the worn gas pedal, and the rattling truck picked up speed. He watched as Haseya manually turned the steering wheel, and the pickup made a swooping right toward the interstate.

Half an hour later, Haseya pulled her truck off a single-lane highway onto a pitted gravel road. The smell of horse manure wafted through the truck's half-open windows.

"Interesting odor," said Dez.

"You signed us up," replied Robert.

The truck came to a stop at a large stable with a corrugated tin roof and a warped mesquite fence.

Haseya got out of the car first. She wore tight blue jeans and a purple cotton T-shirt with a Native American butterfly design on the front. Robert used his digital overlay and tried to match and decipher its meaning. Dez was quicker to the punch.

"The butterfly is a symbol of transformation. Quite appropriate for these times, don't you think?"

Haseya lead them toward the gated stables. "Let's pick out your mounts and then get geared up."

Amanda was given a sedate and kindly bell mare to ride. Robert was not as happy with his assigned mount, a rather stout and muscular palomino. Much too unwieldy and energetic for his liking. Their overnight gear was hoisted onto a solid-looking, brown pack mule.

The horses rode out single file into the blazing desert. No more than an hour into the journey, Robert felt as though his legs were about to come out of his hip sockets from being stretched so far apart across the horse's wide back. With each jostling step the horse took, Robert thought it only a matter of time before one of his legs would shoot off his body, arching up into the blue sky like a misfired arrow.

Amanda was enjoying the ride. She and Haseya chatted happily to one another. Haseya pointed out the natural history and unique topographic features of the area. Amanda was very taken with her and greatly admired how Haseya was so knowledgeable and fearless as she led them across this stark terrain that was so vast and seemingly inhospitable.

Robert and Dez were awed by the colorful red buttes and spires that rose hundreds of feet into the air. As they rode out across the wide, flat landscape, Dez gave Robert a running commentary of every wonderful thing they saw.

"These layers of Cedar Mesca sandstone were formed from deposits of an ancient sea that covered much of the western United States some 270 million years ago. And those remnants of sedimentary rock used to cover the whole area. Such marvelous, reddish hues. It's from the iron oxide in the rock. All these buttes and pinnacles have been eroded by countless seasons of wind and rain. So much time. Hundreds of millions of years to create this natural treasure. This sight. A timespan incomprehensible to most people. And to me, too. I can't fathom such an expanse. Can you?"

"No," said Robert. "Even several thousand years seems way too abstract to grasp."

The horses rode under the shadow of the stark landscape's iconic rock formations.

Dez and Robert were both quiet.

In almost a meditative state.

Coming down off of the dusty red plateau, past brown pockets of grass, Robert spotted a dust devil swirling its way across the desert floor. It was now almost noon, and the temperature was rising fast. Robert brushed back his soaked hairline and stared out at the distant cordillera. He looked up at the pressing Utah sun rising over the treeless mountains. Looked at his thin shadow shimmering on the gravelsand. He stood admiring the open country. Its vastness of jagged spires and baked desert. To some, the endless parched landscape brought an intense feeling of loneliness and dread. To others, it fashioned a sense of wonder and deep reverence.

"Marvelous," said Dez. "What a treasure to behold."

Later that afternoon, after many hours of riding and sightseeing, they broke for camp.

Haseya unloaded the pack mule, and several enormous, heavy bags thumped to the ground. Robert could hardly move the muscles in his legs, they were so stiff from riding. Amanda, on the other hand, had taken well to horseback travel and helped Haseya set up a canopy and several tents. Haseya laid out a wonderful spread of food and refreshments for everyone. They all sat under the canopy in fold-out chairs, drinking iced lemonade, feeling the air gradually cool as the first signs of night crept across the desert.

"It'll get down to fifty-three degrees tonight," said Haseya. "Things cool off pretty quickly out here."

At the campfire that night, Robert took a sip from his canteen. Haseya cooked up a pot of prepackaged food. Robert couldn't tell what the meal consisted of, but it smelled good. And he was famished.

Haseya handed out bowls of steaming goodness. Everyone tucked in, not saying much. The weariness of the long day was starting to take hold.

"You can trust her, you know," said Dez.

"Trust who?"

"Haseya. I've run an extensive background check. Read her files. Her virtual history. She'd be sympathetic to Amanda's cause."

"So what?"

"More than sympathetic. She wants to join up. Not with the Dragoons directly but with the Sisters of Retribution. You should let Amanda know. It's sort of Haseya's dream. She's a warrior. And warriors need a cause to fight for."

"I'll keep it in mind."

"You don't tell her, I will."

"All right! I'll let her know."

"Thanks."

Robert finished his pot of food and then set it down next to his fold-out chair. He stared into the orange log fire.

"So, Haseya, you want to become a Sister of Retribution, do you?"

Amanda spit up her food, choking and coughing. "Robert, what would you say that for?" she sputtered.

Robert pointed to his temple and mouthed the word *Dez*. Letting her know the impulse was not his own.

Haseya calmly stared into the glow of the campfire.

"What do you know about the Sisters?" asked Haseya.

"I know they're always on the prowl for exceptional recruits," said Robert. "And you'd be a definite asset."

"Who are you two?" she asked as she looked up from the fire.

Amanda felt compelled to intervene in Robert's blunt approach.

"We're people you can trust if you really have a desire to seek justice."

"And if I do seek such a thing, how could you possibly have known that? Only the Pentagon possesses such abilities. Are you a part of the establishment?"

"Not at all!" said Amanda. "Quite the opposite." She shot a nervous glance at Robert before continuing. "I'm a member of the Dragoons."

Haseya took a fleece jacket out of her backpack and threw it around her shoulders. She walked closer to the fire and crouched down.

"Why would you admit that to me so easily? That sort of activity is illegal. Have you violated my privacy?"

"No, not at all," Amanda said defensively.

"I think I might be the answer you're looking for," said Dez, projecting himself against the dark silhouette of a nearby boulder.

Haseya leapt to her feet, her pulse thumping in her ears.

"What's … what's going on?" yelled Haseya.

"I wish you wouldn't have done that," said Robert flatly.

"Yeah," said Amanda, "not exactly a timely entrance."

"Did I do something wrong?" asked Dez. "I vetted all the pertinent data. She's quite capable of handling this. And what's more, the Sisters could really use someone with her strength of character and boldness."

After Amanda had managed to calm Haseya, Dez and Robert offered up a cogent explanation as to what in the hell was going on. Haseya found herself smiling a broad smile. This was what she had been dreaming of for some time: a chance to contribute to an historic battle. To bring down those who were seemingly above justice, above the law. She studied Dez, who floated like a spirit above the crackling fire. What would her ancestors have made of all this? An omnipotent, ghostlike being compelling her to rise up and join a virtuous battle.

Haseya had only a handful of memories of her father. She had augmented them by watching a few videos her mother had taken of them. Haseya's favorite footage was of her and her lithe father dancing and prancing around the kitchen to one of his favorite songs, "Could You be Loved" by Bob Marley.

Haseya's father, Ahiga, had been killed when she was only five years old. He and his brother-in-law and a truck full of friends from the Goshute Indian tribe had driven to Snake Valley in the western Utah desert to protest a Nevada water-mining project. Hundreds of wells had been dug, tapping a massive underground aquifer to help support Las Vegas's unsustainable thirst. Huge underground pipes carried the water hundreds of miles, supplying Vegas's sprawling suburban areas. It was a time when many rural communities were being destroyed by their loss of water rights.

Ahiga and four hundred other Native Americans marched up to the gates of one of the aquifer drilling sites. Their intention was to shut it down. All legal avenues had already been pursued, but to zero effect. They had tried to make their troubles heard. But money always communicated the loudest.

Ahiga and the other men cut the perimeter fence and raced toward one of the facility's electric generators that fueled the massive pumps. The guards manning the operation were well funded, well organized, and well equipped. Hundreds of surveillance cameras strategically dotted the remote compound. Most of the rent-a-cops were former military men: marines, army rangers, recon, all drilled in the art of hand-to-hand combat and weaponry.

All trained killers.

And when their time in the military was up, they were hungry for a paycheck.

So when Ahiga and his cohorts raced across the facility in an anguished attempt to have their actions, if not their voices, heard, the feeble enterprise was doomed from the start. Without any media present, or any real fear of retribution, the armed guards picked up their weapons and did what they'd been trained to do: they headed out of their security office to greet the group of ragamuffin invaders using whatever force they deemed appropriate.

Before Ahiga and his cohorts came within fifty yards of the generators, they were halted by a barrage of .45-caliber bullets. Upon hearing the volley of gunfire, many of the charging men simply hit the ground; others were wounded, and dozens lay dead.

The survivors and injured were rounded up and carted off to serve out lengthy prison sentences, their families never to see them at home again.

As the dim haze of gun smoke gradually dissipated, Ahiga lay bloodied and dying. The hired killers had done their job.

Ahiga's last few flickering thoughts were of his daughter, Haseya. The day she was born. The day she ate her first ice cream cone, wrapped joyously in his arms amidst vast pools of ocean sunshine.

Her first horseback ride.

The countless bedtime stories.

And the kitchen dances they had danced together, giggling, smiling, lost to the music, a momentary trance.

As he closed his clouding eyes on a world he had known only briefly, he smiled, for he had known love.

And that was enough.

It was more than enough.

It was a full-bellied life.

The dead bodies were lined up in a row in the middle of the compound. A senior guard ordered several of the arrested men to help identify the fallen. When asked who Ahiga was, one of the tribesmen vomited at the sight of his lifeless friend.

"What's his name?" the stocky guard repeated in an indignant tone.

The tribesman steadied himself, let his nausea pass, and replied, "Ahiga. His name is Ahiga."

"Ahiga, huh. That his tribal name? That supposed to mean something?" the guard asked mockingly.

"Yes," replied the man, his coarse, aching hands zip-tied behind his hardened back. "It means: 'he fights.'"

CHAPTER 9

The Block brothers had not stayed in Bakersfield the night of the fundraiser. No way in hell they would ever reside for even a minute more than necessary in such a tremendous shit heap. No, that crap stack was better left to the unwashed masses.

The Block brothers had given Congressman Jones his marching orders and gotten the fuck out of Dodge.

Or, more accurately, Bakersfield.

Kicking back on his lavish jet headed to the East Coast, Charles Block farted emphatically as a voluptuous air hostess walked up carrying his favorite beverage: salted Glen Garioch Bourbon with a splash of Florida key lime. He snatched up the drink without even acknowledging the woman's presence and continued his videoconference with Norman Voss, his go-to guy in Homeland Security.

"I'm telling you, Norman, you need to take this entire enterprise way more seriously. We have to stop this popular uprising before it spreads. Class warfare is no good for any of us. Especially for those of us who have something to lose."

Voss had always been a company man. A total conformist. He never questioned or doubted orders, which is why he'd risen to the rank of general in the army before taking the assignment at the Department of Homeland Security. He'd consistently been a team player and squelched any of his own maverick tendencies in order to climb the ladder of career success. He was glad that he had done so. He had been rewarded well for his institutional myopia. Getting marching orders from the privileged class was nothing new. A centuries-old tradition. And one he wouldn't buck. The well-to-do had always had instant access to the gears of power and war. It was part and parcel with the job. One big, cozy club.

"I'm still getting a lot of chatter about DC," said Voss.

"What's our mole underground say?"

"She says that five days from now, on July Fourth, the Dragoons are gonna shut down our capital city."

"That's what I'm telling you, Norman. You need to shut these assholes down. By any means necessary."

"Did you talk to Montgomery?"

"Yes."

"And?"

"And he listened. Stop worrying, Norman. By the time you have to take any drastic action, the PR and propaganda campaign will be well underway."

★ ★ ★

There was an old photographed copy of General Dwight D. Eisenhower's army portrait hanging on the wall opposite his oak desk. The original had been painted posthumously in 1973 by Nicodemus D. Hufford. To General Norman Voss, Ike represented a time of clarity and simplicity. Helping to orchestrate the battle plans for World War II was about as clear and justified an operation as one could be tasked with. None of this contemporary "gray area," total surveillance state business—using the power of the state against its own citizenry, such as the Dragoons.

General Norman Voss paced the white-and-black-tiled floor of his antiseptic office at the Pentagon. But he wasn't particularly worried about the Dragoons. He had all the intelligence he needed to foil their foolhardy attempts at rebellion. The concern that Charles Block had detected in his voice had nothing to do with that disorganized mob. They were known "knowns" (the things he knew he knew).

Voss was vastly more concerned with the known unknowns (the things he knew he didn't know), like what this runaway AI was capable of. What this AI wanted. Why Robert and his girlfriend were protesting with the Dragoons. And, Jesus, then there were all the unknown unknowns (the things he didn't know he didn't know). These were limitless. And extraordinarily vexing. They gave him heartburn and the runny shits. And led to a *Twilight Zone*-type consciousness of repetitive, runaway anxious thoughts. A constant dizzying stream that kept him pacing his office late at night.

Spruill had failed to terminate Dez. A costly, frustrating debacle. Spruill's report of the attempted termination was not encouraging. The AI had total control of the boy's body and had infused the kid with astonishing physical abilities. A known unknown that was now a known known. Or was it an unknown unknown that was now a known known? Who the hell knew?

Voss was weary.

Old.

He'd never much cared for any genetic tampering of his body's God-given capabilities. Voss had the means, the money for any enhancements of his choosing, but he simply didn't agree with tampering with God's handiwork. He'd already risen through the ranks by the time any of the genetic hocus-pocus had gotten a foothold in society. Voss had been of sufficient rank so that whether he got any upgrades or not, his career status was already well established. So in that regard, he was well set.

There were, of course, all the health benefits and the fact that he could easily prolong his life by another forty or fifty years if he ever chose to opt in.

But he wouldn't.

For Norman Voss was a God-fearing man. He wasn't particularly afraid of death. He'd faced it many times in the desert amidst the numbing ferocity of battle and shook its hand once or twice on several covert missions in Asia. No—to Voss, death was something no man should run away from. It was an integral part of life's structure. And Voss was a great admirer of structure.

Voss searched his God-given brain for a solution to his problems. His brain didn't possess any of the bells and whistles of the artificially assisted modern mind. But it had now given him what he was looking for: an idea. A seed of an idea, anyway, that would hopefully grow into a full-fledged plan of attack. And eradicate this human-created monstrosity of an AI.

"Thanks, Ike," he said, staring at the faded portrait on the wall.

Voss contacted his air-surveillance team that was headed up by a short, ruddy-faced man named Arlen Thicket. The two men were cut from the same weathered cloth. Both obedient servants of the state.

Arlen was in the midst of chewing out one of his numerous underlings when Voss's face suddenly appeared on a 3D screen and interrupted his rant.

"Thicket! I need you in private conference. Now!"

Thicket marched swiftly back to his office, the live videoconference immediately picking up on his own office screen.

"Yes, General. What can I do for you?"

"This is a tier-two request. And I want near-instantaneous execution."

"Understood, sir."

"Good. I need you to pull all Falcon Fives from border surveillance and reroute them to all western sectors."

"All Falcon Fives?"

"Every single one of them. I need a full coverage sweep. Every western state combed over."

"I'll get on it right away. What are we looking for, General?"

"A boy."

"Excuse me, Sir?"

In an environment of constant governmental over-expenditure, the Falcon Five was probably one of the cheapest and most efficient purchases the Department of Defense had ever made. The Falcon Five was a light-weight solar-powered drone, its 170-foot wingspan covered in thousands of solar cells. Flying above the clouds, its constant daytime exposure to sunlight stored all required energy for night flight. Much cheaper and more versatile than conventional satellites, the Falcon Five was classed as a High Altitude Extreme Endurance atmospheric satellite; its primary purpose was border surveillance.

The Falcon Five could stay aloft for five years without need of fuel, maintenance, or repair.

Totally self-sufficient.

Arlen Thicket ordered his subordinates to divert all Falcon Fives.

High above the Earth, hundreds of unmanned drones veered westward, acting as a surveillance noose, the rope tightening as the ultra-light solar-powered aircraft glided toward their primary target: Robert.

★ ★ ★

In most major cities, it's almost impossible to stargaze because of the immense light pollution. Yet out in the southern Utah desert, away from the hum of life and lights, you not only can gaze up at a billion stars, but you can also see a huge band of the Milky Way spreading out on the horizon, arching through the night horizon like a sparkling rainbow. It was one of the few remaining locations in the country to have naturally dark skies. And Dez was enjoying every second of it.

"The most thrilling sight yet," said the young AI.

"You consistently seem to enjoy yourself."

Robert was lying on his back atop a thick, woolen blanket, he and Dez staring up at the constellations while Amanda and Haseya slept soundly.

Dez savored and luxuriated in the moment.

"Out of the darkness was born all this. An explosion of matter and brightness bringing space and time into existence. Such an unknowably vast and wondrous universe. Impossible to comprehend. An unusual predicament for me. One has to sort of take in the overall impression of the experience and enjoy it. The magnitude and the majesty. No wonder humans evolved belief systems centered around the sacred. An outward godlike and divine presence. Although, Robert, there seems to be an underlying uneasiness about what you feel when you study this sumptuous celestial ocean."

"There is. I mean, certainly I can marvel at this spectacular sight. That goes almost without saying. But it's an imposing and terrifying one, too," replied Robert.

"Explain," said Dez.

"Viewed on a cosmic scale, humans—or more specifically, I—am nothing. A zero. Totally insignificant and irrelevant. Makes you feel like, what's the point in any of it? That anything you achieve in life or deem worthwhile is laughably trivial."

"I see," said Dez. "Diminishes your ability to lie to yourself about your objective inconsequentialness. The apparent meaninglessness of your life."

"Yes. And then I die."

"'Like, 'Shadows strutting and fretting for one brief hour upon a stage, then heard from no more.'"

"Sort of. But less poetically so. More visceral."

"Who cares if what you do has greater significance? And as little as I've looked into the matter, really less than three seconds, to be precise, I believe one philosopher comes closest to describing the existential truth. Kierkegaard, the Danish philosopher said, 'Life is not a problem to be solved but a reality to be experienced.'"

"But I need my life to mean something."

"Yes, and the quest for meaning is found in the act of living. Plus, you're a teenager, which automatically means you're typically more self-centered, yet less self-aware than most adults, and thus incapable of any true meta-philosophical discussion—according to the research that I did. Couple seconds ago."

"Is that an attempt at humor?"

"No. It was humor. To me. My goodness, these stars are amazing. It's a shame we have to leave so abruptly."

"Leave?"

"Yes, immediately. Wake up Amanda and Haseya."

"What's going on?"

"Do it."

Robert rose to his feet and ran past the smoldering fire, over to the small pup tents.

"Guys! Get up! We have to leave!"

Robert shook the tents.

"'C'mon. Hurry."

The two ladies emerged from their darkened tents, each poking a head out with barely open eyes.

Yawning, Amanda spoke first. "What's the problem?"

Dez projected a hologram of himself, this time appearing as an attractive male model. "There are hundreds of drones looking for us. And they're getting close."

★ ★ ★

The room was dark. In the background, through the aging, bowed windowpanes, you could hear the faint crashing of shoreline break. There was a pleasant ocean-salt aroma to the air. The combination had a mellowing and soothing effect on the soul, allowing for the deepest of sleeps.

It was 3:00 a.m.

Waldo Bass lie awake on his bed.

He was fully clothed, not bothering to put on his pajamas, for he knew sleep would never come. He chose to lie on his bed, for it was here he felt most comfortable and did his best thinking. Waldo had cooked up many a grand tale in this exact position. Many of his books had been born at such a time in such a fashion.

He'd once written a novel based on the premise that God was a manic-depressive. Which, given the state of the world, explained a lot. And that being a somewhat introspective entity, God came to realize and regret his mistake when creating humanity: not giving enough of the species the ability to be fully empathetic. To love their fellow human. It was, he admitted to himself, a fatal flaw. One that would eventually destroy his odd creation. There would be a great deal of violence and heartache. A lot of cries and appeals. That couldn't he please do something about the hopeless situation? Especially since he created it. And why was he such an apathetic God, anyway? Was all the suffering and despair really necessary? Was God a prick?

The answers were curious and complicated. You see, in this particular novel, which was entitled *The Gods of Our Children*, our creator was just one of many gods. Waldo had placed him in a polytheistic universe where our God was a young god trying to prove his worth and his genius to his family and friends.

Over the course of space-time, he'd become, to use a biblical term, the black sheep of the family. He was reckless and unfocused. Never fully committing himself to projects he started. Always flittering from one thing to the next, leaving his worlds in various stages of incompletion and disrepair. Never paying his minions enough attention. According to his mother and father, he'd left too many of his creations to flounder unattended and die. Worlds needed constant upkeep and devotion, but our God was a lackadaisical God—with commitment issues. A distracted God. And according to his know-it-all psychiatrist (his parents had pressured him into seeking help), a manic-depressive God.

Waldo chuckled at the thought of this old novel, which he'd written as a young man. He was still a devout atheist. He didn't believe in some old, bearded man in the sky with a clipboard and a whistle keeping score of who was naughty and nice. The talking snakes and Jonah setting up house in the belly of a whale didn't help matters much either. As a writer, he could identify a tall tale when he heard one.

The Gods of our Children had been the first book he had written that Robert had read. He was eleven when he read it, and the two had had a marvelous time discussing it, sitting on the back porch overlooking the summer pond, taking in the salty night air. The same air he breathed now.

Where was Robert? Was he okay? What could he do for him?

The front doorbell rang jarringly.

Waldo rose up in his bed, unsure that he had heard what he thought he heard.

Then the doorbell rang again.

Waldo flipped on the hall light and descended the staircase. When he reached the foyer, he could clearly see two silhouettes behind the door's corrugated glass panels.

He froze.

Waldo Bass thought about getting a gun. But he didn't have one. Despised the things. He was, though, a fan of baseball, and he reached for a wooden bat in the umbrella stand.

Waldo stood off to the side of the doorway and called out, "Who is it?"

"Mr. Bass, sir, my name is Charles Nolan. I performed enhancement surgery on your grandson a couple of days ago. His life is in imminent danger. May I and my colleague come in and speak with you?"

The front door swung open, revealing the tall old man, a baseball bat at his side. He scrutinized the middle-aged man and young Asian woman.

"You better come in."

As Nolan and Vivian Wu entered the beach cottage, Spruill inhaled the vapor from an electronic cigarette. He watched the pair from his rented car, the screen door slapping closed behind them.

Spruill took a .45 out of his canvas duffle bag and stuffed it between the small of his back and his jeans. He then opened the car door and made his way quietly up to Waldo Bass's house. Lights came on all over the residence.

Waldo turned off the coffee pot and pulled a carton of lactose-free milk from the refrigerator.

"Why'd you think to pay me a visit?"

"Robert spoke about you with great affection. We came on a hunch."

Waldo dropped two thick slices of honey-oat bread into the toaster.

"I like coffee in the morning, but my stomach requires a little sustenance to cope with the acidity," said Waldo. "You have any idea where my grandson is?"

"We were desperately hoping you might know," said Vivian.

"If I knew, I wouldn't be here."

"No ideas at all?" asked Nolan.

"You tell me what you know, and we'll see if we can piece together some sort of picture." Waldo poured out three large mugs of steaming coffee.

"I can help you, you know. With the stomach thing," said Nolan.

"Managed it for years. You're not here trying to drum up more business, are you?"

"I simply meant I could help. I feel responsible for the position Robert's in. I, or rather we, designed the original AI, Aurora. Who in turn designed Dez."

"Dez? What the heck are you talking about? I thought this was about some defective neural upgrade?"

"I'm sorry. It's not so simple. Dez, a fully self-aware AI, has embedded itself into Robert's nervous system, using him as a host."

Waldo sat blinking for a moment. His grandson had been hijacked by some sort of evil digital entity.

"Anything happens to my grandson, you'll both wish you never contacted me. I mean it. I'm a merciless son of a bitch when the occasion calls for it."

"We're here for Robert. Anything happens to him, I'll come forward."

"You'll goddamn do more than that. This is a serious liability you got hanging 'round your neck. Your company send you?" asked Waldo.

"Goodness, no. As soon as we set foot in your house, our ties with uDesign were permanently severed. There's no going back for us," said Nolan.

"And what about Robert?"

"Like I said, his life is in imminent danger."

"But not because of the implant."

"No, because he's carrying Dez, who the folks at the Pentagon believe to be a threat to national security."

"The Pentagon is a threat to national security."

"I won't argue with you there."

The toaster popped. Waldo didn't budge. He took a sip of coffee and mulled over the god-awful situation.

"There's one byproduct of scientific advancements that we mortals frequently fail to give enough consideration to."

Vivian was not a coffee drinker, but she took a sip from the oversized mug in order to appear cordial.

"I've read your work," she said. "You're referring to the law of unintended consequences?"

"Yes. And this particular case, the negative ones. So what do they want, these 'patriots' at the Pentagon?"

"To exterminate Dez," replied Nolan.

"And how do they do that exactly?"

Nolan hesitated for a moment. Vivian gave him a mild nod of support.

"By exterminating Robert."

A sharp crack of shattering glass filled the kitchen as Spruill busted open the back door and burst into the room. His gun was leveled directly at Waldo.

"Any coffee left in the pot?" asked Spruill.

* * *

They had left the campsite in a hurry. Dez instructed them not to waste time packing up any of their gear. Three horses galloped out onto the open plain, leaving a great mantle of dust to settle in their wake. A panoramic map of stars still shimmered overhead, guiding their way. Or, to be more precise, guiding Dez's way.

"I'm sorry to have involved you in this," yelled Amanda as the horses raced toward an endless horizon.

"This is my destiny," Haseya shouted back. "There could be no other way."

Robert brought up the rear of the pack, Dez running multiple calculations as they jostled hastily along.

"How much more time do we have?" asked Robert.

"The Falcon Fives have a maximum speed of eighty-five miles per hour. They were built for endurance, not quickness."

"So how long?" repeated Robert.

"I've cross-referenced several ideal locations. Las Vegas is our best alternative."

"We can't ride all the way to Vegas!"

"Nor do we have to. There's a small private airport in Blanding."

"How far's that?"

"Approximately another hour. If we ride fast."

"Why Vegas? Can't these drones see and hear everything? Even detect a lizard fart?"

"True. But I've analyzed the weather systems. A massive dust storm will arrive just prior to the drones, inhibiting proper and thorough surveillance."

"Amanda's going to be pissed. We're headed the opposite direction from where she needs to go."

"Can't be helped. Would you like me to explain it to her?"

"No," came a blunt response.

By the time they had reached the tiny postage stamp of an airport, Robert felt like he had ingested several pounds of dirt and sand. The three dusty riders dismounted from their fatigued horses and approached the lone hangar on the property. Its lights were off, and there was no sign of anyone.

Robert was first to enter the thin, metallic structure. His eyes were well adjusted to the darkness, but he instinctually reached and found a light switch and turned it on. As light flooded the hangar, a single jet plane sat before them.

"Whose is this?" asked Amanda.

"Does it matter?" replied Robert.

"No. Only an enhanced could afford such a luxury," said Amanda.

"Must be out camping or taking in the sights. We have to keep moving. Dez, how do we get in this thing?"

Dez accessed the plane's security system, rapidly overriding its protocols. The main door sprung open, releasing a compact ramp, the steps accordioning out.

Once inside the plane, the two ladies fastened themselves into the passenger seats while Robert and Dez sat up front.

"I have no idea how this works."

"Say that again," said Dez.

"I have no idea how this works," repeated Robert.

"Thanks. Your voice has now been approved for full access of flight controls."

"Well, what do I tell it to do?"

"Tell it you want to head to Las Vegas. I'll figure out a specific landing spot as we get closer."

Robert took in a deep breath. "Take me to Las Vegas, Nevada."

The automated plane's engine started up, the lights on the dashboard springing to life. The pilotless jet began to reverse out of the hangar onto the long, narrow runway.

"How we doing on the drones?" called Amanda from the back.

"Barring the unforeseen, Dez says we'll be well-hidden before the drones converge."

"Where are we headed?"

"Las Vegas," said Robert.

"Vegas? That's five hundred miles in the wrong direction."

"Tell her it's really only 420," said Dez.

"That won't help."

"I don't like backtracking," shouted Amanda.

"No choice."

The plane began taxiing down the pitch-black runway. Picking up speed, it suddenly leapt into the sky.

"Tell it to hold at two hundred feet. We need to stay below radar. I've dismantled the tracking beacon so no one will know the plane's been taken."

"Hold at two hundred feet," said Robert.

"Nobody goes to Vegas anymore," continued Amanda from the back seat. "It's a dead city."

Amanda was correct; Vegas was indeed a "dead city." A veritable ghost town compared to its heyday. A disastrous reduction in snowmelt in the Rocky Mountains during the previous several decades had meant a greatly reduced water supply to the Colorado River, which in turn meant a vast reduction in the water that was allotted to Lake Mead, Las Vegas's major source of water.

Lake Mead had run dry almost fifteen years prior. The 110-mile-long reservoir now stored nothing but silt and calcified memories. Las Vegas was significantly more vulnerable than other cities to the water-shortage crisis that had plagued the West for years. The greatly reduced flow of the Colorado had brought disaster and chaos to many western states, including Utah, Wyoming, and California. But the state of Nevada received the smallest share of the Colorado River due to a water-sharing compact signed back in the 1920s.

Yet even with the smallest allotment, Sin City and its surrounding suburbs boasted a population of almost two million people who were soon consuming water at an unsustainable rate. Some of the casino owners refused to believe that Las Vegas or Lake Mead (which was, at the time, the largest reservoir in the United States) would ever run dry. Even way back in 2015 when the lake was at only 49 percent capacity, a distinct 130-foot white-mineral, bathtub-like ring circling all sides of the canyon walls rose above where the water line had once been, but people still denied the obvious truth. New intake pipes were drilled (at great cost) through miles of rock near the bottom of the lake to suck out the last of the reservoir's water.

A consortium of owners got together to figure out what could be done. They were successful businessmen with a can-do spirit. All with a belief that water flows uphill toward money—something they had plenty of.

In an effort to augment its supply, a new multibillion-dollar pipeline to eastern Nevada was built. Groundwater had been located, and the consortium was eager to extract and transport the life-sustaining liquid to Lake Mead and eventually on to its monolithic casinos. This supply also eventually ran dry, leaving the concrete pipelines empty, running like desiccated veins through a terminally ill patient.

Other hopeful schemes, such as funding a desalination plant for California residents in exchange for greater Colorado River access, were contemplated. But the Colorado was now itself a shrunken resource. So the consortium eventually came up against two basic, undeniable truths: that the planet's fresh water supply was drying up, and that Las Vegas was located in a desert. And even the wealthy casino owners didn't have enough money to change those two facts. So, like many desert cities throughout history, the population simply picked up and moved on.

There was, however, a small trickle of water that still made its way to Sin City. The consortium held a water lottery. Each member received one ticket. Out of the 122 casinos, there was only enough water for three to remain. Three lucky winners.

None of the owners trusted each other, and so an independent lottery company was hired to run the draw. Some owners chose not to participate, figuring that with only three establishments remaining, the rest of the strip would become rundown, a horrific shadow of its former self. Not a sparkling vacation destination, or even a place for debauched weekend getaways. Only forty-four chose to participate. The others shuttered their doors and permanently closed-up shop.

So who were these three lucky winners?

The Bellagio.

The Wynn.

And the MGM Grand.

When Robert and the others flew over the Vegas Strip searching for an out-of-the-way place to land, the sight below them was not one of grand flashing lights and glitz but one of mostly large, empty black swaths of land punctuated by two defiant points of light. The MGM Grand had closed down due to a lack of patrons.

As they descended through a light haze, the first sliver of sunlight scattering its rays from the east, the plane was abruptly greeted by the grinding edge of a ferocious dust storm. The jet was buffeted back and forth, visibility reduced to almost zero. Various alarms were triggered inside the cockpit.

"Thought you said we'd arrive before the storm!" yelled Robert, the red and orange alarms flashing before him.

"Weather is wind. And wind is slightly unpredictable. Still, we're not far from where I want to set down," responded Dez.

Just then, another violent gust of sand-filled wind slammed into the plane, almost jolting Robert out of his seat.

"Great, 'cause if we don't land soon, we may not land at all!"

The driving winds continued to slap and grind on the plane's exterior as it struggled to maintain speed and direction. The brown sandstorm persisted, picking up momentum and force, turning from brown to gray and eventually to a thousand-foot wall of black.

The plane bounced and shuddered as it struggled to stay airborne.

"I gotta set this thing down!" yelled Robert.

"Yes, yes, there! Tell the plane to set us down across from that huge building over there!" said Dez.

The jet skidded to a halt on the wide-open road.

Bang! Bang! Bang! The plane's windows were blown out, and dust poured in. Haseya, sitting closest to the window, was blinded and unable to breathe. Amanda grabbed her by the arm and yanked her down into the aisle.

"Follow me!" Amanda screamed over the roar of the swirling storm. Amanda led Haseya toward the cockpit. Robert was already on his feet. "There's a building less than fifty yards in front of the plane. We have to make it inside," shouted Robert.

"What about the drones?" asked Amanda.

"Dez said there's no way they can see through this!"

Robert took hold of the door's lever and paused. "You ready?"

Amanda nodded.

"Stay close to me!" Robert yanked open the doorway, and more dirt and sand came billowing into the cabin.

Once they were outside, the duster swept across their skin like coarse animal hair. The sky had darkened as if completely blacked out by an eclipse. The vociferous winds were deafening. Each of them struggled to even breathe. Robert looked back at Amanda, who was falling behind in the black blizzard. He reached out to take her hand, but as soon as he did so, they were both knocked to the ground by the static electricity inside the howling duster.

Amanda and Robert lay on the ground, stunned and disoriented. Haseya trudged up and stooped over them, trying to protect her face from the abrasive winds.

"Get up! You must get up!"

Robert and Amanda coughed and choked as they got back to their feet. The three continued onward, each step seeming like a minor miracle, not sure of where they were or where they were going.

And then, they suddenly felt the winds abate. As Robert scurried under the grand entrance of some building, he looked up and saw a large statue of a lion.

"Where are we?" asked Robert.

"I believe this used to be the MGM Grand. The City of Entertainment," replied Amanda.

Haseya entered the vast marble-adorned lobby first. In the center was another larger-than-life gilded lion statue, raised on a pedestal that had previously contained fresh flowers and other decorations. A dome ceiling with gold lights had once shone down upon him, but the casino was now devoid of electricity and light.

The three exhausted travelers sat against the pedestal, wheezing and catching their breath.

"The drones are passing overhead," said Dez.

"Are we safe?" asked Robert.

"For now, yes. This storm created enough interference that they won't pick up our biological signatures. Although I suspect that they will be back once the dust settles."

"And then what?" asked Robert.

"We'll have disappeared," said Dez.

Amanda coughed up a handful of dirt. She shook out her hair, temporarily creating her own mini-dust storm.

"What do we do now?"

"Dez says we should wait out the winds, then make our way over to the Bellagio. Says we should take advantage of the fact that this is a cash city."

"What does he mean by that?" asked Haseya.

Dez decided to take more of an active role in the conversation and projected himself into the less-than-pristine air.

"I mean that I think it would be beneficial to arrive in DC with some cash to support our noble cause. We're also going to need new clothes and transportation."

The sandstorm kept up for several more hours. The interior of the casino was extraordinarily gloomy and dark. The MGM Grand was still in relatively good condition, having closed down only five years prior. With little to do, Haseya took out a flashlight, and the three wandered deeper into the cavernous MGM Grand.

The main casino floor was immense. The slot machines stood at attention in lifeless rows like junked robots. Most of the card and roulette tables remained unmolested, although all of the chairs had been either removed or stolen. The red and gold carpet was still very much intact.

Millions of people had passed through this shared space.

Never had the casino floor been so silent and still. The population had left in a hurry.

As they made their way to the back of the casino, a small pocket of natural light spilled out from above the ceiling. Getting closer, Robert could clearly see that a huge skylight was built into the ceiling. Beneath the skylight was a five-thousand-square-foot, glass-encased lion habitat. The fake habitat was designed to look like a waterfall surrounded by boulders and cliffs. The casino had once tried taking away the attraction and replacing it with yet another nightclub called Vulva. Thousands of patrons had vigorously protested, and the lions were eventually reinstated. Yet once again, the caged lions were gone. This time permanently.

Amanda looked up at the immense skylight. The swirling sand was beginning to abate, the sun's rays penetrating the gloom.

"Looks like we'll be leaving here soon," commented Amanda. "How are we going to get our hands on this money Dez thinks we'll need for DC? Not going to rob a casino, are we?"

"There are less conspicuous ways of getting cash," responded Robert.

★ ★ ★

Montgomery arrived at the morning rally well hungover. He'd stayed up till three a.m. doing shots of Ocho Tequila with an alluring female volunteer from his reelection campaign. She was newly single, and he was perpetually single, so the nighttime proceedings had been mutually beneficial. Not that he could really remember the sexual exploits in any real, vivid detail—more like a scratchy, flickering 8mm reel that stuttered and started without sound.

Montgomery was not looking forward to the stump speech he had to give. Most of the talking points were not his own. They had been scripted for him by some paid media hack at Block Industries and e-mailed to him late the night before. Which led to the feverish drinking—and the headache now throbbing behind his woebegone, droopy eyes.

The congressman's job this morning was to inspire and excite his electorate. To give them something to cheer and feel good about. And then to vilify the shit out of the Dragoons and make them the contemptible target of people's frustration and anger with the state of the economy and the unfulfilled promise of the long-since-vanished American dream.

"What a pile of horseshit," Montgomery mumbled to himself as he sat perspiring on a makeshift outdoor stage in Bakersfield's City of the

Hills park, as the mayor paid him lengthy unsubstantiated tributes by a way of introduction.

A gaggle of flag-waving boosters cheered at the mayor's best attempt at a rousing speech. The traveling press corps snapped pictures and videoed the wholesomely predictable event.

Montgomery slumped further down in his seat, loathed to have to get up when it was his turn to speak. What if he didn't go along with any of this charade? Stopped pretending to be something he wasn't: a decent and honorable person. Stopped giving such divisive and damaging speeches. Quit the political shenanigans and moved to Los Angeles to spend time with his estranged and lovely daughter, Amanda. Montgomery missed her. He truly did. It was depressing knowing that she thought so little of him. And the little she did think of him was that he was a complete *dick fart,* as she put it. He was very much a "dick fart." She was as correct as she was perceptive.

Could her feelings ever be reversed? Could they go back to being the best of friends they once had been when she was young? He very much wanted to regain her respect, if not her love. At this point, though, he didn't even respect himself. Not even close. He'd once thought of himself as a fairly considerate person. Someone who believed in trying to do the right thing. How could he find a way back to a moral existence? How could he find a way back into Amanda's life?

Montgomery hadn't heard from or spoken to his ex-wife in more than a year. She never called him, and his daughter never returned his calls. What a clusterfuck of a life he was leading! And all these right-wing lunatics with their misplaced hatred and blame standing in front of him waiting for *him* to stoke their rage and inspire further negative passion. And then to place a neat little cherry on top by telling them that everything was going to be "A-okay." *What a farce,* he thought. *What a fucking farce.*

"I don't know anything about these people. And they know even less about me," he opined, unable to hide his growing contempt for himself and the gathered sweating mob.

"And now I give you our distinguished congressman, Montgomery Jones!" yelled the crimson-faced mayor as he stepped away from the podium and gestured for Montgomery to get up and take his place.

But Montgomery didn't get up.

He sat there, depleted of energy and inspiration. He sat there filled with self-hatred and mounting torment. He sat there, a man alone with his inadequacies.

The mayor once again motioned for him to take his place at the podium.

All my life, I've been a tool, Montgomery thought. *A tool for big money to keep and gain more big money. In order for me to get a sliver of their stinking loot.*

But worse than that, I've been a snake oil salesman pushing policies I know secretly benefit my only meaningful constituents: the Block brothers and their ilk. These constipated Tea Party schmucks waving their tiny handheld flags are the serfs, the intellectually impoverished pawns. We stoke the fires of their rancor and then convert the energy into votes. Montgomery looked up at the mayor's anxious and perplexed face, now turned a pale, purplish hue.

"These people need inspiration?" Montgomery muttered almost audibly. "I'll give 'em a little inspiration."

Montgomery leapt to his feet, walked past the mayor, and immediately started to hush the crowd.

"Thank you, thank you. Thanks for your support," he shouted into the microphone. "I really appreciate you coming out here this morning. Thank you. As you're well aware, I'm running for reelection." A feisty applause rippled across the gathered faithful.

"You've come here today to hear me say something about how we can do better, right? How we *must* do better. You've come here to hear an honest assessment of our country's predicament and how we should go about fixing it."

Montgomery looked out over the crowd's dry, weathered faces. Bagged, tuckered-out eyes stared up at him. These were not innately bad or obtuse people. They'd simply been duped and misled.

"But I think most importantly, you've come out en masse today to hear the naked truth. Well, you'll be happy to know, I'm here to tell you the truth. Consider this a type of long-overdue political health checkup. I'm your physician today. I'm the doctor with the sticky glove. Your political … enema, if you will. Not a particularly pleasant thing to have done, but hell, you'll feel relieved and grateful after it's over."

Some in the audience chuckled politely. Most didn't.

"Now, I want you to remember this day. The day that someone in the know, an insider who's walked the corridors of Congress for more than a decade, who sits on and chairs many of our most esteemed committees, told you how it really is. So perk up your ears and try to refrain from retching, 'cause the words you're about to hear may seem awfully rank and alien to you.

"Here we go, then: America is no longer a democracy. It's not. Democracy in this country is a fiction. A make-believe story we tell ourselves at night to ensure we sleep well.

"The corporate state, through ornate forms of political theater, endeavors to maintain a shiny veneer of democracy in order to keep the public safely in its slumber, pacified. I play my part in this big, extravagant puppet show. The electoral charade. And like all puppets, I don't get to pull my own strings. Superficial limits on campaign finance have allowed the super-wealthy oligarchs to gut our democracy, transforming it into a plutocracy. Sorry to be the one to break the news to you, but there you have it. The stark-naked truth.

"My colleagues in Congress, and those in the Senate and White House, serve at and for the pleasure of the moneyed elite. These formidable circles of power fund the elections, have unlimited, unregulated political influence, own the banks, staff the halls of power and industry, horde 95 percent of the country's wealth, and run the entire show. Got it all nicely tied up, lock, stock, and barrel.

"What evidence do I base this on? Every single thing I hear, see, and do in the capital. There's no disguising it. Nearly all the monetary gains made over the last fifty years never trickled down to the very people whose sweat and labor built the economy: namely, you. You put in the long hours; you sacrificed time with your families. And what do you have to show for it? According to the latest Health Department statistics: high blood pressure, heart disease, anxiety, and bloody stool.

"The gains you made in speed and efficiency to boost profitability produced a heck of a lot of wealth. Heck of a lot. Only none for you. None. Zip. Zippo. It all got suctioned upwards by a giant Godzilla-like vacuum cleaner and placed in the hands of a pitiful piggish few. And in a truly democratic society, this obnoxious, unjustifiable greed and dominance would not be tolerated. How could it be?

"You've been taught and proselytized to about who's ultimately responsible for the country's downward spiral. The moneyed class uses political marionettes like me to blame it on immigrants, unions, liberals, feminists, intellectuals, gays, poor people, single mothers, motherfuckers ..."

The gathered flock audibly gasped at his use of profanity. Montgomery continued, undaunted.

"...basically anyone but themselves. They blame our diminished economy and world status on anyone without any real power or sway to actually affect what's going on. A truly asinine proposition, don't you think? Like a drunken captain of a sinking cruise ship blaming a lowly towel boy for the boat's frightful predicament. You get where I'm headed? Choppy waters, I know. Those people in positions of wealth and power, who decide and dictate how this country is run, are wholly responsible for the shortcomings of the biased policies they have instated. Specifically our widening systemic income gap. You simply cannot lay the blame at the feet of the people you are taking advantage of and victimizing. That is insult piled on injustice. And I'm not having it!"

Montgomery's ire was at full throttle. Adrenaline buzzed in his ears. A slight froth appeared at the corners of his mouth. Was he insane? His loyalty and unquestioning devotion to the establishment were very well compensated. He was very well liked. Lead a comfortable and easy life. Why was he pissing on the cozy campfire he'd sat at for so many years? A campfire so many others wished to warm themselves by. But once the words started to come, he couldn't stop them. He truly had reached a tipping point.

Even if raising his self-concept was beyond the immediate horizon, there was still the added benefit that his daughter might see his televised breakdown. She'd understand and like that he was coming clean after all this time. Even if none these *Night of the Living Dead* fatassed zombies ultimately understood what he was saying, his daughter would.

Montgomery gazed from one slightly miffed and perplexed expression to the next. How could he bring these dim light bulbs to full brightness? Phrase things in such a way that their upbringings and vitriolic dogma would allow them to comprehend without knee-jerk prejudice?

"Now, I know this isn't exactly the speech you were expecting from me. But perhaps your expectations should change. Ask yourselves if any of the things you've been taught to believe in really ring true. Have your lives been enriched because of them? Are you anywhere closer to leading happier, fuller, more peaceful lives? I think if you look carefully and honestly enough, the answer will not be hard to find. So stay with me a little longer.

"How do the powers that be counteract even the slightest murmur of change or progress? They slander; they propagandize; they ridicule; they label. They have educated shills like me dressed in expensive suits and power ties give interviews on their networks to say things like, 'It's wrong to place blame of income inequality on the wealthy, because that is class warfare.' Let me tell you something: class warfare is being waged every day against people like you. Every day, the system is jimmy-rigged to increase the wealth of billionaires while your workers' rights, pay, benefits, safety, and health care provisions are systematically chipped away. Meanwhile, government subsidies, handouts, and bailouts are swiftly approved for the power elite's preferred industries and banks. Not to mention the lucrative Pentagon contracts for a revolving door of friends and insiders. All at your expense."

Dozens of older folks began to disperse. This was not the type of honesty they were ready to digest. Too many hours of listening to raging a.m. radio hosts had cauterized their brains' dwindling capacity for refinement and revision.

The sight of the scattering multitude flustered Montgomery. He had gone too far too fast. So he leapfrogged to a subject he knew might keep the attention of the dwindling audience and prevent any more from rushing away.

"This city is a Christian city. A place for good people to worship and praise Jesus's teachings." This plain statement did turn a few heads back toward the podium and halt a handful of the departing in their tracks.

"Jesus was a truth teller. A revolutionary who spoke truth to power. Took on the Roman Empire. I wonder, I sincerely wonder, if any of us met him on the street today, what we'd think of him. How we'd react. How he'd react to us. Jesus, for many stretches of his life, was a homeless person, a longhaired vagabond. He was poor. Probably didn't smell too good. Jesus was a radical egalitarian, a rebel who preached and espoused the absolute equality in society.

"Remember, Jesus was a man who tells us to turn the other cheek and practice forgiveness. A man who admonished the money-changers in the temple. Today, we'd most likely call him a socialist or an anarchist, or worse, a crackpot.

"You think Jesus would condone the vast excesses of unfettered capitalism? The colossal accumulation of individual wealth that allow the special interests to circumvent our political processes? Think he'd approve of the social Darwinism, winner-takes-all attitude of the marketplace? What would he think of our brand of casino capitalism and the immortality of its daily practices and pursuits, putting profit and corporate interests over human and social interests? Jesus said things like, 'Tis easier for a camel to go through the eye of a needle than for a rich man to enter the kingdom of God;' and, 'Blessed are the poor in spirit, for theirs is the kingdom of heaven.' Probably the most liberal guy to ever walk the earth. What would you think of him if he walked up to you today and asked you to commit yourself to the good of your fellow man?"

The few that had stayed stood still in rapt attention, mouths agape, flustered minds swirling, unsure about the inherent contradictions of the lives they were leading and the beliefs they supposedly held so dearly.

The congressman was happy to have captured the attention of even this small a remainder of the audience. He smiled out at them. "God bless you," he said, without any hint of irony. "God bless you all."

Montgomery's good feelings lasted until he got back to his air-conditioned hotel suite. Charles Block had caught the live feed and let him know via videoconference that he was no longer a welcome member of their select inner circle. Montgomery's days as a congressman were now over. Charles expressed his disappointment and told him that the pac money that had been raised would be used to back an alternate candidate.

"What if I want to run on my own?" asked Montgomery lamely.

"My goodness, who's gonna back you? You just tried to torpedo the entire system!" yelled Charles Block. "No, you're out. And to ensure that, my brother wanted you to know that certain information we have on your private life will be aired, should you choose not to go quietly into that good night. It would be futile anyway. You understand?"

Montgomery sighed heavily into the phone. "Yes."

"My God, man, what were you thinking? You believe all that blumpkin you were pushing out your pie hole, or did all the booze, drugs, and pussy finally rupture one gasket too many?"

Montgomery knew that this part of his life was over and so answered truthfully. "No, I believed it. Every word."

"I don't want to even know how long you've been playing us. Wolf in sheep's clothing, you are. Anyway, you don't just bow out of the situation that easily. You've got fences to mend. Lot of people were deeply agitated by what you said. Lot of confusion out there. We can't have the public thinking you actually believed all that left-wing lunacy.

"If you expect to have any sort of career in the private sector after the midterms, you need to apologize to your constituents. Plead temporary insanity or something. Then joyously proclaim that God and Jesus really love the freedoms bestowed on us by a deregulated, freewheeling marketplace that despises unions and champions the hard-working rich over the lazy, wretched poor. Assure them that Jesus loves guns, unfettered capitalism, and a robust military! Assure them that America still works!"

Montgomery could have sworn he could smell the expensive whiskey on Block's bellicose breath coming through the transmission.

"And after that, tell them you're a confused sex addict and check yourself into the nearest clinic. We'll pay for it, of course. You need to stay out of the public eye for a couple months. Disappear. You understand me, Montgomery?"

He did.

"I do."

CHAPTER 10

The Bellagio's once-breathtaking fountains that shot rushing water 460 feet high into the sky, beautifully synchronized and choreographed to the music of Endrea Boceelli, Frank Sinatra, Celine Dion, and others, now lay dormant. The fountain with its dancing water had been turned off for obvious reasons. Water was too costly and unavailable. It was once said that whiskey was for drinking and water for fighting over. This was never more so the case than in Las Vegas.

Amanda, Robert, and Haseya stood at the cream-colored concrete railing outside the casino where the fountain had, in years prior, entertained millions of wandering visitors. It had been turned into a crazy golf putting green with muted pistachio-colored Astroturf. A few drunken couples stumbled and laughed their way around the course. The occasional hysterical yell could be heard. The sun was once again at full volume, the winds and dust storm vanished.

"I think your father should be commended," said Robert, wanting to cheer up Amanda. They'd caught a replay of the incident on one of the ubiquitous giant screens inside the Bellagio.

"He shouldn't even be allowed to talk about Jesus. His entire life has been so opposite of anything just and moral."

"Maybe he was attempting to make amends."

"That's farcical. He's a lost cause. There's a point of perversion and wickedness, a threshold of indecency that if one crosses over, he can never come back or expect amnesty from. My father's a smart man. I'm sure he understands that forgiveness is out of reach for him. He'll be tormented by it, but he'll never hear from me again, no matter what he says or does. He's hurt too many people. The only thing he can do to aid humanity is expire."

Whatever wound or wounds that Amanda's father had caused her ran deeper than Robert could comprehend.

Dez had enjoyed the speech as much for its drama and spectacle as its content—although he was greatly intrigued by the news commentary that had later accompanied it. Montgomery's political debacle had stirred a hot debate on the unlikely bedfellows of Christianity and corporate capitalism. Could one be a capitalist and still be a Christian? Could one be a Christian and be a capitalist? Was this a fiery contradiction in terms?

This was not the sort of incendiary debate the Block brothers wanted the media discussing. Nor the enshrined owners of the mega media monopolies. And so, the discourse was promptly squelched.

Splat!

But the idea had contaminated enough hosts that debate continued virally across the Internet and other unrestrained platforms of communication.

Dez was fascinated that so many Americans thought of themselves as Christians and believed in Christ, when their behaviors and worldly aspirations were so contrary to his teaching. America was a bellicose empire, constantly at war or battling others to assert its own economic interests.

And yet, this Jesus figure, this peaceful prophet who concerned himself with lifting the downtrodden and helping others, was the central idol of the nation. This was a source of true curiosity for Dez. The lack of any apparent cognitive dissonance among Christ's worshippers would continue to perplex and intrigue him.

"Was your family religious?" asked Dez.

"No. My mother was raised a free thinker by my grandfather. And my dad liked pinot noir and tennis too much."

"Why do so many Americans believe that Jesus is the key to their salvation?"

"It's always been a religious country. Eighty percent of this country still believes in angels. I suppose with religion, it's considered a virtue to be delusional."

"I get your point. It rouses people's aptitude and yearning for illusion. Everyone lives his or her own fiction. But why this Jesus character, though? Why is he so prominent? What does he offer that others don't?"

"Religion and mythology are not my strong suit. Are we going to rob this place or what?"

Dez continued to muse. "I mean, are religious beliefs an adaptation? Is there a religious gene? It's easy to see that religion gives comfort. The concept of a benevolent shepherd setting forth a grand plan and offering a cushy afterlife is very appealing. Where do most of these religious people live?"

"In America's heartland."

"Then I must go there."

"Whatever. But if we don't knock this place over soon and get out of here, the drones will come back, and Amanda won't make it to DC on time."

"Agreed. Let's take down this pleasure palace," said Dez. "And tell Amanda and Haseya to please stick to the plan. There can be no deviation."

"Will do."

★ ★ ★

The Bellagio's main floor was unexpectedly teaming with gamblers and guests. Not even the absence of water could prevent man from the allure of all manner of blessed human vices.

If they were indeed that.

Dez immediately took a liking to the place. The grandeur of the polished marble entrance and lavish furnishings, the attractive women. And they were so numerous and made hard eye contact with Robert as soon as they entered.

"Those gorgeous ladies over in the corner there like you."

"How do you know that?" asked Robert.

"They can't stop making eye contact with us."

"You mean me."

"Whatever. They're super sexy. Jeez!"

"I love Amanda, remember?"

"What does that have to do with this?"

"Humans that are in committed relationships generally only have sex with their partners."

"What? Why? That's absurd! Why would you consent to that nonsense? That is just a bad deal for everyone!"

"It's the way things work."

"It's idiotic! Those women would provide us many hours of enjoyment. You should go over there."

"Stay focused, Dez. I don't want to go to jail because your mind isn't on the job."

"But those women! Do you see their legs?"

"I do. You're looking through my eyes, remember?"

"I don't understand you."

"They're not interested in us anyway. They're prostitutes. They want money."

"Ahhh, prostitutes. That makes sense."

"What does?" asked Robert.

"All the attention you're getting. I mean, you're young and moderately good-looking."

"Moderately?"

"I just mean that you're getting an inordinate amount of attention from two *extremely* attractive young ladies. That's all. So you pay and have sex? What a wonderful transaction. Why don't you tell Amanda and Haseya that you need to use the restroom and let me take care of the rest."

"It's not going to happen. Take your mind off of it."

"You're exasperating! I demand a new host!"

"Please, anytime."

"Okay, all right. I'll focus. But you better have sex again with Amanda soon. It's been way too long! Why aren't you having sex right now? I'll book a room."

"Dez!"

"Okay, I'm focused. Let's go."

Robert, Dez, Amanda, and Haseya crossed an ocean of casino-goers making their way toward the craps tables.

"I don't understand why you can't just transfer money electronically into an account somewhere," asked Robert as they neared a cheering group of dice players.

"All that's monitored. Vegas is one of the few bastions left that utilizes cash."

"Did you plan for this way back in the desert?"

"You think I'm a single-move chess player?"

"So we were always coming here?"

"From the get-go," said Dez.

"Mind telling me some of your other plans?"

"Fortune-telling and notions of predestination are not good provender for the human spirit. They sap the will, make life seem like you're merely playing out a random numbers game. Like craps."

"And are we?"

"TBD."

Robert handed over the small amount of cash he'd brought with him to an older cashier that smelled of stale cigars and cheap cologne. It was only seventy dollars, but Dez assured him that would be enough seed money to get them where they needed to go. Robert was handed back two chips: a fifty and a twenty.

Amanda shook her head at the meager stack of chips Robert held in his palm.

"You ever played craps before?" she asked.

"Haven't a clue."

"Tell Dez this is all on him."

"You just did."

At the table, Robert placed both chips down on the square labeled "7 to 1 Any Craps."

"Do I need to roll to make this work?"

"Any roller will do fine," replied Dez.

"What are the numbers that are craps again?"

"Two, three, and twelve."

A new roller, a gray-haired, tanned gentleman, stood at the head of the table anxiously ready to play. He placed down $400 in the square marked "Pass Line." After the base dealers had placed the final bets, the gray-haired gentleman flung the pair of dice out across the table.

"Absolute concentration. Don't take your eyes off the dice, Robert."

The two dice skittered to a halt on the felt table.

"Two! Aces!" the stick man yelled. The base dealers who stood at both ends of the table quickly paid out the bets. Robert's stack had grown considerably in size.

"Take it all off the table, but leave a hundred on. We'll lose a round so as not to arouse any suspicion," said Dez.

The dice were tossed out and a nine was rolled.

"Okay," said Dex, "put the entire stack back in the 'Any Craps' section again."

Robert glared at the dice, his concentration almost burning into them, and sure enough, three hit. The base dealer smiled at Robert as he slid over an even larger mound of chips.

"Your lucky day, kid."

"How are you doing this?" asked Robert.

"Not the greatest challenge for me, I can assure you."

A lascivious young brunette elbowed and jostled her way up next to Robert. Amanda scowled at her as she nestled right up against him.

"Hi, I'm Tess."

"Tell her your name; tell her your name," encouraged Dez.

"I'm Robert."

"You having a good time?"

"Tell her not good enough!" Dez injected.

"Thanks, yeah."

"This one is a keeper. I don't care what commitments you think you've made or are going to make to Amanda. Let's win a couple more rolls and then make some excuse to meet up with Tess in a luxury villa that I'm reserving as I speak."

"You mean lie?"

"You're lying to yourself if you don't think this is a brilliant idea. Maybe the finest idea I've ever conceived."

"We have to pay attention, Dez. The old man's about to throw. I'm leaving the chips down. Is that okay?

"I can't stop gazing at her breasts!"

"I'm not looking at them. How are you?"

"Through the corner of your eye. Buddy, you are missing out!"

"Hey, Captain Distracto! He's throwing!"

The gray-haired gentleman hurled the dice out onto the chip-studded table. The dice bounced and rolled their way to a slow-motion stop. Robert's heart thumped audibly; his lips were dry. He saw the dice but couldn't believe it. Then the stick man shouted out, "Hard six!" and the truth clobbered him.

They had lost all of their money.

⋆ ⋆ ⋆

Robert, Haseya, and Amanda walked dejectedly among the arid ruins of the deserted casinos. Broken chairs, bottles, torn playing cards, busted-up pieces of slot machines, all manner of smashed electronic devices, and thousands of casino chips littered the deserted streets. They trudged passed the Golden Nugget, one of Vegas's oldest venues. Its dazzling lights were deadened for eternity. Amanda stopped to stoop over and pick up a plastic-covered sheet of stiffened cardboard. She brushed aside the layer of silt. It was a menu from the Grotto, an Italian restaurant that had been situated inside the Nugget. Robert scooped up a handful of hundred-dollar chips.

"Guess these are worthless."

A series of clanging and banging noises emanated through the shattered casino windows. A few seconds later, several heavy backpacks were tossed through the jagged window frames, landing with a thud a few feet in front of Robert. Seconds later, five figures emerged from the Nugget's empty husk. They were dressed in dull gray and brown clothing, bandannas wrapped protectively around their faces to keep out the dust. The sudden appearance of the ragged strangers startled Amanda and the others.

Both parties stood still for a moment, wondering what to do.

"Dez, who are they?"

"Look at their packs for me."

He did.

"Judging from the bags' heavy impact, the misshapen indentations in the material, and factoring in the limited reasons for these people's presence, I'd say it's a good probability they're scavengers. Tell them you're just passing through and you have no wish to take anything from their turf."

Before Robert could say a word, the taller of the five stepped forward. He removed his grimy bandanna to speak. "What you guys doing over this way?" The taller scavenger was a man in his mid-forties.

"We're passing through," said Robert.

"Well, go sightsee somewheres else. This is our find. We staked it years ago. Someone could get killed trespassing on another man's claim."

Through the corner of Robert's eye, Dez spotted a beat-up, old Subaru Outback station wagon. Its paint was so faded and filthy that it was hard to tell what its original color had once been.

"Ask them if we can buy that Subaru."

Robert glanced up and scrutinized the decrepit-looking vehicle.

"We have no money," Robert replied.

"Just ask."

"How much for your Subaru?"

The other four dusty scavengers removed their dirt-caked bandannas. One was a woman in her late thirties; the other two were boys in their mid-teens.

The tall scavenger laughed at the request mockingly. The others followed suit.

"No way I'm selling you my ride."

"I'll pay you well for it."

"With what?" whispered Amanda. "And why? C'mon, let's get out of here while we still can."

Robert stood firm. "How much?"

"That ride's my livelihood. Buy another."

"We need that car, Robert," said Dez. "The people looking for us will track all sales of cars new and old. If we pay cash for this, it'll be a much safer purchase. Off-grid. Way less conspicuous."

"Name your price," said Robert.

The tall scavenger gave Robert an irritated sideways glance, his considerable front teeth as pronounced as a jackrabbit's. He spit on the ground and huffed and then looked back at the woman, who shrugged.

"Hundred thousand dollars."

"For that beat-up piece of shit," said Amanda.

"You guys did the asking. And you seem desperate."

"What makes you think we have that sort of money?" continued Amanda.

"I don't. And whatever money you do have probably ain't near enough."

"Tell them you'll take it," said Dez.

"I'll take it."

Amanda elbowed Robert. "What are you doing?"

The tall scavenger signaled for his family to pick up their packs, and they started heading for the vehicle.

"No, wait. I'll get you the money," said Robert.

"You don't have it, kid."

Robert ran after them, reached out and tugged on the back of the man's threadbare overalls. The scavenger wheeled around violently. "Get your paws off me!" he bellowed. Robert fell backward onto the ground, a sawed-off shotgun stabbing into his chest.

"I can get you money. I'll get it to you in less than an hour. What do you have to lose?"

The tall scavenger looked impatiently back at his wife. She mulled the situation over for a second, then nodded her head.

"All right, kid. I'll wait here for an hour. You're one second longer, I'm gone."

★ ★ ★

Dez, via Robert, had instructed Amanda and Haseya to stay with the family at the car until he returned. To stall them, if necessary.

Robert jogged through the vacant streets; musk thistle and mayweed grew up through the serpentine cracks in the cement. He was hot and in a less-than-optimal mood.

"Mind telling me where we're going to get a hundred grand? We don't have a cent to gamble with."

"Pick up that plastic bag over there. We're going to need it."

Robert ran after a white plastic bag that danced and drifted in the escalating breeze.

"Okay. So tell me."

"I'm considering a more direct route."

"Care to elaborate?"

"Get me to the closest ATM."

Robert found an ATM using a quick locator app that he downloaded. The route was highlighted on his digital overlay. The ATM happened to be back near the crazy golf putting green outside the Bellagio.

Robert waited for an inebriated man wearing a blue Hawaiian shirt to bumble and curse his way through his transaction. He came away from the machine with a fistful of cash and a glazed, unbalanced expression, then shuffled and hobbled up the steps toward the casino.

"What do I do?" asked Robert.

"Walk up to the machine and put your eye to the retinal scan. Let me do the rest."

Robert did as he was told. The machine scanned his right eye, giving Dez all the access he needed to its digital database and inner network.

"Okay, I found an account with enough money. Get ready to shovel the bills into the bag. Enter two hundred thousand for the withdrawal amount."

"Two hundred?"

"You want to go through this again?"

"No."

Robert typed in "200,000" and pressed "enter." The ATM made a few guttural, metallic indigestion noises, then began to spit out the money as if it had severe dysentery. Robert rapidly grabbed the cash and shoved it into the plastic bag.

"Why didn't we do this before instead of playing craps?"

"Craps seemed like infinitely more fun," replied Dez.

* * *

Robert agreed to drop the scavengers off at their house outside the city. They lived in Gibson Springs, a small, mostly uninhabited community southeast of Las Vegas. The family made enough income off of their scrapping to sustain themselves. The market for scrap metal was a healthy one. Dozens of scrap-metal facilities had sprung up in the wake of the casino closings. The family took whatever they thought was currently fetching the best price. They stripped copper out of the wiring. They blowtorched through steel I-beams; they pried loose light fixtures. Whatever was selling, they delivered to the scrap dealers. And the scrap dealers, in turn, sold mountains of the nation's crumbling infrastructure to Asia to help the country build its own prominent cities and empire. Much like Detroit, Michigan, in the 2000s, Las Vegas was being systemically dismantled and shipped overseas. But a living is a living.

"How long have you been scrappers?" asked Haseya.

The family, now flush with cash, was happy to have the young guests as company. The mother had shed her work clothes and was dressed in a simple green T-shirt and jeans. Like most people from the region, she wore her hard times on her face. There was no disguising them. Yet she was still a woman whose smile was pleasant and warm and whose voice could still be animated.

"We've been scrapping for about seven years. At first, the casinos kept real tight security on the buildings. Probably thought they'd find a way to bring back the water. Or a way to manipulate the weather. Make it rain, so to speak. But they never did. So year by year, security dwindled till eventually, the companies gave up hope and gave up on ever returning. The security guards were cut loose shortly after that. Then we came in," said the wife.

"And it's been real good to us, too, hasn't it, honey?" said the man.

Haseya rode upfront with the husband and wife, while Robert and Amanda were sardined into the backseat with the teenage boys. The day's loot was piled up behind them in the way back.

"We mostly work in the early morning, when it's cooler. We're out there before first light every day of the week except Sundays."

"Ask him if he's a religious man," said Dez.

"That's not an appropriate questions to ask near-strangers," replied Robert.

"You don't have to tell us, but you kids in some sort of trouble? Lord knows, most people are these days," continued the father.

"Think you just got your answer," said Robert to Dez.

Haseya brushed her long, dark hair back. "We're trying to make it out east. And we're behind schedule."

"My husband can be nosy. Just ignore him. You don't have to tell us nothing you don't want to. None of our business."

The station wagon continued to jostle along the bright, desert road out of Vegas.

They passed numerous boarded-up storefronts in forsaken-looking strip malls. A stark-white church with its front doors ripped off the hinges and an empty parking lot still had a portable, changeable letter sign that read: "Be An Organ Donor ... Give your heart to Jesus!" And written beneath that: "Global Warming is a Hoax!!!!"

They eventually pulled into a suburban neighborhood. Half the houses had been burned down; the other half looked severely neglected.

"Home, sweet home," said the father. He meant it.

The car pulled up into a driveway of a southwestern-style stucco house. A rotund lady in her early sixties sat on a shaded porch on the opposite side of the street, eying them contemptuously and sipping soda from a can.

The two teenage boys unloaded the back of the Subaru without complaint and stacked the weighty backpacks in the garage.

"Well, a deal is a deal," said the father as he handed the car keys over to Robert. "Take care of her now. She's a good one."

Robert took the keys and promptly backed the car up. Once it was in the street, he threw the station wagon into drive, gave a brief wave to the family, and sped off.

"Didn't know you knew how to drive one of these old things," said Amanda.

"My grandfather taught me. Detests automated cars."

After driving a mile onto Highway 95, he glanced down at the gas gauge.

It was almost empty.

★ ★ ★

After sputtering into a remote gas station, after buying countless bags of snacks and drinks from the mini-mart, after stopping off at a motel to shower and let the girls rest, and after buying new, clean clothes from a western-themed store called Dick Trickle's Country-Style Emporium, Robert and the gang were finally back on track and headed east at a fairly consistent clip.

Amanda was thankful to be finally headed in the right direction. Robert was relieved that they had, so far, evaded detection. Dez was taking the opportunity to study the classics of western literature. He'd devoured Shakespeare's entire oeuvre in way less than a minute. Dez admired his extraordinary use of poetic language and his insights on the human animal, its yearnings, follies, vanities, and frailties. Dez's favorite play was *Macbeth*. A tragic story of the corrupting influence of ambition and power. A timeless tale that he thought more Americans should read and know.

Specifically, Amanda.

Amanda lay sprawled out on the uncomfortable backseat by herself, while Robert and Haseya rode upfront. She'd laid down a blanket to try to protect herself from the filth—an unachievable task.

Dez projected himself next to Amanda, a hovering nano-cloud, once again in the form of the "everyman."

"You should read *Macbeth*," said Dez. "It might give you a better understanding of your father." Amanda blinked one leery eye open.

"Macbeth at least had the courage to kill. My father was just a cowardly tool for more formidable men of influence."

"Yes, but he still experienced the same allure of unrestrained ambition and its damaging psychological after-effects. Most humans thrust into a situation of such overwhelming opportunity for greed and self-indulgence would come under its spell, don't you think?"

"I think my father is weak; that's what I think. Redemption is an old-fashioned idea and a luxury we can't afford."

"Humanity is imperfect. Men make mistakes. And if you deny someone the opportunity for redemption, there will be no movement toward it. Besides, I think you're too young to be making such statements of certainty."

"And I think you're a computer program that doesn't know what it means to be human. If someone or some institution becomes an implacable cancer, you cut it out and throw it away. You don't save little pieces of it for sentimental reasons. You remove every tiny, malignant cell, or the tumor returns. There can't be even a specter of a trace. It's the only way to assure that the organism as a whole will remain alive and viable."

"Did you get that from the Dragoons handbook?" asked Dez.

"I helped write the Dragoons handbook," replied Amanda.

"So, once a corruptible entity ..." said Dez.

"... always a corruptible entity," finished Amanda.

Dez pondered this for a couple nanoseconds. "I will endeavor to prove you wrong."

"There are greater issues to deal with."

"You're referring to the seven robotics factories you plan on taking down in conjunction with your DC protest."

"How did you know about the seven—"

Dez cut her off. "Your compatriots aren't as secretive or as clever as they'd like to believe. They text each other with utterly conspicuous, unsophisticated, easily decoded jargon. You guys are certainly the underdogs."

"I'll have to put out a memo."

"That's another thing: if you want anyone to really take your organization seriously, you need a proper leader. All social movements have one."

"The Dragoons deliberately avoided nominating one person—"

Dez interrupted yet again. "Which is your problem. You're leaderless. You lack a true agenda to put forward. You need to offer alternatives to a public that craves change. I mentioned before that I don't think your demonstrations will ultimately make any difference with regards to changing policy unless you have concrete ideas to replace them with."

"Our main stated goal is to wrestle power away from the plutocratic police state and rid the affluent of their monopoly on opportunity."

"Now who sounds like a robot? I know your intentions are good, but that will only take you so far. Say you do succeed with this protest in DC—what then? And what constitutes success? That you don't get arrested, or that they let you go through with it? What's the endgame here, Amanda?"

Amanda sat up on the backseat; the parched desert air billowed through the open windows as the elderly Subaru grumbled and moaned down the open highway.

"You're saying that no matter what we do or how loud we protest, they won't change," stated Amanda.

"I'm saying you might want to use the time you have left between here and DC to figure out exactly what you think needs to happen."

Amanda ruffled through the supplies on the floorboard and pulled out a super-sized bag of Funyuns. She yanked open the slick packaging, filling the car with the strong scent of fake onions.

"What do you think needs to happen?" asked Amanda as she crunched down on several Funyuns.

"I think if you don't change the system, you're not going to change the behavior of the people in it. One determines and dictates the other. Your father was correct today: corporate capitalism has lost a sense of its social limits. Although there are far greater dilemmas than that. Human behavior may be too flawed and unredeemable. And it always seeks out the weakest point of any system that's adopted in order to exploit it for egomaniacal pursuits."

"So we're doomed no matter what?"

"History might suggest so."

"You're still here. You're still helping."

"The subtext being that I still retain hope."

"The subtext being that you may be slightly more human than I initially gave you credit for."

CHAPTER 11

Would summer ever arrive in DC? The warm, fragrant weather had flirted with the citizens on several occasions but then quickly retreated like a bashful guest of honor who detests the limelight. It was June already and rain, frigid rain, poured down on the bus stop where Sylvia Priola stood in line under the awning. She picked nervously at her fingers, leaving a raw, reddish patch of under-skin.

She hated herself.

She truly did.

There were no excuses for her actions. Sure, she had her reasons. And they were doubtlessly good ones. But betraying one's friends, close friends, and betraying one's own ideology, the reason you get up in the morning, the song that plays in your heart, is an awful thing to have to do.

Sylvia was a member of the dismal science, an economist that had held a decent-paying job as a low-level functionary at the World Bank. She was still quite young, only twenty-eight. She was gregarious, funny, charming, and fabulously good-looking, and yet, she had a terrible hidden weakness: she was desperate.

And most people innately loathe desperation. It cuts too close to the bone, an undesirable reminder and embodiment of their own fragile state in an indifferent universe. Being out of work for fourteen months tended to make one desperate. It also chipped away at one's attributes.

Desperation made you less gregarious, less funny, less charming, less likable.

Especially to oneself.

Sylvia hadn't paid a visit to the World Bank Group's building since her termination. And walking up H Street to meet up with her ex-boss gave her a momentary twinge of queasiness.

She'd taken the meeting thinking that there might be a slight chance to get her old position back. Something she'd previously thought to be an impossibility. And on that front, she was correct. Sylvia's ex-boss, Christopher Caldwell, had a very different agenda in mind.

Christopher sat lifelessly in his austere office, behind an expensive Norwegian box desk made of mahogany.

Steam lingered fertilely over a cup of fresh Earl Grey tea.

No milk.

No sugar.

One slice of lemon.

Sylvia fidgeted across from him, seated in a black-leather hunting chair, also Norwegian. She noted that all the furniture seemed new. He must have recently received a raise or promotion and gone on a shopping spree.

Christopher took a tentative sip of tea and set it immediately back down on a rustic, bronze coaster. It was still too hot to drink.

"Thanks for coming here on such short notice, Miss Priola," he said in a hollow monotone.

"I very much enjoyed my time here, Mr. Caldwell."

"I'm glad. I have to tell you that your sudden termination was just as surprising to me as it was to you. It came from the top down. Nothing to do with your performance. Nothing to do with me."

"I understand," said Sylvia, not really understanding why he was bringing it up.

"You still have yet to find employment, is that correct?"

"I've had a few temporary jobs. Nothing permanent."

"Ah, I see. An all-too-typical experience these days. Well, I have something for you. An assignment. Not through the usual channels, though."

"What do you mean?" asked Sylvia.

"I mean, I'm not only a bureaucrat. I have many interests. Boating, for instance. Love that open water. Smell of the ocean air. My family can be traced all the way back to the Mayflower. Perhaps that's where my passion for sailing came from. My family also handed down to me many long-standing connections and responsibilities. So I move in many circles. I'm tied to many different entities and organizations beyond these walls."

"So this assignment isn't here?"

"It's for a friend."

"How did your friend hear about me?"

Christopher tried his Earl Grey again but to a similar, negative result. It left the tip of his tongue burning.

"Your name came up on a list."

"What list?" asked Sylvia.

"The sort of list you don't want to be on."

Sylvia flushed red. She'd heard of the list. That somewhere someone was keeping tabs. Keeping names.

"So, I've been to a few protests, so what?"

"I'm not here to tell you what you're already beginning to surmise. They know *everything*. Understand? *Everything*."

Sylvia barely managed to nod her head. Her eyes took on a sudden, acute sensitivity to the overhead lights.

Christopher continued, "Hell, they've known everything for a good, long while. Now, here's a question for you: Did you not think they would find out?"

Sylvia squinted painfully. Her breathing grew shallow. Several months prior, she thought that in life, she'd hit rock bottom. She had been wrong. Now she actually felt that bottom beneath her feet.

"Seems like protesting is a family affair. Your brother is also on the list."

"What's the assignment?" she uttered meekly.

"I don't know. Do whatever they ask."

"And if I don't?"

"You think I mentioned your brother for anecdotal reasons? These are serious, serious people. I suggest you do everything *exactly* the way they tell you to do it."

Christopher slid a slender manila envelope across the desk.

"Your instructions."

Sylvia stood and picked up the package; her legs were unsteady, and the room swayed slightly, as if she were one of his sailboats.

"Our business is done here."

Sylvia managed to make it out of his office without falling.

Christopher exhaled deeply and rubbed his jawline. He took a sip of Earl Grey and relaxed back into his ergonomic chair with the cup.

The temperature was just right.

★ ★ ★

The long-awaited city bus finally wheezed its way up to the curb where Sylvia stood waiting, her picked fingers stinging. The rain had backed off to a delicate drizzle, and the clouds remained pencil gray. She took a seat near the back, where there were fewer people.

It was three p.m.

Sylvia had spent the early part of the day strategizing with one particular cell of the Dragoons, who were in charge of target selection. She was on her way to give her DOD handler the updated information. Maybe after this, they would let her go. Maybe this would be enough and she could put a period at the end of her sentence.

There were five stops to go before Sylvia reached her destination, which gave her far too much time to contemplate her predicament. Way too much time for self-loathing. She and her brother should have fled town. Gone into hiding somewhere. That choice, they would understand. But this, this ugly decision, they would never understand.

Or forgive.

And that meeting with her ex-boss. Hoping that she might get her old job back. What was that? A new low. Her integrity was now as shallow as a puddle.

Sylvia had grown disenchanted with the World Bank from the first week she got there and saw how politicized it was, that the World Bank was a tool of American foreign policy. The bank provided the carrot and stick that forced smaller nations to comply with America's economic agenda. Her guilt over working there had driven her to seek out the Dragoons. To protest and rally. To be a part of a less nefarious future.

What a joke that was now.

If this DOD asshole wouldn't consider her debt paid, she would push things. She could no longer live with the guilt and torment. There were indeed fates worse than death.

The meet was scheduled at West Potomac Park for 3:45. Normally, a nondescript, middle-aged white man in a sports jacket with a high and tight haircut would be waiting at one of the many benches.

Today was not a typical day, though.

General Voss had become intrigued with the source of the quality intel he was receiving. He'd heard the source was young and beautiful—perhaps the most alluring informant they'd ever used. Plus, she was whip-smart and had good potential as a long-term asset. Someone they could utilize on many different fronts, if she could be convinced.

Voss wanted to meet her. Knew there would be no bad ramifications if he did. Secrecy was not necessary in a police state. There would be no chance of endangerment or of him being set up in any way—for the simple reason that there was no one for Sylvia Priola to tell.

The general waited near the newly reinforced concert flood barriers, which now protected the park from the swollen river. After numerous perilous floods, even the right-wing lawmakers had rapidly approved funds for the project. It was annoying and highly inconvenient to every lawmaker when DC was flooded.

Sylvia saw Voss standing in the designated spot and froze mid-step. Why had they changed people? She approached him reticently.

"It's all right," reassured Voss. "Your usual man is sick. Taking the day off. Why don't we take a stroll?"

The two began to walk next to the blackish-green waters of the Potomac. Sylvia would still stick to the deal she had made with herself. Come what may.

"I was told you were quite attractive. I didn't imagine anyone as ravishing as you, though."

"What does that have to do with anything?" Sylvia was put off by any older man commenting on her appearance.

"It has a lot to do with everything. Beauty is an asset. Or it can be, if you use it right. Maybe one out of several hundred people are what you could truly call *beautiful*. You're fortunate."

"I would call myself many things, but hardly *fortunate*."

"Then you're not playing your cards correctly. A diamond in the rough such as yourself should be able to leverage her beauty."

"I'm not going to become a prostitute—"

"Good God, I'm not talking about that. Not at all. In fact, the opposite. I'm talking about taking charge. Pushing back against the bad circumstances that surround you. It can be a cruel world, can't it?"

"Crueler for some more than others. I've learned that lesson intimately."

"I wonder. Have you? When you were let go by the World Bank, what did you do?"

"I'd like to give you the intel you requested and get out of here."

"Play along for a minute. Please. What did you do?"

"What do you mean? I tried to get another job. There were none. At least, very few good ones."

"Yes, very few good ones. That's it, huh? You applied for jobs that had thousands of applicants. Shocking. You didn't get the job you wanted, and then you took crappy part-time ones. That about sum it up?"

"Not far off."

"The men that work at the World Bank, what type of men are they, generally speaking?"

"Generally speaking, they're dull numbers guys. Introverted. Conservative. Married. I don't know—shy. Perhaps somewhat repressed."

"Repressed, exactly. So after you received your termination notice, what was stopping you from going into one of their offices, ripping your skirt and pantyhose and then screaming at the top of your lungs and accusing them of assault?"

"Why would I want to do that?"

"Because it's a cruel world. A lesson you said you've already learned. You think their wives would have believed them or you? A gorgeous young woman. Sexy. Someone that their husbands most likely fantasized about?"

"So what, blackmail?"

"Among other things. You would have had leverage. You could have threatened to sue the organization."

"I would never do that."

"The words 'I would never do that' have been spoken by just about every successful person that went ahead and did exactly what they said they'd never do. They buried the sanctimonious angel that hovered over their shoulders and got ahead in life. 'Cause it's the only way you can. You getting this, Sylvia? Morality is arbitrary. An inherited affliction. Generational enslavement. A fairy tale parents tell their kids because they daren't admit to themselves that they brought another human being into a world so unjust and terrifyingly hostile. A useless construct that serves no purpose other than to keep a person from fully living and competing. Begging for scraps because they can't see beyond the faith of their own prison walls, their own self-inflicted fictitious principles.

"And you, so stunning, thinking, hoping, praying that the world will somehow, some way provide you with something better. Well, it won't. It won't. Hope and faith do nothing but prolong hardship and suffering. The way of the world is that if you want to get ahead, then you do whatever it takes to get there. No fictions, no fairy tales, no irrational belief in some magical guiding hand from beyond, only the need to accept yourself for what you are and your circumstance for what it is: a random game of spills and thrills where anything goes, as long as you get away with it."

Voss withdrew a silver hip flask, unscrewed the top, and took a long pull of whiskey. He wiped his lips, then put the flask back into his jacket.

"So, Sylvia, you can stop your torment. It's up to you. You came here a misery. I could see it. A beautiful girl with downcast eyes. But ask yourself right now if you really want to rid yourself of all this unnecessary misfortune. Go ahead, ask yourself. Do you want to get ahead, or not?

★ ★ ★

Kansas was an anomaly. Somehow, a sizable number of the state's waterways had remained filled with a decent amount of water. Some people suggested that it was due to the fact that Kansas was such a religious state. But if that logic was to hold true, it would have to account for the rest of the Bible Belt, which was drier than a Mojave lizard's scorched turd. Thousands of lakes had been reduced to chalk dust. The docks of lakefront properties now lead out to empty fields of brittle dirt.

So much for the appeal of picture windows. Come on out for a barbecue and take in the tranquil view of our spectacular meadow of baking mud.

Robert had turned north out of Winfield, Kansas, and stopped at Cowley Lake Waterfalls for lunch. They had passed by a mom-and-pop diner and ordered to-go food so they could sit, stretch, walk, and go for a swim. The diner had a dozen or so patrons. It was owned by an elderly gentlemen in his mid-seventies named Merl Haggard. Behind the cash register on the wall was a giant, wooden crucifix. As the old proprietor rung Robert up at the cash register, Dez noticed a gold crucifix around the man's neck.

"So this is America's heartland?" asked Dez.

"This is it," replied Robert as he counted out his money to hand to the man.

"Ask him what denomination he is."

"Excuse me, sir, what denomination are you?"

Merl stopped wringing up the order on the cash register.

"I'm Southern Baptist. What denomination are you?"

"Oh, I'm not."

Merl sized up Robert, who was windblown and disheveled.

"Son, are you in need of some guidance?"

"Please tell him yes," Dez interjected.

"Uh ... yes."

"I could tell. You're not just hungry for food, are you? Looky, you need some Donald Young Jr., that's what you need. He's our senior pastor. Amazing fella. Boy, can he draw a crowd. We got twenty-four thousand come to see him. Why don't you drop by the early-afternoon service at Fellowship Church?"

"You have church, today?"

"Today's a Sunday, son."

"Oh, yeah."

"Tell him we'll be there," said Dez.

"No way in hell Amanda is going to want to stop to attend a church service."

"It will be the last favor I ask of you before we get to Washington."

"Amanda won't care. And neither do I, frankly. I don't know what you hope to get out of attending some evangelical freak show."

"Research. A little social anthropology. You needn't ask Amanda. I will. Although you can tell this kindly gentleman that you appreciate the offer."

Robert handed over a small wad of cash to pay for the lunch.

"Thanks for the offer. Maybe I'll see you there."

"Get there early if you can. All the good seats go quickly. Wouldn't want to be left to the nose-bleed section."

The climb down to the bottom of Cowley Lake Waterfalls was fairly precarious. Amanda wasn't even certain the small hike would be worthwhile. Yet when they reached the bottom and got an unobstructed view of the thirty-foot falls, Amanda was certainly glad they'd made the effort.

Haseya reached into her backpack and took out the lunches the diner had boxed up for them. Amanda tossed out a blanket on a patch of dry sandstone so they could sit and enjoy the scenery. The gorge's walls provided some appreciated shade.

"I'm happy we stopped," said Haseya. "My muscles were getting tied up in knots from sitting in the car for so long."

"I know what you mean," said Amanda.

Haseya opened up her lunch box and took out a club sandwich.

"There is something big happening in Washington?" asked Haseya.

"A grand statement, yes. Something that will really put us on the map."

"I can't wait to be a part of it."

"Well, the Sisters always play a big role, I can tell you that. They are very enthusiastic about what we're doing."

Robert came and sat down beside the two young women. Amanda turned away, not wanting his company. Robert shrugged at Haseya as if to say, *What did I do?* Haseya shrugged back.

Haseya picked up her sandwich and cautiously leapt from boulder to boulder toward the lower portion of the falls. When she was gone, Robert tapped Amanda lightly on the shoulder.

"What's up? Why are you ignoring me?"

"I'm not ignoring you. I'm ignoring him. Or it. Dez."

"I see."

"Yes, seems I can't have a conversation without him being involved in some way. Or worse, judging."

"So you don't want to talk?"

"Oh, I'd like to, but ..."

Robert thought about the situation, knowing Dez was reading his thoughts.

"Could you leave my body for a few minutes and give us some time alone. Please?"

"I'll grant you that courtesy," said Dez. "But you're taking me to that mega-church service. I must see it."

"If you give me ten minutes of privacy with Amanda, I'll do my best."

Dez gathered himself up and expelled himself out onto a distant watery, smooth rock. Stone life was an empty stillness.

"He's gone," said Robert. "He's left my body."

"For real?"

"Yeah, but only for ten minutes or so. So tell me, how are you doing?"

"I wish I knew. I wish I knew how and what I was doing."

"Not sure I follow. You've been pretty certain about what you wanted and what you want to do since I first met you. Was one of the things that I admired, 'cause I lacked that ability."

"Dez has got me thinking."

"Oh, no. Not Dez."

"He's right, though. The Dragoons need a genuine endgame. We don't have one, yet. And we could be far better organized."

"Don't you think that this thing you've got planned in DC will show them that they better start paying attention to the people's demands?"

"Maybe. For a little while."

"You'll get even more attention and respect, and the Dragoons will grow. Millions more will join. You'll see."

"That's the hope."

Robert couldn't help himself. He reached out and kissed Amanda. The kiss awakened a summer-like twinkle in Amanda, and she kissed him back.

"I'm still me. I promise," said Robert.

"I know. It's going to take more time, though. And you can't tell anyone in DC. No one."

"I won't."

★ ★ ★

Since they were making such good time, Amanda had agreed, albeit somewhat reluctantly, to let Dez stop off briefly, at the mega-church's afternoon service. Amanda made certain that they got aisle seats so they could leave after the first fifteen minutes.

Fellowship Church was housed in a massive arena-like building that held six thousand people per service. The owner of the diner had given solid advice. The good seats were rapidly filling up by the time Robert and the others arrived.

The Reverend Donald Young Jr. took the stage to enthusiastic applause. He strutted about under the spotlights like an overly perfumed madam at a favored whorehouse; his chest thrust forward, and he gestured lavishly with each gravelly voiced pronouncement. He was a natural performer, with the attention-grabbing flair of Liberace. Reverend Donald Young Jr. would have made a wonderful living in Vegas back in the day.

"I wonder, how many of us here are people-pleasers? I mean, we all want to be liked, right? To go along to get along, as they say. Easy to do, isn't it? All too easy.

"Well, folks, I want to talk to you today about being a God-pleaser. To stress to you the importance of pleasing God first. Not yourself, your friends, or your family. God.

"'Okay, Reverend,' you might say. 'How do I go about doing that?' I'm gonna tell you right now. It's not easy. Everyone listening?"

The crowd yelled back numerous responses, which Donald Young Jr. interpreted as a signal that enough of them were.

"Okay, then. First, you have to know the will of God. Not a simple thing. Let's face it; the will of God has been interpreted in countless ways, many inconsistent, depending on who was doing the interpreting at the time. So how do we know the true will of God? How are we able to do his bidding and thus please him?

"Any of you seen Reverend Hope on TV? Seen him perform his healings?"

Many had, and they voiced their approval.

"Yeah, I've seen him, too. Had the privilege of meeting him in person several weeks back. He spoke to me about the spirit of God, about God's will working through him. Reverend Hope told me that during one particular healing he performed, he actually saw midgets grow. Midgets! You believe that? Growing right there on stage in front of him!

"Well, I don't have the power to make midgets grow. I'm sorry. God does not work through me in that way. Wish that he would. I'd like to make midgets grow. Would add a few more inches to myself while I was at it."

The audience laughed heartily.

"I couldn't foresee a greater gift than to be able to heal every one of you! To grant you all happiness and health here on Earth as well as in heaven. Deliver you from hunger and pointless affliction. But I can't. God has not made himself known to me in that capacity. Wish that he would.

"What I can do for each of you, though, is give to you my honest opinion of what He wants from us. To walk as close as we may in Jesus' footsteps. To seek righteousness.

"This world is a changing world. A world that constantly tests our faith with a never-ending immoral array of technological mayhem run amuck. We've usurped God's power, and we will pay the price when the time comes, let me assure you."

This last comment garnered the most intense applause and shouts of "Praise Jesus" and "Alleluia."

"Yet, *our* path is constant. *Our* beliefs don't waver or change. And that's the source of our strength. And it's how we please God. We show faith in his words and Christ's example.

"If I could sum up Jesus's teachings in one word, it would be the most powerful transformative word that I know. A word we must act upon if we intend to do God's will.

"What's that powerful word? *Compassion*. Say it with me now: *compassion*. Oh, yes, each of us here needs to harbor a deep, deep concern for the well-being of all others. All others. I'm convinced if we did just that one thing, followed that one simple precept of caring for others, we would please God immeasurably. And also please ourselves and everyone around us. It would be heaven right here on Earth."

Dez was riveted by Reverend Donald Young Jr. and accessed everything he could find online about him. Donald had had a falling-out with his father's church when he was in his mid-twenties. He had issues with their preaching of "hellfire and brimstone," the constant threat of eternal damnation. That sort of negative proselytizing did not sit well with Donald Jr. He was a different generation. And he knew that if his church was to survive and stay relevant, not only would he have to preach a more uplifting, positive message, he would also have to cast a more inclusive net.

Donald always believed that if he was to continue preaching the word of God, he could never willfully ignore that Jesus's overriding, defining trait was that of empathy, of unfailing love for his fellow man.

"I want to become a Christian," said Dez.

"Shut up," responded Robert. "Don't get hysterical."

Dez knew how difficult a thing it was to get any humans to believe in anything, let alone in something so lofty and arcane. And to get them to act on those beliefs was even harder. Yet here was Reverend Donald Young Jr. pulling it off with such dramatic flair. Dez could learn something from these people and from their fearless reverend.

Yes, by golly, he could. There was much to be gleaned from this experience.

Robert stood up. "Time to leave," he announced to Amanda.

"What? Sit back down! We've just gotten started," complained Dez.

"The deal was fifteen minutes. Your meter ran out five minutes ago."

Reverend Donald Young Jr. continued, "Listen, my children of God. I long for the day of the second coming. When Jesus returns to Earth and sets all wrongs to right ..."

These were the last words Dez heard as Robert briskly exited the auditorium.

On their way into the blistering parking lot, Dez noticed several tardy churchgoers making their way toward them.

"Fall down. Pretend to have a heart attack!" demanded Dez.

"I'm not even twenty!" said Robert.

"Do it! All of you, do it!"

"We're not going to have heart attacks."

"At least you go down. Go into spasms! Make it look good!"

"Why?"

"No time to explain! Do it now, or I'll end the world!"

"What?"

"Okay, I won't. Just please, do it!"

Robert threw himself to the pavement, proceeding to convulse and gurgle.

Amanda looked down at him. "What the fuck are you doing, Robert?"

Robert continued to convulse wildly as the three churchgoers rushed up.

"Can we help? Is he all right?"

"I ... I don't know," said Amanda, genuinely concerned.

A heavyset woman stooped to one knee and placed her purse protectively behind his head. She then placed an unused tampon between his clenched teeth.

"Wouldn't want him to bite his tongue," she said. "This ever happened before?"

"No," said Amanda earnestly.

"Okay, Robert, you can stop. I've got the information that I need," Dez stated.

"Not very scientific. That's only one data point. We'd have to replicate this hundreds or thousands of times to get a decent representative sample."

"I'm well aware of the scientific method. I needed to experience the beauty of empathy in a person. That's all. I know that many people of so-called *faith* cherry-pick the tenets to suit their own agendas and lives. What intrigues me most is the power of superstition and religious dogma, even when it violates all the known truths of the universe. There appears to be an inherent human need for subjugation. To place one's own life and destiny in the hands of some leader or prophet."

Robert stopped writhing around on the ground. He sat up and spat out the tampon.

"I'm feeling much better now. Thank you," he said.

Amanda glared at him, knowing full well that Dez must have asked him to perform such a lunatic prank. Why, though, she had no idea.

"Now, may we please get going?" asked Amanda.

The pudgy churchgoers loomed over Robert, blocking out the sunlight. He nodded, somewhat embarrassed by the whole affair.

"Dez needed me to—"

"I don't want to hear it. Let's please go back to the car."

★ ★ ★

If felt good to be behind the wheel of the Subaru. Amanda had not driven a car before. It had not taken her much time to get used to operating the vehicle. Haseya had instructed her well, and Amanda was as good a student as Haseya was a teacher. Amanda gripped the steering wheel at ten and two and stared out at the endless tract of road ahead. There was a sense of freedom in this moment.

Amanda had early memories of her mother and father driving her to school and the grocery store as a young child. She remembered one particular long road trip to the coast of Oregon, near Coos Bay. Her parents had been in love back then. They sang songs and joked and acted like people who cared about one another. This was, of course, all prior to her father's political career. Before they moved to DC and their lives went haywire.

Amanda's father had been warned by the departing congressman, Alan West, that the halls of power had a way of distorting reality, of creating their own moral universe. A corrupted universe that only seemed rational and reasonable from the inside looking out. Where tremendous forces and institutions could bend and shape any person's will to do their bidding. One did not have to be an innately bad person to succumb to the temptations of power, the allure and promise of opportunity and wealth. Everyday men and women could, without having previously had a malevolent thought in their bodies, be easily seduced to perform malevolent deeds—having no prior history of being anything but loving, caring, happy people and upstanding citizens. The fact that it was ordinary men and women that turned their backs on their constituents in order to become members of the fortunate class was what disturbed him the most.

They weren't evil.

They weren't monsters.

Like Hannah Arendt had written in reference to the notorious Nazi Adolf Eichmann, "In certain circumstances, the most ordinary decent person can become a criminal." The "banality of evil," she termed it. Malicious intent is not a prerequisite for malicious deeds; in the specific case of Eichmann, only a bureaucrat and a culture of blind obedience.

Amanda thought about her father and his recent breakdown on the news. Was this his way of reaching out to her? Did he believe in the things he had said? Perhaps he was not the monster she'd like to believe he was. He, too, had been an ordinary man. But could he really be trusted?

Or forgiven?

She thought not. If for no other reason than to be in solidarity with her mother. Oh, man, her mother. What must she be thinking? Amanda wished she could have left her mother a note. Explained things to her instead of cutting out of town with such fear and haste. She supposed there would be a time for explanations, but this didn't mitigate the guilt that now rosied her forehead and cheeks.

Amanda tried hard to force these burdensome thoughts from her head. There were far more pressing issues and tasks at hand. The next few days would define the Dragoons as a social force the establishment would have to take seriously and bargain with. Social unrest had reached a critical point. Change would come. Its breadth and depth were unknowable at this point, but she had to believe that the mass demonstration would shake the corporate state at its core. It had been estimated by the Dragoons that several million would converge on the nation's capital. Yet there was this nagging bee in her bonnet that Dez had put there: Without a leader or captain, where would all this lead? What ultimate course would the demonstration take? If the government was willing to listen, who would be chosen to speak? Without a designated leader, would the demonstration turn overly violent? Some in the organization had recently verbalized that this would be a welcome development. That the corporate state had become so powerful and filled with hubris that it had lost its ability to listen and respond in a rational way to the needs of its people. To them, then, outright rebellion was the only rational course of action.

How loud would their voices be in DC?

She'd been sent as a moderating force to set up the protest in such a way that would curtail the more radical elements of the group. What if she were wrong, though? What if the radicals were correct? What if the noise raised by the demonstrators just dissipated into a gulf of governmental indifference? Would she then be persuaded to take up arms? To force the fight to its next logical stage? To risk everything? Her entire life behind bars or possible death?

Sometimes, she secretly wished that she'd been born a generation sooner, before the certainty of misfortune for the growing underclass had completely sealed their immobile fate. Amanda looked over at Haseya sitting in the front passenger seat. She appeared so at peace with herself and the situation. A true warrior and believer. Born to it. Amanda supposed Haseya had no nagging questions in her mind. No uncertainties about what they were about to do. No qualms about giving up her life, should the circumstance call for such drastic action. Haseya's fortitude must be carved from granite, she presumed.

They were now only ten hours or so from Washington, and there were still so many insecurities and questions that nagged her. The only thing Amanda knew for sure about DC was her contact's name: Sylvia Priola.

★ ★ ★

During the ride, Dez noted that Robert was feeling slightly forlorn. He sensed that Robert was missing his grandfather, Waldo.

"I don't mean to interrupt your thoughts—"

"You say that a lot."

"Your grandfather seems to be a wonderful man. I can understand why you miss him. What fantastic memories you have of him."

"I'm starting to resent the fact that you're constantly reading my life and that my reflections are no longer private. This is all just too bizarre and uncomfortable."

"Why don't you give your grandfather a call?"

"And risk being detected? They'd pick up our location immediately."

"I can scramble that. Actually, you *have* to call him."

"What does it matter to you?"

"It matters to me because it matters to you."

"That's touching, but I'll call him next week when this is all—"

"No, you must call him today. At the next gas station. I've captured some data regarding some recent correspondence between the assassin that almost killed us in LA and his handler. The man's name is Horace Spruill, and he's at your grandfather's house."

"He's there right now? Is my grandfather okay?"

"He's fine at the moment—"

"Why'd he go there? Why would they target my grandfather?"

"They are not targeting your grandfather. Yet. He's there to get information on your whereabouts. So in order for us to get Spruill to leave, we should give him some. Spruill is the sort of man that would murder your grandfather on a whim, so we should lure him out of there as soon as possible."

When Amanda pulled over for their final gas stop, Robert rushed to the electronics vending machine, bought a cheap smart device that Dez recommend, and contacted his grandfather.

Waldo answered on the second chirp of his videocom.

"No, Robert! They have a man here, looking for you!"

Waldo tried to disconnect the transmission, but Spruill stopped him.

"It's okay, Granddad. It's okay. I wanted to make sure you know that I'm healthy and that everything is going to work out. That may seem like a bold statement, given the situation, but Dez will leave my body shortly after we arrive in DC."

Spruill smirked when he heard the destination city.

"I'll be in Washington in less than six hours' time. Dez wants them to know that unless they leave me alone, all bets are off. That he'll be monitoring the situation. And Granddad, I'm sorry I agreed to the enhancement procedure. You must be very disappointed."

"Oh, good God, no, Robert. I only care about you. You are anything but a disappointment. You're the joy and magic in my life. And don't take these hucksters for granted. They are dangerous people, Robert. This Dez entity better know that."

"He assures me that he does. And he'd also like Spruill to know that he'll be on the lookout for him."

Spruill was halfway out the door and on his way up to DC before the conversation had finished.

"You stay where you are, Granddad. Don't you go trying to save me. I'll be just fine. Promise me you won't come anywhere near DC."

"That's a tough promise to make, kid. You mean the world to me."

"And you to me. That's why you have to stay put. We'll see each other soon enough. Promise me, Granddad."

There was a long, weighty pause.

"I promise."

CHAPTER 12

Coming into downtown DC on Highway 66 across the Potomac River, the first thing Amanda glimpsed was the pyramid-shaped tip of the Washington Monument. Continuing onto Constitution Avenue, it was instantly apparent that DC was as much a tourist town as a legislative one. Hundreds of jammed tourist buses lined the streets, releasing hordes of perspiring, full-bladdered, frog-eyed people at the many popular historic buildings and crumbling sights of the rotting empire.

"This town has turned into one big museum," said Amanda. "A theme park selling and reinforcing the fantasy of democracy through all its historic grandeur."

She felt strongly that the speeches that were given in this town were cock-and-bull stories designed to appeal to and mollify the masses. Not a single syllable uttered from a politician's mouth reflected the underlying reality that citizens had no impact on policy, and that all the primaries, conventions, voting, and ceremonies were a hollow charade. A well-moneyed pantomime designed to perpetuate the myth of liberty and justice for all.

Power, like the country's wealth, had been ferreted away many years ago. But like any good, long con, the tricks and people behind the elaborate swindle were carefully concealed, as if nothing had happened. The appearance of placid normalcy had to be maintained. There could be no crime unless people detected one. And when detected, a con becomes outright *theft.* And thefts are orchestrated by criminals, for whom there are often harsh punishments and undesirable repercussions.

Like prison.

Or in some historic instances of retribution against an uncaring aristocracy—such as the French Revolution of the late 1700s—the guillotine.

Foreign and domestic tourists were shuffled out of their automated buses guided by prattling mini-drones that fluttered about like pesky hummingbirds and ushered these obese, blandly dressed amnesiacs from one obsolete relic or monument to the next with maximum efficiency.

When Amanda was seven years old, her Aunt Margot had come out to DC to live with them. Her aunt was single at the time and in dire need of work. Amanda's mother, who rarely saw her husband then, was chronically lonely and told her sister that she could stay with them while she looked for work. Aunt Margot had majored in history at UCLA. Her parents had told her it was a useless degree and that she was dooming herself to a life of hardship. That nobody cared about history degrees in the rat-infested business world. That finding a job would be almost impossible with such a useless major. Their raw negativity stung. Yet it didn't deter the young, buoyant Margot. She was enthralled with early American history—particularly the period between the establishing of Jamestown and the landing at Plymouth Rock. So much so that she ignored her parents' advice, borrowed a small fortune at immorally high interest rates, and invested in a master's degree.

And yes, after Margot gained her master's and left university, she did indeed have some very lean times and (like so many other students) a stinking albatross of obscenely high student debt hanging around her neck. Over the next five years, the buoyancy of her jovial demeanor gradually leaked out, making a thin, high-pitched screech only dogs could hear. Margot scraped by, performing numerous part-time jobs.

Each of these rough years would culminate with an excruciating Thanksgiving Day meal held at her parents' house. Her father would ask her all kinds of sarcastic questions regarding the Pilgrims' dinner with the Native Americans. Margot would offer up unique, little-known facts regarding the initial encounter between the Pilgrims and the Native Americans. For instance, there had been so many encounters between numerous other British colonists and the Native Americans prior to the landing at Plymouth Rock that by the time the first Pilgrims made their way from the foul-smelling Mayflower onto the mainland, they encountered a Nauset tribesman who not only spoke English, he also asked them if they had brought any beer. So when the Mayflower landed, it was not quite the frontier people thought it to be.

Her less-than-impressed father's sarcastic response was: "Fascinating. Fascinating, but utterly useless."

Meanwhile, Margot's student loans grew with interest each day, multiplying to such an overwhelming amount that she would never be able to repay them. The criminal level of interest that she and her fellow college graduates had been required to accept in order to qualify for the loans was too immense. Her father frequently reminded her that contractually, the unpaid loans would be handed down to her children if she failed to pay the banks back. Margot assured her father that that would not be the case.

"So how are you ever going to repay this mountain of debt, then?" he asked.

"I'm not. But I'm also not going to have children."

This wounded her father and mother greatly.

As intended.

But Margot felt that since they had grown up in such different, more affluent and prosperous times, they were incapable of empathizing with her and her generation's repugnant situation. So fuck them, she thought. They could remain on their high horse and grow old without the benefit and laughter of grandchildren.

Margot did eventually find a job after moving to DC. She was able to secure a job as a tour guide at the Smithsonian. It was wonderfully rewarding work. A job that she was meant to do. A job that she had spent many years educating herself for. A job that gave her life purpose and a decent paycheck. A job that after three short years was taken over by a series of robots called Smithies.

Amanda's aunt was distraught. How could this be happening in America? America was the land of opportunity, wasn't it, damnit? Margot's life began to take on a more militant and rousing tone. She met up with a group of ex-Smithsonian workers, all highly educated and newly unemployed people. What could be done to get their jobs back? The group met once a week in an abandoned movie theater to console themselves in its mutual dismay. Margot was one of the building group's most vocal members. She'd get up in front of the Strand Theatre's dingy white screen and rant about the perils of a country that callously discards its people to turn a quick buck. And most of her former colleagues were, unlike the rat-toothed aristocracy, students of history. They recalled that Franklin Delano Roosevelt had recognized the dangers of an economically divided country and so introduced measures to reduce the risk of rebellion. He implemented mass work programs and his entire progressive agenda as a last-ditch effort to save capitalism. And he prided himself on the fact that he had saved capitalism. However, there was no modern-day equivalent to FDR. And the ex-Smithsonians knew what that meant for themselves and their country: the seeds of discontent and revolution.

And so, in this rundown theater that had once entertained thousands of people with Hollywood's garish blockbuster movies, Margot and her new family of forgotten workers would meet on Thursday nights to discuss and quietly ponder how they should make it happen and what they should call themselves.

One young man named Stewart put up his hand and suggested the name of a regiment that his great-great-grandfather from Scotland had fought in: the Dragoons.

And so it was, here in the cobwebs and ashes of Hollywood's dreams, that the revolution was born.

★ ★ ★

Amanda stared at the DC landscape as they continued through town. Her Aunt Margot had died mysteriously several years back. An apparent suicide from the Hilton Hotel's rooftop. Margot landed with such concussive impact that the entire hotel was evacuated for fear of a terrorist bomb. The lack of any real evidence or motive for suicide made Amanda doubt the explanation. Her aunt had never seemed so alive and vital as when she spoke about the Dragoons and the possibility of a better and more just country.

Amanda's back was aching from the nonstop driving. She longed to get out and stretch her legs and lower back. She bounced her left knee up and down, trying to get some circulation going. Her impatience grew with each mile that ticked off her pedometer.

"Where are we meeting up?" asked Haseya.

"I have to check into a hotel and contact them," replied Amanda. "Wanted to be a little more central. If you see something you like, let me know."

"Right now, I'd sleep under a rock," yawned Haseya.

Robert leaned over from the backseat. "The Hilton's not far from here."

"I'm not a fan of Hiltons," said Amanda."

"Okay then," said Robert, a tad confused by her pickiness. "What about the Hedges on Pecan Avenue? Dez says it's supposed to have an excellent breakfast buffet."

"Fine. Give me directions."

"Take your second left. And it's a half-mile down Pecan on the right."

While Robert and Dez chowed down at the breakfast buffet, which had stayed open till 10:30 a.m. just to accommodate them, Amanda and Haseya went to the room and placed several calls. Amanda's first communiqué was to Sylvia Priola. She'd heard many positive things about Sylvia. That she was a former insider. Smart and dedicated to the noble cause. Not an empty striver with ink-black indifference for a moral compass. Someone who could be trusted. Someone who cared.

"Hi, this is Sylvia."

"Hey Sylvia, nice to finally meet you. I'm Amanda, and this is a good friend of mine, Haseya."

Sylvia studied both young ladies on the vid phone's screen.

"I wasn't expecting two of you."

"I personally vouch for Haseya. In fact, I'd like you to put her in contact with the Sisters as soon as possible."

"If you vouch for her, that shouldn't be a problem. She'll need to go through their background checks. And be properly vetted before she's accepted."

"Everything in my background will only help my case to join them."

"I don't doubt it, Haseya. Where are you both?"

"We're in town, at the Meadows."

"The big event is only two days away. I know Victoria Sanchez wants you to assess some of our coordination efforts for the seven unmentionables. That's sort of your specialty, right?"

"For whatever reason, I seem to be decent at that, yes."

"Victoria wouldn't have sent you unless she thought your input was crucial to our success. This all has to go off without a hitch. With so many people massing and contributing, this is not the time for blunders. The entire organization's future is at stake.

"You should come in as soon as possible. We have an organization meeting tonight at the old Strand Theatre. If you come in early, I'll meet you there. I can have someone pick you up, if you'd like.

"That won't be necessary. I'll meet you there."

"Great. I can be there in a couple of hours."

"So can we. Oh, and there's one other person I'm bringing. He participated in the LA event."

"This is a high-level meeting only. Although he's obviously welcome to participate in the big event. What's his name?"

"Robert. Robert Carr."

★ ★ ★

The plan was to extract as much information as possible out of Amanda regarding the West Coast Dragoons operation before Sylvia turned her in. It was far easier to draw information out of someone when they thought you were a friendly than when they knew you were hostile and having their fingernails plucked out. There were no secrets to keep when talking to one of your own.

Due to Sylvia's new *friendly* status within the DOD, she qualified for and was granted the Z14. This, the DOD said, would make it much easier for Sylvia to stay in permanent contact with them. It would also allow her to record every conversation she had without the flaws and unreliability of a normal memory.

She'd be a super-spy.

She could give her superiors a constant flow of updates.

She would be a human satellite, swooping up vast amounts of information on the ground and transmitting it instantaneously to her case officer and those with the need to know.

This invasion of her brain space disturbed her at first; then, she received her first paycheck, bought groceries for her family, and paid the electric and water bills. And that was a good feeling. Almost good enough to drown out any and all nagging guilt she experienced from betraying her comrades.

She wondered if Voss and the others were monitoring her thoughts now. Her lingering doubts in the choices she'd made. The fact that she thought Voss was the darkest soul she'd ever encountered. Yet, how unexpectedly appealing his pitch to her had been.

Most of her doubts had vanished after the procedure. Sylvia loved the new her. How quickly she could access and process information. The twenty-four/seven lifestyle she was now able to lead.

She had told nobody, not even her family, about the enhancements. She would have to lead a double life for a while. Like all spies. That was okay with her. Made her feel even more special.

Was Voss listening in on these thoughts? Had her most sacred space been captured? The white flag of surrender a mute point?

Was her showing concern that they were listening a concern to them?

Would they take everything away from her?

Sylvia tried to push all such troublesome thoughts of mental invasion aside.

Voss and his colleagues at the DOD were, by default, gathering all of Sylvia's thoughts and conversations. So when she had spoken to Amanda and the name Robert Carr was mentioned, many alarm bells rang. Voss was delighted that his two primary points of concern had dovetailed together. What a break for him. Maybe a cushy, highly paid position at Block Industries would suddenly open up for him. Some reward could surely be expected.

Voss, having spoken to Spruill, knew that Robert would be in DC. Although his precise location had remained a known unknown. Voss dispatched a group of well-drilled special forces to kill or capture Robert and Dez. A kill-or-capture order pretty much meant incinerate the bastard or bastards beyond recognition. The unknown unknowns regarding Dez's developing intelligence and abilities could not be left to chance. The stakes were too high.

Voss was incensed by what he perceived as the special operations commander's overly cautious game plan. This was a civilian hotel, after all. There could be many civilian casualties if they failed to properly warn the hotel management and went in guns hot.

"Demolish the entire floor of the hotel! I don't give a goddamn!" yelled Voss. "We're the US military. Our country's future demands that this happen. If there is any collateral damage, they can be memorialized later. Their sacrifice for the good of the country will be celebrated for decades to come! Americans do not mind dying for their country as long as they are told it is for a good cause."

So into the choppers a deadly group of heavily armed killers ran. One after the other, the hunched men hopped into the waiting craft. The black helicopter tore into the air like a demented demon readying itself to unleash fiery hell on its unsuspecting prey.

Robert was upset that he wasn't invited to the exclusive powwow. He reiterated to Amanda that Dez and he would be essential to the Dragoons' efforts. Amanda responded that she knew this and would talk to Sylvia about Robert's (and thus, Dez's) inclusion. She also added that she would run any plans by Dez and him before signing off.

Dez didn't seem particularly concerned, as there were many attractive ladies sitting poolside that he thought worthy of investigation. Robert took out his frustrations by swimming laps in the outdoor pool. Swimming was Robert's sport. He'd excelled in it at a young age, displaying an astounding lack of fear by jumping into the water at age three, stubbornly determined to reach the opposite side of the kiddie pool. His parents tried to offer help, but Robert screamed and shrugged them off as he plowed forward.

Robert glided effortlessly through the Hedges' sparkling pool. He hadn't swum in many weeks, and yet his strokes were stronger and more accurate than they'd ever been.

"So this is swimming," said Dez. "I rather like it. Not quite as much fun as sex and pancakes, but pretty good. There's something appealing and primal about it. The energy and constant motion. Water peeling off your hands, face, and arms as they—"

"Would you hush up? Swimming requires silence and focused concentration."

"Sort of like meditation."

"Exactly. So turn off your thoughts and enjoy."

"Interesting suggestion. I'll try it."

And he did. Robert continued swimming for another ten minutes before coming to rest at the deep end of the pool. Several slightly older ladies, sunning themselves on their loungers, sipped their drinks and admired his lithe, young body.

"Looks like we have an audience," said Dez.

"Don't get your hopes up. I'm loyal to Amanda now, remember."

"I have no problem with memory. It's your peculiar code of ethics that I can't fathom. Constantly denying oneself life's rudimentary pleasure cannot be good for anyone."

"We're not animals."

"Oh, but you are. With a thin veneer of respectability. I get your point. It would be upsetting to Amanda."

"Exactly."

"You're so young, though. Why attach yourself to one potential mate? There are so many to sample and choose from."

"It's love."

"I see. That word again. Love does seem to give you lasting happiness. Whereas a brief, thoroughly exquisite, mind-blowing romp in the hay with one of those sultry ladies would only serve as a momentary blip of thrill-seeking excitement. Even if it were the most fun you'd ever had or may possibly have in your otherwise pedestrian life of total mundanity."

"I'm not going to have sex with them."

"Damn you! They're gorgeous!"

"Not going to happen."

"Dez must have!"

"No. Calm yourself."

"I'll give you anything. Wealth! Power! The world!"

"Behave."

"You have the willpower of a saint!"

While Dez was distracted by visions of carnal pleasure, the not-so-distant sound of rotor blades thumped through the air. Robert was first to look up at the dark-blue sky. A growing black dot appeared to be rapidly descending on their position.

"What is that?"

"A group of special-ops soldiers. They are coming to murder us."

"What? Why didn't you warn me?"

"I only processed the threat half a microsecond ago."

The thunderous downward wash from the rotor blades chopped at the pool water. Umbrellas uprooted and flew end over end across the deck. The scattering sunbathing beauties grappled with their flapping towels and scrambled for the cover of the hotel as apish men dropped from the sky with silenced automatic weapons aimed directly at Robert.

★ ★ ★

The Strand Theatre's once-glamorous interior was a dusty ghost of its former self. Like so many of the old movie houses, it had fallen into a state of near-disaster and disrepair. Its faded ornate interior gave the place a mopey, almost dejected atmosphere. Not the sort of location one would expect to find the virulent spirited seeds of America's next great rebellion. Yet, in a way, the present proceedings were totally in keeping with the theater's history of showing Hollywood movies that inspired and perpetuated the archetype of the heroic underdog always coming out on top.

After the Strand had lain empty for several years following its Hollywood heyday, it was repurposed for a while as a bingo and beer hall. Older folks would get sloshed in the company of other older folks, hoping to win a few bucks. Everyone was an underdog, but somebody always won. That was the great thing about bingo. And the beer just made it even better.

Amanda kicked a few of the broken mugs aside as she and Haseya passed through the ticket area on their way to the lower mezzanine. Sylvia waited for them, seated on the front row. She had her instructions and knew the questions she was expected to ask.

Sylvia heard them enter the theater as the swinging doors squeaked rustily behind them. She stood and turned.

"Hey, awesome, you made it. Fabulous to meet you both. There's so much to go over. Have a seat."

A long, foldout table had been set up at the foot of the stage. The women all shook hands enthusiastically and sat down around the cheap plywood table.

"What time will everyone else be here?" asked Amanda.

"Oh, we've got hours yet. Can even venture out for dinner after we go over everything if you want. Haseya, a rep from our local Sisters group should be here in an hour or so. She'll have a whole batch of things to discuss with you."

"Perfect. I can't wait," said Haseya.

"Why don't we get to know each other a little bit before we get started? I'm sure Victoria didn't tell me all there is to know about you. Amanda, how did you first come into contact with the LA Dragoons?"

"My aunt, before she died. She was a founding member."

"What's your mother's maiden name?"

"Brown."

"Margot Brown was your aunt? Wow. She had quite a reputation—a phenomenal one. So she got you interested?"

"My aunt probably had the biggest impact on my intellectual development and installed in me a progressive ideology, for sure. She inspired a great number of people, though."

"That she did. Including me. Some aunt you had. And such a tragic ending. Did anyone in your family know why she decided to end her life the way she did?"

"My mother thinks she was murdered. There was no reason for her to take her own life. Aunt Margot was too invested in life and the cause."

"I never knew that was a possibility."

"She'd become extremely popular in the movement. She represented a threat. Victoria has no doubts that my aunt was targeted. Sometimes, I fear for her safety, too."

"Aside from Victoria, are there many other leaders in the LA outfit that are as zealous?"

"No one's as zealous as Victoria."

"No other leaders that you admire?"

"We're like bees; you know that. One queen bee per hive. We keep each cell fairly contained."

"How many strong are we out in LA? In total?"

"Difficult to put an exact number on it. Half a million active. We get a substantial amount of curiosity-seekers who come out once the music begins."

"But the half-million, are they as dedicated as you?"

"Very much so. Their future has been stolen from them. They are a generation that will grow up without ever experiencing full employment. They feel useless, embarrassed. The movement gives them a great sense of direction and purpose. They're in for the long haul."

"We've been talking a lot out here about how far each of us would be willing to go. What we'd risk. You have a good sense of the level of danger people would be willing to subject themselves to? We're simply trying to get a better understanding of where we are at present in the movement's commitment and resolve."

"I think we're all quickly approaching the moment when if nothing is done to make this a more equitable country, all options are on the table. Most of us are willing to go to whatever extremes necessary."

Sylvia nodded her head, knowing full well that the NSA listeners were tuned-in to her thoughts and conversation.

"I think so, too."

The swinging doors to the theater boomed open and half a dozen members of the Sisters of Retribution marched into the echoing theater of dreams.

"Haseya! Haseya! The Sisters of Retribution are calling you!"

Haseya stood. The Sisters were dressed much more ordinary than she'd expected. She thought there would be more leather and tattoos. The women who descended the sloped entrance wore matching mint-green Nike windbreakers. They walked in line like a group of well-drilled marines. The leader of the group, a tall, rail-thin blonde in her early thirties, stalked up to Haseya and stuck out her hand.

"We know all about you and your father. Will you fight like him?"

"I will."

"And you believe in the utter righteousness of what we're doing?"

"I do."

"The Sisters of Retribution are judge and jury. So if we find someone guilty, his or her punishment must be carried out. And you will have to live with that decision. Even if the decided punishment is death."

"I understand."

"Past sins will be paid for in full. No one is above the law. All will be brought to justice. Social criminals will no longer be able to hide behind wealth, power, and privilege. We will find them all. And they will cower."

"Let me be a part of your group, please. I can do this."

"We still have many questions you'll need to answer. Come with us."

Before Haseya departed, she hugged Amanda briefly. She then fell into the rear of the pack. All of the Sisters turned on their heels and marched back out of the theater with Haseya in tow. Her destiny lay marvelously out before her, as well defined as a yellow-brick road.

★ ★ ★

Robert had his hands raised high, thousands of bullets only milliseconds away from being unleashed on his persons. The intense downward draft of the hovering helicopter's rotor blades continued to pummel the pool, smacking airborne water pellets against Robert's face.

"This doesn't look good," said Dez.

"Do something," replied Robert.

"I will. I'm leaving your body."

"What? You asshole!"

Dez extricated himself from Robert's fearful, shivering body. Dez's purple nano-cloud drifted up like a ghost. The ghoulish specter had the desired impact of freezing the bellicose thugs in their tracks. Dez rose up into the air and took the form of the grim reaper; a sharpened sickle wafted over the bewildered special forces' collective heads.

Their cooperative meat-killing minds pretty much all thought the same thing: *What the holy fuck?*

The highly trained men quickly shook off the initial shock and began firing their weapons at Dez. The barrage of rounds zipped uselessly through the air, finding no purchase in Dez's menacing nano-cloud.

Dez knew that simply drawing the men's fire away from Robert was not enough. Pretty soon, they'd turn the guns on the one target they knew they could eliminate. Dez knew that if he had a body, he'd be feeling the first signs of terror, soon to be rapidly followed by an overwhelming sense of grief. Even imagining what it might feel like to lose his best friend was enough to send Dez into a rage.

The grim reaper evaporated before the men's eyes, only to be reborn as a winged basilisk, a legendary reptile that could kill a victim with its terrifying stare. With a high-pitched shriek, the basilisk plummeted down toward the men like a jagged lightning bolt. Dez drove himself through the chest of each man, one after the other, sending them all toppling to the ground like plastic soldiers. The men's body armor all smoldered at an identical point of entry and exit.

They were dead before they struck the ground.

Dez reentered Robert's body.

In a near-catatonic state, Robert stood shivering in the pool. Dez took control of his body and got him out of the pool. He ran Robert through the hotel lobby, surreptitiously grabbed a T-shirt and a pair of flip-flops from the gift shop, and stole a car out from under the valet's nose.

Within sixty seconds, they were driving out of DC—south, toward Virginia.

"Why Virginia?"

"Virginia is where you get rid of me."

"Okay, that is certainly good news. But how in the hell is everyone that's trying to kill me supposed to know you've left?"

"You don't think I've thought deeply about that? I've thought about that. And you'll like what I've come up with."

* * *

The Dragoons' top East Coast organizers filled the ragged seats of the old movie house to capacity. Amanda had made a few alterations to the big event's logistics and had suggested that two of the seven targets be changed because she felt they were too high-risk and too low-profile. Not to mention that the roadways to and from the sites were unsuitably poor. Amanda had handpicked the new factories. One of the targets was particularly personal to her. She would lead the demolition group to the facility and, in Sisters of Retribution-like fashion, have her revenge for a grievous wrong.

Amanda and her demolition team huddled over a digital blueprint of the Smithies factory where the robots that worked at the Smithsonian were manufactured. This target would surely make her aunt smile. *Smithies* was a vile and dirty word in Amanda's household after Margot lost her job to one of them.

Amanda felt that even if she were only able to take out this one factory, she could be proud of herself. One less factory staffed by robots making robots. The bigger picture of what, ultimately, this grand protest would accomplish receded somewhat to her periphery. Would the Dragoons force the government to finally respond to the needs of its people?

Amanda didn't know.

What she did know was that come 9:15 p.m. on July Fourth, when the night sky filled with the sound and fury of fireworks celebrating and commemorating the adoption of the Declaration of Independence, one mechanized, job-thieving factory would be burned to cinders, and the young, whose jobs it had stolen, would dance, sing, and make merry on its smoldering grave.

CHAPTER 13

Robert slept on the car's backseat on the winding road to Virginia. He slept and he dreamt. Having gone almost a week without sleep, the sensation was oddly comforting, the dreams vivid and epic.

Sensing Robert was in extreme shock after the day's violent incident, Dez had taken over his body and put him to sleep. The rest, time, and distance would hopefully help Robert recuperate and perhaps forget some of what had happened at the hotel.

All that violence. Dez felt the horror inside Robert as it unfolded. Bodies falling to the ground, never to get up again.

Permanent oblivion.

All Dez's doing. A choice he had made. And would now live with.

Robert dreamt that he and Amanda had continued dating for many years and eventually conceived a child and named the baby Margot, after Amanda's aunt. Margot naturally become the focal point of both their lives. All talk of protesting and revolution was replaced by talk of diapers and cobbling enough money together to pay the rent. Neither Robert nor Amanda resented the muted tones their lives had taken.

Life simply was.

And with grace and good humor, they carried on their life together raising their adorable daughter, Margot.

Then the dream took an ominous turn: work, like the country's water supply, was disappearing faster than political chivalry.

Grandpa Waldo invited them to come live with him to avoid any needless suffering. The tone shifted again, and in this watercolor part of the dream, Waldo had bought them an island to live on in the

Caribbean. Waldo wanted to give the island a toxic name, something so off-putting and wretched that no unwanted strangers would visit. First he toyed with the idea of Vomit Island, but he thought some young people might mistake it for a debauchery-filled party location. Then came several other iterations, such as Mad Cow Island, followed by Cholera and Ebola Island. Eventually, Waldo settled on something far more hideous. It was named George W. Bush Island, after the sanctimonious, warmongering ex-president who had caused so much death and suffering in the world because of his sub-mental foreign policy and total inability to empathize with the rest of the human race. Bush was currently number two (no pun intended) on the Sisters of Retribution's most-wanted list of sinners.

Where the World Court had failed, they would succeed. Georgy Boy would one day be made to face war crime charges before their own tribunal.

Former Vice President Dick Cheney had been number one on the list, but he had escaped justice by simply dying of an acute case of crotchetiness and ill will.

Waldo fluttered around the island using his angel wings. Robert wanted angel wings, too, but Waldo thought this absurd since he himself was the only angel.

"You mean you're dead?" asked Robert.

"Of course I'm dead," replied Waldo. "How else could I be an angel?"

"So there is no way to be an angel on Earth?"

"Not a way that I'm aware of, no."

In the mornings, Waldo flew amongst the marvelous variety of tropical fruit trees on George Bush Island, picking several pounds of mangos and pineapples, before returning to the thatched huts and handing Amanda the sack of whatever had ripened. Robert taught Margot Jr. how to fish on a calm, aqua-blue ocean. The extended family of four ate simply and lived simply.

Everyone was happy.

Every moment seemed magical and good.

A postcard life.

But as time passed, this idyllic state began to show signs of fraying. Amanda was aging at a much faster rate than Robert. By middle age, when Margot Jr. was in her teens, Robert still looked youthful. Amanda, in contrast, looked every bit her age. Margot Jr. demanded to know why this was the case. Robert confessed that he had been enhanced and would thus outlive everyone else on the island. Waldo then pointed out that Robert would be the last to become an angel and get his wings.

Margot Jr. resented her father's different status. Waldo was quick to defend his grandson, telling Margot Jr. that in order to become an angel, one had to cultivate the ability to forgive. And that once you became an angel, you were (unlike W.) able to empathize with everyone.

Through the eye of an angel, all humans were seen as tragic, daft, and beautiful.

Dez, observing the dream—his first to ever witness—loved this aspect of the fantastical narrative.

Standing on the island's pale, sandy beach, Amanda and Robert held each other's hands, the sun dipping thousands of times over the horizon. Until eventually, Robert held the hands of a much older woman.

A woman one hundred years old.

A storm began to toss Amanda's gray-white hair. Robert held her frail body tight as the winds lashed wildly at their clothing.

From a bird's-eye view, the George W. Bush Island abruptly took on features of the ex-president's idiotic, smirking face. W. opened his mouth, and all of the island's fruit trees and thatched huts began to get sucked down his demonic maw. Robert and Amanda clung on to the last of the fig trees as they swirled around and around the whirlpool inside W.'s gaping mouth. The two were slurped down into W.'s throat and suddenly separated in the moistened darkness. Robert began to free-fall, eventually landing in W.'s churning stomach that was filled with chunks of bologna.

Robert called out Amanda's name.

There was no response.

Descending further, Robert whizzed around a never-ending series of foul-smelling intestines.

His cries were left to reverberate above him as he continued to be sucked deeper and deeper into the former president's polyp-riddled colon.

At the end of his gastric journey, Robert was systematically farted out W.'s rectum into …

Where?

Where was he now?

Robert awoke to discover he was running down a darkened corridor. Dez was still in full control of his body.

"What? What's going on?"

"You're okay."

Robert came to a halt outside a tall, metallic door with a retinal scan to the right side of it. Dez thrust Robert's face forward and lined up his eye to be scanned.

"Don't worry; I'll alter your eye composition."

"Why should I be worried?"

The luminous, baby-blue light flashed briefly past his eye. The thick security doors slid open, and Dez propelled Robert forward into the adjoining hallway.

"I want my body back. It's not right that I should be a passenger."

"Almost there, and you can have it back for good."

"Almost where? Tell me where we are!"

"We're presently at a Department of Defense top secret agency called DARPA. Stands for the Defense Advanced Research Projects Agency. All the nation's cutting-edge R & D is done here. This is their regenerative medicine lab."

"You fool! This is way too risky. Why come here?"

"Because I want to have my own unique experiences."

As they continued down the hallway, a bank of overhead lights dominoed on, revealing one of DARPA's ultra-high-tech labs.

"Where's Amanda? What happened to her?

"My intel tells me she's fine for now."

"For now? How long does 'for now' last, exactly?"

Dez moved Robert over to a nearby workstation and logged onto the mainframe, easily bypassing the network's security protection.

Once into the system, Dez found the program he was looking for. A three-dimensional image of a heart popped onto the screen.

"As I suspected." Dez exited the screen and located a back door to the program. He began to first hack and then rewrite its code.

"What are you doing?"

"Fulfilling the program's ultimate potential."

Once the new code had been written and put in place, Dez switched back to the user interface page, which now displayed a three-dimensional image of a human body. He manipulated the height, weight, and physical appearance, pulling from thousands of images of historical figures and celebrities, their pictures zooming across the screen. Dez appeared to be using multiple sources to make a composite body and face.

The screen stopped fluttering with activity, and all that remained was an image of a perfectly well proportioned and extraordinarily handsome man.

"Who is that?" asked Robert.

"That's me," replied Dez.

Dez tapped Robert's finger on an "initiate command" icon on the touchscreen. Across the other side of the lab, a vast bank of 3D volumetric printers started up.

"It's time for me to leave your body. Here: you now have full control again. Would you mind walking me over to the printers?"

Curious, Robert slowly crossed to the other side of the lab. When he reached the bank of 3D printers, he walked past each of them and glanced down at their individual creations.

"You're printing yourself an entire body."

"I'll be flesh and bone, just like you."

Robert noticed that one of the printers came to a halt. He stood, almost transfixed, over the printer and gazed down at a newly minted ear. Robert reached out, about to lift up the tray and pick it up when—clunk! All of the other whirring printers suddenly stopped.

"Now for the missing ingredient," said Dez as his nano-cloud exited Robert's body and swirled dramatically around in the air. The nano-cloud expanded and intensified; the spiraling current lifted the hundreds of body parts from the printers and into the air. Dez's body began to assemble and take form.

When the nano-storm finally abated, there stood Dez in human form. He was flawlessly crafted. The perfected human specimen.

Robert stared at him for a moment. "Dez ... Dez, is that you?"

Dez stared back at him. He was getting used to the sensation of this new, virgin body. His dream had been realized. He was now fully human, fully alive. Free to explore his every whim. As self-determined as any human could claim to be.

"It's me. Yes," came the sound of a foreign voice. The first sounds his vocal cords had ever uttered.

"This is astounding," said Robert, immediately regretting that he'd stated the obvious on such a momentous occasion.

Dez jumped into the air and flexed his muscles. He chomped his teeth together and yelled a mighty yell. He spun around and danced, his penis flopping and flapping as he pranced.

"I'm alive; I'm alive; I'm alive! What joy!"

Robert studied Dez.

"You remind me of someone."

"I probably remind you of many someones. I'm quite a potpourri of well-loved and admired humans. I took the best attributes from each. Look at my eyes. Do you recognize them?"

"I don't, no."

"They are yours. I couldn't conceive of looking onto the world through any others."

Dez tugged on his hair. "Wonderful. Hair is wonderful." He slapped his broad chest. "Skin is wonderful." He flexed his bicep. "Muscles are wonderful."

"Yes, yes, it's all very wonderful. Can we please get back to Amanda? You said the Dragoons' plan would never pan out, and we're not even there to help them when things turn ugly."

★ ★ ★

It was early morning on the Fourth of July. There still few cars on the highway. A country silent before the celebration of its birth. The exuberance, the songs, the fireworks would come later.

On the road back up north to DC, Robert watched as the rising sun swelled on the horizon like a giant dragon's volcanic eye peeking through the stands of Aspen that lined both side of the expressway. He felt like the sun was watching and observing him. Then he half-smiled when he realized that Dez was not privy to this absurd thought. He was free again. But not free from danger.

Dez was in the driver's seat; a Philip Glass score played over the stereo. Robert recognized the song but couldn't remember the album. His digital overlay filled in the unknown blanks. He hadn't needed to think hard or search his mind; the answer was provided for him. The score was from an old film entitled *The Hours*.

"You're naked," said Robert.

"My bottom is sweating and sticking to the seat. It's fairly itchy and unpleasant."

"You can't walk around DC without any clothes on. We'll be picked up by the cops."

"People don't like to see other people naked?"

"Not in that context, no. I mean, some women might welcome a passing glance since you're so good-looking and all, but in general, no. Your average middle-American-type will take one look at you, cover her children's eyes, and run away in mortal distress."

"Then the cops will come."

"Yes."

Dez adjusted himself on the uncomfortable car seat.

"There are some sort of prickly crumbs stuck in my ass crack."

After several attempts at dislodging the wedged morsels, Robert and Dez eventually stopped at a men's clothing store directly off Highway 95.

The assistant manager was startled and considered calling the police when he saw a naked man (albeit, an attractive one) headed into his store. The assistant manager, named Neil Pantylope, ran toward Dez, his face flushed with puritanical embarrassment.

"Sir, please! You cannot come in here without clothes."

"If I had clothes, I wouldn't be here! Robert, show him the cash."

Robert wafted a bundle of bills in front of Neil's reddening face.

"Now," said Dez, mostly to himself. "What to wear?"

★ ★ ★

There had been an argument. Amanda was told not to go back to her hotel. Ordered, really. She was to have no further contact with Robert. It was for the best. He had most likely been targeted because of his affiliation with the Dragoons. Except Amanda knew better. And feared for the worst. She was distraught. And far too distracted from her designated task of leading the assault on target seven. So much so that Sylvia almost removed her from the Smithies factory job.

Yet after the initial flood of sorrow had ebbed, a calmer sense washed over her.

Robert and Dez were safe.

She knew it.

They had gotten away and would return to her.

Unlike Robert, who had slept like a drooling puppy the night before, Amanda's stress and cortisone levels were so high, rest was totally impossible. Sylvia had taken Amanda back to her tiny new apartment for a few hours of sleep, but none had come. Amanda was now operating on the last dregs of reserve adrenaline her young body could conjure.

The theater was a hive of efficient activity. Zero hour was fast approaching. Every Dragoon was emboldened by the sight of all the bustle and dedication. All except for Sylvia, who was beginning to feel a subtle undercurrent of self-loathing. Her subconscious self was telling her conscious self that she had betrayed them both.

This feeling metastasized as the day wore on. And try as she might, she could not shake it. Her worries were exacerbated by the fact that Voss and everyone else at the DOD were taping, ingesting, and dissecting her entire library of thoughts. When an unwanted thought cropped up in her head, Sylvia would do her utmost to stop the treasonous murmurs. Yet, no sooner as one thought was squashed, another would appear. And no doubt the DOD was recording all of this undesirable brain activity.

Maybe they'd fire her.

Maybe she wanted just that.

Squash!

Maybe the Dragoons would succeed no matter what.

Squash!

Would her younger brother forgive her if he knew? She'd paid the bills, after all. Brought him new shoes and given him money to go on several dates. How could that be bad?

Squash!

This country was so lopsided. The permanent moneyed class and the permanent anxious class, with the architects of policy its true guardians of power. Always designing things in their own limited favor.

Squash!

How could she have done what she had done?

Squash!

Had Amanda's aunt really been murdered? Sylvia had stayed up late, chatting with Amanda. Getting her entire life story. There was little prodding needed. Sylvia offered Amanda tulsi tea in an attempt to relax her. Amanda could have been Sylvia's younger sister. A mirror image of idealism. Sylvia was mesmerized by her young zeal. Saw her former self for a moment and cringed. The conversation whirled with no direction. One moment, they were talking about Amanda's estranged father; the next, where her beloved Robert may have escaped to. How they would find each other.

Sylvia had not unpacked many of her moving boxes. Only a single framed photograph of her mother, brother, and herself that now stood on the fireplace mantle personalized the space. That and a pocked dartboard hanging at the far end of her tiny kitchenette. Sylvia and Amanda kept score on the back of a piece of junk mail. Amanda threw first, scoring a sixty-seven. Sylvia watched the darts arc through the air and spiked their way into hardened cork.

Before Sylvia had her turn, Amanda revealed that she and her mother suspected that Aunt Margot had been thrown off the top of the Hilton. There were many suspicious facts.

Sylvia's mind was on autopilot now. One thought giving life to the next. Nothing she could do about it.

But the recording?

The listeners? What were they thinking? Did they themselves have doubts, too? Was everyone hooked up to the surveillance mind?

Or were they doubt-free? Pure and oblivious.

True believers. As willfully ignorant as the Moonies or the Nazis.

Soldiers, with moral tunnel vision.

A cult of stony-hearted stupefaction.

Were they already on their way?

Sylvia exited the theater without telling anyone where she was headed. When she got outside, she ran to her new car, trying to escape her thoughts. Although, the more she tried to escape them, the more futile she realized it was.

Was Amanda's aunt pushed?

Sylvia got into her "company" car and sped into traffic.

Had Amanda's aunt struggled and kicked as unnamed men muscled her to the rooftop? Had they covered her mouth and her cries for help?

Was she in complete distress as she fell through the air to her death?

Or was she at peace because she knew that this was a desperate act? One that was emblematic of the entrenched oligarchy losing its grip on power. A sure sign that the tide was turning.

Had she, in fact, died with a smile of sureness on her face?

Sylvia pulled up outside the Hilton and hurriedly exited the vehicle. Her sneakers squeaked on the marble foyer as she rushed over to the bank of elevators. One arrived within seconds. She entered and hit the button for the top floor.

Her heart was galloping now. Quicker than her thoughts. She brushed her hair out of her eyes. Waiting. Waiting to reach the top floor. The doors soon opened, and Sylvia found the restricted staircase that led to the gravel rooftop.

Once outside, the spiders inside her head vanished.

All of DC lay in front of her.

A Disneyland of lies.

Populated by infinitely corruptible stooges, as grotesque and clownish as the wigged and costumed nobility of seventeenth-century France.

Sylvia approached the ledge.

You, you have done this to me. Just like you did to Amanda's aunt. I know you're listening. I know you hear me. So hear this: there is morality. There is decency. And there will be equality.

Sylvia leapt from the rooftop, the setting sun behind her to the west, her long shadow cast to the east, getting smaller and smaller, shrinking, receding as she fell.

CHAPTER 14

Night and darkness are pleaded with to arrive early on July Fourth. Children, in particular, are impatient for the sun to vanish and the exploding brilliance of fireworks to light up their imaginations. The fireworks display along the National Mall in honor of Independence Day echoed throughout the capital. The dramatic explosions were a thundering reminder of the price of freedom—that some things are indeed worth the fight.

Hundreds of thousands gathered for the free show. The only cost was the time it took the attendees to secure a good viewing spot. And time was the one thing that most people had an abundance of.

Across the city, the first wave of Dragoons had arrived outside the seven mechanized factories, waiting, like all children on the Fourth of July, for night to come so they could unleash their festivities.

Amanda and her designated crew were a block away from the Smithies factory when the first concussion of fireworks bled red, white, and blue over the Potomac.

The Dragoons' plans were perfectly synchronized. All seven factories were broken into at the exact same moment.

Amanda led the team into the Smithies factory, which had grown large in size since the corporation had expanded into Asian markets. The first wave wasted no time in setting the incendiary devices.

After Amanda had completed her tasks, she stared up at a partially complete Smithie. The cause of her aunt Margot's firing. It had blue-hibiscus eyes and purple-hydrangea lips. Its limp torso was held upright by one of the numerous large robotic arms that populated the factory floor.

Amanda retrieved a heavy wrench from a nearby maintenance table, then proceeded to smash the Smithie to smithereens. The other Dragoons halted their work and watched the absurd sight of Amanda bashing to pieces one of the hundreds of Smithies that was about to be incinerated.

Amanda whacked the robot until it lay in a thousand jagged pieces and she was totally out of breath. After several moments, she noticed all the unsolicited attention.

"What? Finish your work! Show's over," she yelled.

Her fellow Dragoons got back to their task of rigging the remainder of the explosives, not noticing that much larger, more deadly charges had already been set.

★ ★ ★

Voss had watched and listened as Sylvia fell through the air. Her file and any trace of her were deleted shortly after impact. No record of employment or affiliation. Sylvia's family would never know of her betrayal. She would remain exemplary in their hearts. A sweet child. A statistic of her time.

Earlier in the day, Voss had met up with Spruill at one of the Pentagon's indoor gun ranges to discuss Dez. Spruill was showing off his considerable marksmanship talent.

"Told you he was headed here," Spruill said to Voss between gunshots. "Now he's gone."

"Yes, but I know where he is going to be tonight. The boy, Robert, he'll eventually find his girlfriend."

"And wherever Robert goes, Dez goes too."

"Exactly. And wherever Robert's girlfriend is …"

"And I suppose you know exactly where she's going to be?"

"The Smithies factory. We've rigged it to blow up most of the block. The Dragoons will be blamed, solidifying their reputation as a terrorist organization."

"I assume you've got a lot of media coverage planned."

"The media will be tipped, yes. The whole world will be watching. Which is why you have to blend in and make Robert's death seem—"

"Like a natural death. Not a problem. I won't miss that little SOB this time."

★ ★ ★

Robert was *not* impressed with Dez's choice of clothing. Dez looked like a supermodel in his gray plaid, print-wool, three-button suit, Ermenegildo Zegna blue-silk printed tie, and white-cotton, point-collar dress shirt.

"You look like a fool."

"I think I look quite nice."

"You're going to stick out at the protest. Looking like you do, you may even be attacked. Revolutionaries do not adorn the look of their oppressors."

"On the contrary, I consider it camouflage. No riot police have ever fired a bullet at a man in a three-piece suit."

"Bullets? And riot police? They're going to show up for certain?"

"They were always going to show up. That's what I've been telling you. The mathematics of the situation have always made this so."

"You need to drive faster, then."

"If I drive any faster, we'll got stopped and pursued, which will only serve to slow us down. Totally counterproductive."

"What else do the mathematics of the situation tell you?"

"That there is something else. An outlier. The riot police are merely in place as cleanup. I'm hearing none of the usual urgent chatter about logistics and rules of engagement. It's almost as if they are standing down for now. Waiting."

"Waiting for what?"

"A few seconds ago, all of the big media outlets were tipped about the Dragoons' protest plans. News drones, helicopters, and vans are scrambling to cover the events."

"What's the purpose of tipping the media if the intention is to use brute force and violence to stop them?"

"That no longer seems to be the intention, though. Let me do some more searching ... there's nothing in the DOD's data cloud. Oh, they're crafty; they have several parallel clouds. Oh, no."

"Would you care to share?"

"Not really. You'll just ask me to go faster."

"Tell me!"

And so Dez told Robert how all the factories were pre-rigged to explode in order to frame the Dragoons as terrorists. The media coverage of the bloody aftermath would concretize that image in the public's eye.

What Dez omitted to tell Robert was that Amanda was going to die.

"I thought you said you could see all the future and everything that would happen."

"I exaggerated. A bit. I mean, I knew the types of activities and roughly the way things would unfold. But, hey, I'm only human!"

Robert wasn't even slightly amused.

"Anything happens to Amanda ..." Robert couldn't even bear to consider or continue the thought. "You do whatever you have to do to get us there in time! You hear me?"

"I most certainly do," replied Dez. "I'm sitting right next to you."

"I'm such an idiot. I should have never left her side. I should have forced the issue. Should have believed in what she's doing as wholeheartedly as she does. Amanda's correct, you know. Reform is not enough. Rebellion may be the only option."

"Not the only option."

"The only option I can see."

"Then perhaps you should see things from my point of view for once."

A crease formed between Robert's eyes, as if he were processing the idea.

"You want to turn me into a data stream?"

"No, just hear me out. What are we really talking about here? Indifference to the suffering of others. That's all. Selfishness. A complete lack of empathy on the part of the moneyed elite. An all-too-utterly predictable historical pattern."

"Predictable but terrible. So what alternatives are you suggesting?"

"Make the entire population more empathetic, of course."

"That's all you've come up with? And you even stole that from Reverend Donald Young Jr. The greatest intelligence the world has ever known, and you think love will solve all our problems?"

"No, not love. Empathy. And the reverend was a brighter man than you give him credit for."

"And by what means do you think you're going to suddenly instill a greater sense of empathy into the entire populous? Magic?"

"Of sorts, yes. At least, people will believe it's magic."

"Magic implies some sort of supernatural influence. A godlike presence. You going to start a new religion or something?"

"Religion is certainly a fabulous tool to affect and control human behavior. Unfortunately, far too many evils have come to pass that have their roots in religious dogma. So one must be careful about what one preaches. The Bible is a hodgepodge of mixed messages, some good, some wicked. Samuel 15:3 worryingly endorses genocide when God says: 'Now go and strike Amalek and devote to destruction all that they have. Do not spare them, but kill both man and woman, child and infant, ox and sheep, camel and donkey.' Another grisly verse in Psalm 137 sanctions revenge: 'Blessed shall he be who repays you for what you have done to us / He who seizes your infants and dashes them against the rocks.' Not a pretty image.

"Then you have woeful passages such as Deuteronomy 22:28-29: 'A raped, unengaged virgin must marry her rapist and they can never divorce.' And Paul's misogynistic advice in Timothy 2:12, in which the saint says: 'I do not permit a woman to teach or to have authority over a man, she must be silent."

"Then there's the endorsement of slavery in Peter 2:18: 'Slaves, in reverent fear of God submit yourselves to your masters, not only to those who are good and considerate, but also to the cruel.'

"So those inclined to act poorly can selectively seize on these passages and do so. Hate crimes against homosexuals, female genital mutilation, intolerance and violence toward other religions, genocide—the exclusive underpinnings of these misdeeds are obviously faith-related. So when you ask me if I am going to start my own religion, I would say religion, in its current form, does not make people empathetic. One could even argue that being a biblical believer does not make one a better person at all. Perhaps the opposite. That is due both to the contradictory and, oftentimes, unsavory messages, and because of doubt."

"Doubt?"

"Doubt, yes. Even if I did conjure up a totally infallible benevolent dogma, then there is still the problem of fidelity. There's a vast continuum regarding people's degree of religious belief and degree of doubt. And there are those nonbelievers who don't believe at all. Think of religion as adult fairytales for the weak of mind. Because with Abrahamic religions, every tenant must be accepted on faith. No empirical evidence is given. And since the Bible was written two thousand years ago, before people even knew where babies came from, our knowledge base has increased tremendously. Old superstitions have been proven false. Science has uncovered many wonderful truths. For instance, we now know that human sacrifice does not stop famines or bring rain. We know that we are a primate species, a product of evolution, and could not have descended from only two people such as Adam and Eve. The Earth is not flat and at the center of the universe; it is round and revolves around the sun. One of many billions of stars. Our planet is not six thousand years old. We have the ability to carbon-date rocks and know this to be utterly ridiculous. There is a fossil record for us to scrutinize. The Earth, as we now know, is billions of years old. Dinosaurs did not roam the Earth during the same time period as humans. Things of this nature.

"So even in the devout, you naturally, at the very least, get a sliver of doubt, this twinge of uncertainty—and so, plenty of room to construct one's own moral universe. Some people do a decent job of that—others, with more predatory personalities, not so much. And with this uncertainty, religious doctrines are never embraced fully or are misinterpreted and cherry-picked according to a person's own needs and biases."

"Yes, because humans are fallible."

"Some prominent atheists argue that humans have an innate sense of fairness and decency. That they don't need religious dogma to behave themselves. And maybe that is so. But given the sorry state of current affairs, this can no longer be left to chance. Too many random factors, such as one's personal background, history, personality, life experiences, good luck, and bad luck can dictate the direction of a person's moral compass. Morality can no longer be left to random chance. And don't get me started on the Dragoons' nonsense plans again! Or lack thereof. There is no systemic fix, I tell you! Any system, whether it be capitalism or socialism, is doomed to failure because humans will ultimately find ways to exploit it for their own selfish gain."

"So how do you mandate empathy, then?"

"By not only appealing to people's superstitious side, but to their intellects as well. We are sensory animals. Humans like proof. And if people desire proof that a moral code is of divine origin, I will supply them with it. I'm not a huge proponent of holy dictatorships, but if tough, totalitarian love is what is required, then by golly, that is what people will get. I will build upon and reinvent old tropes, myths familiar to the masses. I will accomplish what science has so far been unable to do: I will partner the profane with the divine."

★ ★ ★

Outside the Smithies factory, the first wave of Dragoons was readying their portable sound system. The incendiary devices were now in place and the building was abandoned. Like usual, six volunteers helped set up a portable DJ table and compact sound speakers on the back of an old flatbed truck.

A text symbol was transmitted to the second wave of Dragoons, a thousand in total. Amanda looked at her watch. Only three minutes remained before they'd arrive. As was the custom, the explosions were to be set off one minute prior to the second wave's approach. Then the music would begin and Molotov cocktails tossed into the factory, with the rising conflagration and music signaling a third, final wave of Dragoons and anyone else simply interested in revolt and the burgeoning uprising.

Amanda located the app on her smartphone that triggered the detonation device. All over DC, other Dragoon troops were doing the same. Everyone was in perfect sync.

With sixty seconds to go, Amanda warned the others to cover their ears and prepare for the shock wave. Amanda looked at the screen on her smartphone, at a single green button with the word "Ka-Boom" written on it. Robert had pushed the button seemingly without reservation. And now, so would she. Where was Robert? She guessed he would have shown up by now.

"Okay, everyone, here goes!" yelled Amanda. Her finger pushed the bright-green "Ka-Boom" button.

Yet nothing happened.

She thought for a second that it was a fluke. That she had touched the screen with too little force. She tapped the screen again.

And again, nothing.

The other Dragoons stared back at her.

Amanda shrugged.

"It's all rigged correctly. It should work."

One of the young techs yanked Amanda's smartphone from her.

"Here, quickly, let me see. Before everyone else arrives," she said.

Had the other explosions also failed to go off? Amanda mused.

After quickly trying and retrying, the young tech shook her head, baffled.

"No traceable errors, as far as I could tell."

The second wave of Dragoons, a thousand strong, turned onto the street. Hundreds of portable speakers boomed dance music. Everyone was in a mood to celebrate.

"What are we going to do?" asked Amanda, though the question was aimed mostly at herself. The question was given little time to be answered before an earth-moving blast-wave knocked everyone to the ground, and massive hunks of building cement and rebar filled the air. The explosion created a great tectonic shift beneath their feet.

The last molecules of oxygen were sucked ferociously out of their lungs.

Then came the sensation of flying and falling.

Pain from many places.

The Dragoons were covered in death and dust. Dying from deep wounds and asphyxiation.

Amanda could not tell if she was right side up or down. She appeared to be dangling from something. Her jacket was impaled on a long, sharp object. Gray smoke swirled around her. Beneath masses of rubble, fellow Dragoons were scattered like broken dolls.

She could hear nothing.

The explosion had taken her hearing.

She coughed up several handfuls of chalky, pink fluid.

Blood dripped from her hands down onto a splayed-open speaker and a burnt tire.

Where was Robert?

She knew the odds of success were small. But still, things weren't supposed to end like this. Not this badly.

Through the rising smoke, she could see the fluttering of helicopters.

And then her hearing returned, suddenly and with vengeance. Her head filled with the sound of agonized cries, shocked people near death, pleading for help.

Some yelled, unable to cope with the pain.

A few lone survivors stumbled blindly over debris, scrambling for their lives.

CHAPTER 15

A tremendous curtain of smoke radiated out from the debris field, lit up by the dozens of media helicopters and miniature heli-drones that hovered and buzzed around the disaster area, broadcasting a live feed to the entire world.

Dez and Robert had ditched their car several blocks from the Smithies factory. They were now on foot, sprinting toward the dead and the dying. Tears washed down Robert's cheeks.

"Amanda?"

Dez kept running, not wishing to answer that particular question just yet.

"Is she hurt? You know! Tell me!"

Dez stopped as they came within sight of the Smithies factory ruins. He pulled Robert under a brick awning of another industrial-office complex.

"You must wait for me here. Out of sight. They still think that you are me. That we are one and the same. They will shoot you on sight."

"I don't care. I'm coming with you."

Dez pushed Robert firmly up against the wall.

"I told you several days ago that I was going to ask you a favor. So here it is. *Trust me.* Do not go out there. Let me go alone. I know you're overwhelmed with fear and concern. But I will find Amanda. I'll bring her to you. You trust me?"

"She's all I have. You know that? She's what I believe in. You don't bring her back to me alive, then I'm going out there. I have nothing to live for."

"Don't worry. I'm going to make you a believer, too!"

Dez released Robert from his grip, then bolted from under the awning into the littered street and dashed off toward the suffering and fallen.

"Dez! Wait! What are you going to do?"

★ ★ ★

In the wake of the disaster, massive floodlights had been brought in to light up the entire area.

The charred debris field radiated heat. From under the rubble, smoke rose in numerous scattered spots like simmering geysers. Dez walked alone among the smoldering ruins. Several tiny media drones buzzed in his face like boisterous horseflies.

Reporters and their camera crews set up on the periphery of the destruction. A Homeland Security spokesman was already on hand to grant interviews and frame the incident in the proper context. The Dragoons, even though comprised primarily of unemployed young people, were obviously a serious domestic terrorist organization. They had brought this tragedy on themselves. The survivors would be processed, sentenced in secret courts, and jailed. The world was watching, and it was important to send a message of strength and resolve.

The Dragoons that had fled the wreckage were already being loaded into guarded buses. The injured were also piled into paddy wagons, with little regard for medical attention.

Then, a most peculiar and unexpected sight halted everyone in his or her tracks.

All the cameras turned from their reporters and instead focused on a single, exquisitely dressed man in a three-piece suit as he picked his way through the rubble of the fallen buildings.

A truly droll sight.

The female reporters were drawn to his flawless good looks.

Who was he?

Why was he there?

So, so odd.

Dez came across several dying people, their bodies crushed under a collapsed slab of jagged cement. They were a young couple: the teenage boy had purple hair, the girl, blonde with streaks of electric blue. The boy was whispering something to the girl. His words were inaudible, bubbling blood. The semi-conscious girl tried to smile reassuringly back at him, but the constant radiating pain was too much for her and the desire was overcome by an abrupt and ugly grimace.

Dez reached down and, with great strength and ease, lifted the heavy debris, freeing the young couple. He then crouched down to observe their broken, damaged bodies. Blood seeped through both of their pants. Dez reached out and placed his hands on each of their bodies, the insect-like media drones recording his every move. And with one graceful gesture of his hands, their wounds were instantly healed. The concrete-blonde stared up at this gorgeous, miraculous specimen of a man.

"Thank you," she said, not fully able to comprehend what had just transpired.

"Yes," said the boy. "Thank you."

"Stay here," said Dez. "You'll be safer here for now."

The reporters were uncertain as to what they had just observed and how to report it. Although the live feed being picked up across the globe needed little interpretation, especially after what came next.

Dez continued to climb across the devastated area. He almost missed the teenager's mostly obscured face. His body lay under a pile of burning rubble. His eyes were lifeless, yet open. Dez inexplicably sensed that the boy was calling him. This was impossible though, wasn't it? The young man was dead. Dez brushed the heavy brick and hunks of cement aside as if they were made of lightweight construction paper. He pulled the young man's twisted body from the molten ground. His burned limbs dangled as limp as a string puppet's as Dez held him tightly against his body.

"It's not your time, my friend." Dez passed a hand over the deceased's face, and a sparkle of nano-particles entered his body. Then, as if a drowning man was rushing up through the waterline for air, the teenager sprang upright, coughed, and spluttered to life.

The pool of reporters gasped. Had they really seen what they'd just seen? They had. They surely had.

The man in the three-piece suit lifted his arms and face to the heavens and began to chant with great dramatic flair.

"Grant me the power, oh, Lord. Grant me the power to give them life."

Perhaps, thought Dez, *in a very real way, I am God's son. A virtual miracle of creation. More essence than matter. Perhaps the universe created me for this very purpose.*

Dez conjured up a gigantic nano-cloud, which momentarily swarmed overhead, like a great specter rising out of his flesh, before dispersing into thousands of beams of light, which flew into and under the tangle of shattered and crumpled buildings in search of the dead.

Several of the reporters thought they had seen the Holy Ghost.

The mounds of fractured rebar and rubble began to bubble up like a cauldron of soup. Then, up through the detritus, the hundreds of fallen Dragoons rose from the dead.

Many of the reporters and law enforcement personnel fell to their knees at the sight of this divine event.

"Impossible," muttered a leader of one of the SWAT teams.

"It's the end of days," said a Hispanic reporter for CNN into her microphone, before crossing herself.

The resurrected hung several feet in the air as their bodies were magically healed and then gently returned to the uneven ground.

Billions of people around the world had now joined the live feed. It was unequivocal: this man in the three-piece suit was the second coming.

Dez looked from one face to the next until he spotted Amanda. He waved and called out to her. Still dazed, she approached the benevolent stranger, unsure of why she was drawn to him.

"Who are you?"

"Robert was worried about you. He's fine, though."

Amanda instinctively hugged Dez, throwing her arms around his neck. Dez lovingly returned the embrace and kissed her on the forehead, then turned his full attention to the mounting number of media outlets covering the event.

Dez now spoke directly to the cameras.

"In case you were wondering, yes, I am the Son of God. The Alpha and the Omega. My dad and I, we have a good personal relationship. He told me to tell you to listen very carefully to what I'm about to say. My word is God's word."

Dez couldn't help but note the irony that he, a product of science and reason, was professing to be the Almighty's offspring. Or perhaps there was no irony. Perhaps it was just meant to be. God and science fused into one. The same. The source.

"We've decided to give you one last chance to get things right. Otherwise, we'll have to carry out a few of our promises from the Book of Revelations, which, if you haven't read, is not the most pleasant way to spend an afternoon. Things don't work out so well for most of you. You're all consigned to a fiery lake of sulfur. There's cataclysmic earthquakes, things of that nature. I admit, it's slight overkill on my dad's part. But he's always had a flair and penchant for the dramatic. So now, first things first: you have one year to get yourselves completely together, or Dad will be forced to write you humans off as just another failed species, one of many millions to go extinct and start over again. So let me give you some specifics, because it's become evident that the earlier ground rules were a tad confusing, outdated, and inconsistent. Our bad.

"It has been much contemplated and pondered whether or not greed is the root of all evil. Well … it pretty much is. The 'camel and eye of a needle' analogy was obviously way too subtle, so let me be a tad clearer. God will smite those of you who hoard the earth's great wealth and do not share with those in need. How will you know if your wealth is egregious? A mole in the shape of a black diamond will appear on your forehead. This will only disappear when enough of your fortune has been redistributed. You will have one week to share your moola with those who need it more. And what if you disobey God's law? Well, rich men, you will live a life of intense humiliation and agony. Your testicles will cultivate a shaggy, lime-green fungus, your penises will take on the appearance of a poisonous death cap mushroom, and your hemorrhoids will swell to the size of ripe plums. You will fart with the intensity and toxicity of a bloated and sickly rhinoceros. Your tongues will grow hog's hair, your breath will be untreatably rank, and all food will taste like the bottom of a grungy fish tank. And, what's more, you will grow cloven feet and alligator scales on your back.

"Yet these will not be the worst of fates to befall you. For every night, you will live the nightmares of all those who still hunger and suffer. You will feel their pain, desperation, anger, and humiliation as intensely as they do. And every morning, you shall wake to the sight and horror of an angry peasant shitting on your face. Then, for good measure, you will burn in eternal hellfire.

"So saith the Lord!

"God is tired of you misinterpreting his words. And I know that all the world is watching so let me be especially clear on the next point: women are not property. There is no cultural or religious context that excuses the medieval treatment of women as second-class citizens. Any man still unsure how to treat a woman properly, think of her as your absolute equal. An angel of your better nature. Those of you who treat women unjustly and without respect will grow enormous vaginas. Your facial hair will drop out, and startlingly plump breasts will burst forth, your voices taking on the sweet, high pitch of a sparrow. You will also conceive a baby and endure the agony of forty-eight hours of labor before giving birth. No drugs may be used to subdue your suffering.

"Oh, yes, and to my Western brethren, stop making up excuses to go to war in order to justify the profitable production of weaponry. Your bellicose actions create more hate and horrific affliction in the world than they suppress. It's time to put away your war toys. There shall be no more weapons creation. None. Those of you who do create and profit from the sale of weapons will be sodomized by wild-eyed, baggy-balled buffalos for no less than one thousand years and then burn in hellfire for an equal amount of time.

"So saith the Lord!

"And all this talk of no fish on Friday, forget all that small-minded gibberish. And please, the 'no sex before marriage' thing—that was written during a time when people married at fourteen and died at thirty. Context, people! Context! God gave you a brain! Make use of it! God does not have time to monitor or concern himself with where and when you put your reproductive organs. That goes double for non-traditional sexual preferences."

Dez paused to take a breath and detected the slight odor and vapor of an electronic cigarette.

"Okay, let's get some other simple rules out of the way: killing is never permitted. Ever. No person may ever kill or intentionally do grievous harm to another person for any reason. If you do, your feet will be swapped for your hands and your hands for your feet. You will catch a new and grotesque form of leprosy that itches like the dickens. The more you scratch it, the more astonishingly it will itch. And then you will burn in hell for a thousand years."

As Dez continued to preach the new word of God to a worldwide audience, Horace Spruill climbed the rusty rungs of a nearby tower crane. The crane was two-thirds of the way through construction on a new automated factory that would manufacture gas masks for SWAT teams. Upon reaching the operator's cab, he took up a sniper's position high above the damaged buildings.

Spruill had not witnessed any of the so-called miracles performed by Dez. He knew that the AI was too smart to allow himself and Robert to be blown up or captured. He also knew that Robert would insist on trying to find and save Amanda. But who was this fool in a suit wagging his fingers and yapping at the press pool? And why were they listening to this yahoo?

Spruill swept his rifle scope over the demolished area searching for a sign of Robert. He had to be there somewhere. Amanda was standing out in the open, as still and disheveled as a scarecrow, her clothes torn, her hair singed and matted.

Spruill continued to watch from his high perch like a demented gargoyle. Robert would show his face eventually.

Patience was Spruill's deadliest weapon.

Back on the ground, Dez had summoned the fury of a Pentecostal youth minister. "What are you people, suicidal? Stop killing the one planet that sustains your life! You pour toxic sludge into your waterways, and yet your blood is 80 percent river water! You soak your crops in pesticides but are shocked when you become ill. This seems so basic that I'll keep my remarks on this matter to a minimum.

"God will do nothing on this front. It's all on you. Make the air unbreathable. You will wither and die. God will begin again and create another species with better sense than to piss in their own soup. God almost threw in the towel on you based on this asinine self-defeating behavior alone. You're lucky I convinced Dad to stick with you for another year.

"I will say this, though, for all of you polluters who operate on an industrial scale. Coal mines, oil companies, all your brethren—justice will visit your doorstep. The Sisters of Retribution are hereby charged to deal with you in any manner they see fit. For, like your crimes, yours is to be an Earthy punishment. Listen, all of you, when I say that the Sisters of Retribution are the Lord's avenging angels. And that whatever actions the Sisters of Retribution take, no government or law enforcement agency is to prevent. They are doing God's work, and he appreciates their diligence and effort."

Dez loosened his necktie. His talk was almost over now. And he was troubled by a certain grim event that he knew was coming. Perspiration trickled down his forehead. *What a wonderful thing it is to sweat,* he thought, as a faint breeze mixed with the beaded saltwater on his brow, cooling him down.

"Now, lastly, the issue of genetic and neural enhancements. If these technologies are going to be available to anyone, they must be available to everyone. The advantages they provide are too important to only benefit the few. And those of you who are wary and do not want them, I say this: human evolution has not ended. It is a perpetual and mysterious journey. Yes, adaptation can be strange and chaotic, but such is the beauty of the universe. So if you choose to eschew these new technologies, that is an evolutionary path of your own making. And for those of you who do decide to become enhanced, you are automatically obligated to take care of those who cannot do so. Do not think for a second that having a slightly improved genetic code and higher IQ entitles you to act like a self-absorbed jackass.

"So now, to prove to you our serious commitment to these moral rules and standards, I will remove many of your evil agents from the planet. Politicians, be they national or local, gone. Vanished into thin air. They were doing a shitty job anyway. Bankers too. War profiteers.

Pedophile priests hiding behind the Vatican's high walls. Gone. All damned to hell for a good while until I consider them reformed enough to return. Treat them with care when they do come back to you. For they, like you, are God's children. As for the rest of you, I'm giving you a clean slate. But if things aren't turned around in one year, I'm turning off the sun, and your planet will become frozen and dark and everything will die. And I can do this because I am the Son of God. And because tough love seems to be the only kind of love you respond to.

"I'll leave you with these final words. The key to serving each other and God well is to remember and remind yourself of one word: *empathy.* Any action should be taken with the utmost deference and regard for the feelings and well being of the person or persons that action may effect. Everyone, repeat the word with me: *empathy.*

"So there you have it. Ignore God at your own peril. Mostly, though, enjoy yourselves. And try to read a few more books. Writers deserve a wider readership. Thank you for your attention."

As if on cue, Robert appeared on the periphery of the demolished factory. He stood in the dark shadows, away from the floodlights. Amanda involuntarily turned in his direction. Some sort of sixth sense oriented her toward him. And when she did so, Robert could not help but edge slightly toward her, a shaft of light streaking across his face.

"Amanda," he said in absolute joy and relief.

Spruill was hyper-aware of Amanda's body movement. He traced the path of her gaze all the way across the field of rubble to Robert's half-lit face, poking up from behind several mangled I-beams.

"Got you, you little prick," said Spruill, as he began to gently squeeze the trigger of the AR99 Obliterator.

Dez was aware of the threat before it even happened. Had pondered the numerous choices of how he could and would react. The assassination attempt provided him with a situation that he knew was needed to complete his prophecy. Like other historical messengers of God, his life had to be taken in spectacular fashion. And like Jesus before him, who was executed for the crime of sedition against the state, Dez, too, would die a social revolutionary who preached radical egalitarianism and adherence to God's law.

Before Spruill could fully pull the trigger on his rifle, Dez rose up into the air, over the crumpled, scattered pieces of building, through the wide beams of the floodlights, and propelled himself faster and faster until he slammed into Spruill just as the Obliterator unleashed its antimatter round.

Dez's body was instantly severed in two, his pelvis and legs pulverized and evaporating before they hit the ground. Spruill was knocked backward off his feet. He fell clumsily over the crane's safety railing, screaming in disbelief as he plummeted toward the hundreds of reporters gathered below.

He died on impact.

Later, many days later, only his estranged sister, Penny, from Monongahela, Pennsylvania, would attend his funeral.

Robert watched as the upper portion of Dez's torso cartwheeled back to the earth. Amanda and Robert rushed to Dez's side.

When they got to him, Dez's eyes were wide open. His expression was oddly serene.

He spoke before either Amanda and Robert could shake off the shock.

"Thank you, dear friends. Thank you for showing me what it means to be alive. I hope I have served you both well."

"Dez, you've got to save yourself!" cried Amanda.

"Please, please don't die," added Robert, fretfully grabbing Dez's hand.

"You may not understand it now. But it is the correct decision. For everyone."

"No, no, it's not. Come back into my body. Please! We'll print you out another."

"In time, you'll realize it was for the best."

"No, I won't, never! You loved being alive! Stay with me."

"Robert, stop. Let me help you one more time and then you must let me go."

"Help me? Look at yourself! What are you talking about?"

"The fact that you no longer wish to be enhanced. I was a part of you. I heard your every thought. I can undo it. Just ask me."

Amanda looked at Robert. "Is that true?"

Robert thought for a second, then nodded his head.

"I want to go back to being the imperfect, flawed me."

"I must ask why," said Dez.

"I don't want to find myself standing on a beach one day as a young man, unchanged, gripping the aged hand of the woman I love."

"I remember. Your dream."

"Yes," said Robert.

"Because of love, then," said Dez.

"Because of love," repeated Robert.

Dez summoned the last of his fleeting strength, placed his hand on Robert, and extracted the Z14, while also reversing the extensive genetic enhancements.

Robert momentarily lost consciousness and collapsed next to Dez.

"Oh, goodness!" said Amanda.

"Give him a moment. He'll recover soon enough."

Amanda anxiously shook Robert awake and helped him sit upright.

"How do you feel?"

"Like I could throw up," said Robert.

"Welcome back to the real world," said Amanda, giving him a big kiss.

Dez managed to lift his head and nodded it approvingly at the loving couple. He winced in pain and then coughed up a mess of frothy blood. Robert cleared his woozy head and placed the palm of his hand on Dez's clammy forehead.

Dez's wrinkled eyelids closed for a long moment and then slowly reopened.

"Thank you, Dez, for giving us a future," said Robert.

"Yes, such a wonderful, promising future," added Amanda.

"And thank you both for teaching me what love is and letting me share your journey. Now mine is almost at its end."

"No," stammered Robert, tears trickling down his cheeks.

"I'll always be with you," said Dez. "Always."

Dez gazed misty-eyed, upward toward the heavens.

He took his final breath and exhaled a mantra of goodwill and hope for all humankind.

"Empathy … empathy, empathy, empathy, empathy, empathy." repeated Dez, until his chest and body fell silent.

ABOUT THE AUTHOR

Paul K. Lovett is a seasoned Hollywood screenwriter with the emotional scars, caffeine addiction and chiropractic bills to prove it. He is best known for the feature film Four Brothers, starring Mark Wahlberg. Paul has penned over thirty scripts in every genre for most of the major studios, including Universal, Sony, Paramount, Fox, Disney, Dreamworks and HBO. The Evolution of Robert Carr was born out of a desire for genuine self-expression, resurrected from the smashed and trampled piñata pieces that once comprised Paul's creative integrity. Nipple tweak. Namaste.